Wendy hadn't retu... hall, so Rita and I head... inside what amounted... lone, lost paper-towel ... Wendy crouching over something—or should I say, *someone*—on the floor.

"What did you find?" Rita asked.

"I'm not sure," Wendy said. "He's pretty good." She lifted the man's hand and opened it, but he wasn't holding anything. She let his arm fall to the floor with a heavy thump. "He hasn't moved since I came in."

"Are there any clues?" Rita asked, joining her. "I can't believe they tried to cheat like this. I bet the solution to the whole mystery is here." She paused. "What *is* that?"

"Coffee, I think."

I swallowed a lump the size of my fist. I could place the smell now. Coffee and caramel and milk. "Who is it?" I asked. My feet were rooted in place, and no matter how hard I tried, I couldn't make myself step into the room to see past Wendy and Rita.

"One of the actors." Wendy paused. "I think it is, anyway?"

I crept into the room and moved so I could look down on the man they were busy frisking.

"Don't touch him," I said, my voice coming out as a whisper. "That's not an actor." The man's head was turned to the side, and a coffee-wet towel had been draped over his face so you couldn't see his features, but I knew who it was. The empty to-go coffee mug lying next to his hand told me everything I needed to know. "It's Scott. And I'm pretty sure this isn't part of the game . . ."

Books by Alex Erickson

Published by Kensington Publishing Corp.

Death By Caramel Macchiato

ALEX ERICKSON

Kensington Publishing Corp.
www.kensingtonbooks.com

All Kensington titles, imprints, and distributed lines are available at special quantity discounts for bulk purchases for sales promotion, premiums, fund-raising, educational, or institutional use.

Special book excerpts or customized printings can also be created to fit specific needs. For details, write or phone the office of the Kensington Sales Manager: Attn.: Sales Department. Kensington Publishing Corp., 900 Third Avenue, New York, NY 10022. Phone: 1-800-221-2647.

The K and Teapot logo is a trademark of Kensington Publishing Corp.

First Printing: December 2024

ISBN: 978-1-4967-4552-1

ISBN: 978-1-4967-4553-8 (ebook)

10 9 8 7 6 5 4 3 2 1

Printed in the United States of America

1

The man lay unmoving on the floor. His head was turned slightly to the side, tongue poking between blue-green lips. His shirt was pulled down over one shoulder, exposing a pink scar or mark of some kind. The lights were dim, leaving much of the room in shadow. A hammer, two bags of herbal tea, an empty cloth sack, and a comb painted gold lay on the floor next to the man.

"Murdered." The word came out as a harsh whisper. "Or was it an accident?"

The speaker's eyes scanned the crowd of onlookers, as if one of us had the answer. Beside me, Rita Jablonski tittered, hand hovering just over her heart.

"The night is dark, cold. No one was in the room at the time of death, no one but the dead man before you. What happened to him? Why was he here in the first place? What reason did anyone have to harm him? Or was his demise caused by something . . . otherworldly?"

The speaker, a man named Oliver Quick, grinned. The shadows made him look sinister. If I didn't know better, I would have pinned him as the killer and called it a day. His hair was light brown, cut short, with eyes the same shade of brown. A tiny mustache decorated his upper lip. It was so thin, it looked like someone had drawn it on.

Across the room, Detective John Buchannan leaned over and whispered something to Officer Becca Garrison. Neither were in uniform, but they still held the commanding presence of those trained in law enforcement. Becca scowled, nodded once, and turned her attention back to Oliver.

"Take a good look. The only way to solve this mystery is to absorb everything. What here is important?" Oliver motioned toward the odd objects surrounding the downed man. "Which ones are mere distractions?" He fluttered a hand past his head, spun around as if following it, and turned back, that horrible grin still on his face. "Who will uncover the truth?"

I half-expected the last question to be followed by a sudden burst of organ music and flashing lights, but the room remained dark and silent. Oliver looked over each of us once more, soaking in the attention as though he was starved for it, before he straightened to his complete five-foot-two height and the dim lights came on full.

"Oh my Lordy Lou," Rita said from beside me. "This is going to be fabulous!"

The dead man on the floor opened one eye and then popped to his feet. "How was I?" he asked Oliver. "I swear my chest didn't even move once that entire time."

Oliver sighed, "It was . . . adequate." He spun and walked away, which caused the room to erupt in conversation.

"It was a bit overdone, don't you think?" I asked Rita. "Like a bad play."

"Overdone? A bad play?" Rita's eyes widened. "Krissy Hancock, how could you think such a thing?" She turned to the third member of our team—and member of the Pine Hills Writers—Wendy Wilcox. "Can you believe her?"

Wendy's gaze was still rivetted to the spot where the "dead" man had lain. "That was so real. I was starting to wonder if they'd brought in a real dead person." She shuddered.

"See!" Rita said, triumphant. "Wendy thinks it was well done, and so do I." She shook her head and muttered, "Overdone. Really?"

We were gathered at the local bed-and-breakfast, Ted and Bettfast, to solve a murder. Or an accident. Or whatever this was supposed to be. The event had been organized by Oliver and had originally been planned as a Pine Hills event, complete with local actors playing all the juicy parts. Something happened along the way, and Oliver had brought along his own troupe from Levington, cutting the Pine Hills actors out before they could even get started. I didn't know why.

All I knew for sure was that it was supposed to be a big production of, as Oliver had put it when we'd first arrived, "movie-like quality." Teams had been gathered to solve the mystery, though there wasn't a prize for winning. Local fame, maybe?

The actual event began tomorrow morning, with this little scene a prequel to the full production later. We were supposed to remain at Ted and Bettfast all night, something that didn't make much sense to me, but since Rita had asked me to join her team, I went along with it without complaint.

I recognized quite a few people who made up the other teams of three, though there were a few people I didn't know. Members of the Cherry Valley book club were huddled together, discussing the scene. A trio of local doctors stood near them, likely discussing the physical clues. And, of course, Buchannan and Garrison were there, teamed with Lena Allison, who was an employee of my bookstore café, Death by Coffee, when she wasn't shadowing the police.

Rita must have seen my gaze land on Lena because she tsked in my ear. "I asked her to join us, but she insisted on coming with them. You'd think after everything you've done for her, she would have jumped at the chance to work with us."

"No, it's better this way," I said. "She wants to be a cop. This will be a good learning experience for her."

A stocky man with glasses approached the evidence on the floor. He hesitated and then reached for the cloth sack, but was stopped by a harsh, "Scott Flanagan! Don't you dare touch that!"

The man—Scott—jerked back, nearly losing his glasses in the process.

Oliver marched across the room to stand over the props. "Everything is to be left untouched overnight."

"If we were truly investigating, we would be allowed to inspect the evidence." This from one of Scott's teammates. A tattoo poked up from the collar of the woman's shirt. Unrecognizable, with just a small bit visible, it just barely touched her neck.

"You'll have the opportunity to investigate everything tomorrow," Oliver said. He spun in a slow circle. "Is everyone still present?" He hesitated a heartbeat before going on. "Good. I'd like to thank everyone for being here. You will be experiencing a movie-quality thrill ride that will have you guessing right up until the end."

There was a muttering from one of the two groups from Levington, the one that Scott and the tattooed woman *didn't* belong to.

"Nothing like this has ever been attempted before," Oliver said. "The entire town will be involved in my production. Everyone." He grinned, though I knew for a fact the local actors wanted nothing to do with his production after he'd dismissed them. "My performers are obvious targets, but are there others sprinkled throughout town who might have a clue or two for you. Asking questions of everyone is the only way to find out."

Two people approached Oliver, flanking him like bodyguards, though, if they were, they didn't look like they'd be of much help in a fight. The woman was thin, actress-pretty, while the man looked to have just finished his awkward teen phase.

"I, along with my assistants, Mr. Richie Husted and Ms. Lydia Ray, will be off limits after the prologue has completed," Oliver said, indicating the two behind him.

"Tonight, we will be setting up for tomorrow's production. Then, bright and early, and once we've established the story, we will become watchful ghosts, nothing more." He paused as if to let that sink in. "You have one hour to mingle, and then you will be confined to your quarters for the night. In the morning, we will recreate the scene one last time, and then we will begin!"

Oliver clapped his hands, spun on his heel, and marched away. Richie and Lydia looked at one another, as if wondering if they should follow, before hurrying after him.

"Well, I think I'm going to go ahead and head to the room," Rita said as soon as they were gone. "We managed to snag one of the actual bedrooms, thank goodness. I heard Vivian complain that she's being forced to sleep on one of those blow-up mattresses in a closet or some such. Can you imagine? At her age?"

Vivian Flowers, one of the Cherry Valley book club members, *was* on the older side, but was still spry for a woman in her eighties. She might even have put on a little weight—*good* weight, considering she'd once weighed no more than eighty pounds. She was currently laughing with her teammates, Sara Huffington and Albert Elmore. I hadn't seen any of them for years and planned on making it a point to see how they were doing before they went back home.

"I'll go with you," Wendy said. "We can start making plans."

"That's a fantastic idea," Rita said, turning to me. "What about you, Krissy? I figure with you helping us, we've got this in the bag. What with all the murders you've already investigated and solved."

"Sure. I don't have—" My phone buzzed in my back pocket. I checked the screen and frowned. "Give me a minute. I should take this."

Rita nodded, and both she and Wendy headed for the stairs that led to our room.

"Hello? Jules?" I said by way of answer. "Is Misfit okay?"

Jules Phan, my neighbor and owner of the candy store, Phantastic Candies, had promised to feed my orange cat, Misfit, while I was running around playing detective with Rita. I couldn't imagine why he'd be calling, other than that something had gone wrong.

"I'm so sorry to bother you, Krissy," he said. "But I can't find the key!"

It took me a moment to realize what he was talking about. "My house key?"

"I left it right on the kitchen table. Maestro"—his white Maltese—"must have knocked it off, though I can't imagine him jumping up on the table like that."

Neither could I. "Lance didn't pick it up, did he?"

"No, he's not here. I suppose I could have moved it while cooking, but if I did, I did it without thinking. Is there any way you could stop by and lend me another key? I promise I won't lose that one. I'll put it on my key ring the moment it touches my fingers."

"Sure. Let me talk to the guy running this thing, and I'll be there. Give me twenty minutes."

"Thank you. I'm sorry about this."

"Don't worry about it," I said. "I don't mind getting out of here for a little while." If Oliver would even let me leave. Not that he had much say in the matter, to be honest. If he disqualified me, so be it. My cat came first.

I clicked off and scanned the room for Oliver. He'd vanished in the back with his assistants, but one of them, Richie, was hovering near the office door. I decided the middleman might be my best bet.

"Hi," I said, approaching.

Richie looked startled when he answered. "Uh, hello."

"I'm Krissy Hancock. I'm one of the contestants." I stuck out my hand.

"Investigators," he corrected before shaking my hand. "I'm Richie Husted, Oliver's assistant." He said the last with pride. "Is there something I can help you with?"

"I hope so." A quick glance at the office door to make sure it was still closed. "My cat-sitter lost the key to my house, and I need to go give him another. I'll be back before our hour is up."

Richie was shaking his head before I'd finished. "No one is supposed to leave."

"I know," I said. "But this is kind of an emergency. My cat needs food and water. If it was just overnight, he'd be okay, but I'll be out investigating all day tomorrow too. This will only take a few minutes. I'll drive out, drop off the key, and come straight back. Promise."

Richie bit his lower lip. "If Oliver finds out . . ."

"I'll take full blame," I said, already inching toward the door. "I won't even tell him I let you know."

Nor did I give him a chance to tell me no. Before

Richie could stop gnawing on his lip to answer, I slipped away, hoping to be out the door and back before Oliver was the wiser. On the way, I passed by Lena, who was standing alone.

"Did Buchannan abandon you already?" I asked.

Lena made a face. "He told me to stay put and keep an eye on things while he called his wife. Becca went to check out our room, which, thankfully, is upstairs. I can't believe they're forcing us to stay here."

"Tell me about it." The out-of-towners, sure, but the rest of us? Would it be so bad to let us sleep in our own beds? Then I wouldn't have to worry about a cat-sitter.

Lena ran her fingers through hair that was fading from purple to a more natural brown. I wondered if she planned on dyeing it again, or if there was some rule in the police handbook that prevented her from keeping her hair unnatural colors.

"I was hoping this would give me a chance to show off my skills, but I have a feeling I'm just going to be a gofer throughout this thing," she said.

"Buchannan?"

She rolled her eyes. "He treats me like his personal assistant. I get that I'm just learning and I'm not an actual police officer or anything, but every time he sees me, he has me doing all the stuff he doesn't want to. How many papers does one man need to be stapled together?"

I tried to hide my smile, but failed. "Maybe with you around, he won't hound me as much."

Lena laughed. "You wish."

And if by magic, Buchannan appeared, tucking his

phone into his pocket. His button-up plaid shirt and jeans looked out of place on him since I only ever saw him in uniform. It made him look almost normal.

"Are you bothering my deputy, Ms. Hancock?"

"Deputy, huh?" I asked. "Impressive. Lena's moved up quickly. She'll be gunning for your job by next month."

The joke earned me a scowl from Buchannan. "I don't want you bothering her during the investigation. I get that she's one of your employees, but she's working for me now."

Another snarky remark was on the tip of my tongue, but I swallowed it. No sense making things more difficult for Lena. "I won't bother her," I promised.

Buchannan didn't look as if he believed me, but he let it go. "I can't believe Chief Dalton made us do this." He glared around the room as if he suspected everyone here of doing something illegal. "I told her it was unnecessary, but she thought it would be good for public perception if we showed the town that we're just like everyone else." *We* being the police.

"It's not a bad idea," I said. "There are some people who look at cops like you're the bad guys."

He grunted. "Someone parks in a no-parking zone or speeds through a stop sign, and somehow it's *my* fault they got a ticket." He sighed. "I suppose she might be right." Though I could tell he thought Chief Patricia Dalton should be the one here and not him. "I'm going to walk around, have a listen." He nodded to Lena, who fell in line beside him. "I could use a coffee," he told her as they walked away.

I suppressed a chuckle as I started for the door. Just as I reached it, someone else called out from behind me.

"Hey, Kris. One sec?"

I bit my lower lip so as not to snap at my ex, Robert Dunhill, for calling me by a shortened version of my name, something he knew I hated yet continued to do nonetheless.

"I need to drop off something at home," I said, but stopped anyway. "Make it quick."

Robert nodded. "Yeah, sure, sure. I just wanted to let you know that I'm here if you need anything."

I waited for him to say more, but when he didn't, I asked, "And?"

"You know I plan on buying the place." The place being Ted and Bettfast. "And while I don't own it yet, I told the Bunfords"—the current owners—"that I'd help out tonight. You know they aren't as mobile as they once were, and they almost didn't agree to host this thing, but I was there and talked them into it. I figured it would be good publicity."

"I'm glad you're helping," I said, not quite sure why he needed to stop me to tell me that. "Where's Trisha?" His wife.

"At home with R.J." Their son wasn't quite a year old. "She wishes she could be here, but—"

A commotion caused us to turn.

"It's true!" Scott was saying. "I swear to you I'm not making it up."

A doctor I knew, Carl Clay, was standing with a small group consisting of members of the two Levington teams. He met my eyes and shook his head with a smile that had likely melted quite a few women's hearts, though, last I heard, he was still married.

"I call BS," one of the men in the group said. He had a thick neck that looked as if it had tried to swallow his chin, which made it seem as if he was always looking down his nose at everyone.

"It's true," Scott said. "Oliver heard stories of others who've done it and tried it himself. He doesn't want anyone else to know."

"Know what?" I asked, unable to help myself.

"Scottie here claims Oliver bathes in blood," one of the other men in the group said with a smile.

"He doesn't bathe in it." Scott shook his head. "But he has a bottle of blood that he keeps at his bedside. He uses the blood on his face, almost like a night mask, in the hopes that it will keep him young forever."

"And where does he get this blood?" the chinless man asked, taking a step toward Scott and jabbing him in the shoulder with a finger. "You're always doing this, making stuff up."

"Ow." Scott rubbed at the spot where the man poked him, which only caused the man to do it again, harder.

"Leave him alone, Drew," the tattooed woman said, stepping forward.

"I'm okay, Shari," Scott said, adjusting his glasses. "I can prove it to you," he said, turning back to Drew, the chinless man.

"Oh? I can't wait to see this." Drew crossed his arms and waited.

Scott swallowed, eyes roving around the room. "Ask Richie. He can tell you."

Richie had been joined at the door by Lydia, who'd just stepped out of the office. They were both oblivious to what was going on.

"Can he now?" Drew asked with a laugh. He spun to face the assistants, raised his voice. "Hey, Richie. Come on over here a sec. Scott's got some juicy gossip he'd like you to share about your boss."

Richie froze while, beside him, Lydia scowled.

"That's what I thought." Drew turned back. "I heard what you said about me earlier." He poked Scott again. "And now you think you can pull one over on Drew MacDonald, like I was born yesterday? Do you think going around lying about everyone will somehow get you what you want? Do you think it'll make people *like* you?" Another poke.

Another man, this one with shaggy, light brown hair, stepped forward. He looked like a former athlete gone soft around the middle. "Come on, Scott, let's get to our room."

"What do you think he's said about you, Austin?" Drew was shouting now. "Told me that you and your neighbors have become awfully familiar with one another. Is that what Scott is hoping will happen tonight? You and Shari maybe? You *are* sharing a room."

"All right, that's enough," Carl stepped forward before Drew could deliver another lancelike finger jab to Scott's shoulder. "Let's all calm down." He put an arm around Drew and led him away. To my surprise, the other man went without complaint.

Scott looked absolutely mortified. His gaze moved around the room, to all the watching eyes. "I . . ." He cleared his throat, wiped at his mouth with the back of his hand. His gaze lingered on Lydia, as if he feared she'd run off to tell Oliver that he'd been talking about him.

"It's all right," Shari said. "Let's take a break, okay?"

Scott nodded, then muttered, "It's true. I swear it."

Austin and Shari shared a look, one that told me that neither of them believed him. It made me wonder how they'd ended up teammates.

"Wow," Robert said with a shake of his head. "Can you believe that?"

"I'm sorry, Robert, I really need to go." I shot a look toward the office door, but Oliver had yet to emerge. "I'll talk to you later, okay?"

"Yeah, sure." He scuffed a shoe on the floor, like I'd just rejected a request for a dance. "I'll cover for you."

A part of me wanted to roll my eyes, but, hey, if it kept Oliver from yelling at me for sneaking out later, I'd take it.

With one last glance toward where Scott appeared to be pleading his case with Shari and Austin, I slipped out the door and into the night.

2

"I'm sorry about this," Jules said as I climbed out of my car. "I swear I looked everywhere. The more I think about it, the more I'm afraid that Lance took it with him when he left this morning, and he won't be back for three days!"

"It's all right," I said. An orange, furry face appeared in the living room window and then vanished as Misfit rushed to the door. "I needed the break."

"Still . . ." Jules heaved a sigh. His dark hair was cut short and made a faint rasping sound when he ran his hand through it. "How was the . . . what was it exactly?"

I unlocked the door and used my foot and leg to block the gap when I opened it. Misfit pressed his face against me for a moment, before backing up and heading for the kitchen, where I kept his food dish.

"It's some sort of play, I guess. A big, interactive one."

Jules followed me in, shaking his head. "I don't get it."

"Neither do I. We're supposed to run around town to look for clues to solve some guy's death."

"Sounds familiar." He chuckled. "You'll likely excel at this little play-thing."

I glanced back at Jules. He looked stressed, which I suppose wasn't much of a surprise, considering the lost key. "I suppose I might," I admitted. "Buchannan's there, and since he's a trained detective, I figure it'll give him an advantage."

"We'll see. The police here don't have the best track record at beating you at solving murders." Jules leaned against the counter as I filled Misfit's food and water dish. "If I catch wind of any clues at Phantastic Candies, I'll let you know, just in case. With Lance gone, I could use the excitement."

"I didn't know he was leaving," I said. "Did he need to do something for work?"

"Family." Jules made it sound like a lament. "A cousin is having a crisis of some sort. He left it rather vague, but made it seem like the world is ending. Lance went to Colorado to see if he can help."

"You didn't want to go?"

"Not particularly." There was a lot said in those two words, mostly in tone. I didn't pry, but I figured that said cousin wasn't a fan of Jules and Lance's relationship.

As quietly as I could, I removed Misfit's treat bag from an overhead cabinet while he ate and poured a small handful into my palm. Despite the fact I'd not made a sound, the cat's head whipped around, and he gave me a wide-eyed stare, like he knew exactly what I'd done.

"Not until you finish your dinner," I told him. Misfit stared at me a moment longer before going back to his food.

"They can sense it," Jules said with a laugh. "Maestro just knows when I'm about to grab a treat for him. I don't even make it into the kitchen before he's prancing around between my feet. I keep telling him that if I fall and break an arm, he won't be getting any treats, but it always lands on deaf ears."

I could just imagine the excited Maltese's legs pumping as he waited to be pampered. I gently set the treats down on the counter and secreted the bag back where it belonged. Misfit wasn't supposed to jump up onto the counter, but try telling a cat not to do something. As soon as he finished eating, he'd be up there to wash.

"I should get back," I said, removing my key from the ring and handing it to Jules. "Lockdown begins in a half an hour."

"You sound thrilled." He removed his own set of keys and added mine to the ring. As soon as it was back in his pocket, he patted it, as if making sure it was still there.

"I'll be okay. I just hate not staying here." I glanced back at Misfit, who'd already inhaled most of his food.

"Think of it as an adventure," Jules said, following me out the door. "A break from the norm."

I locked the door from the inside before closing it. I tugged on it a few times to make sure it had latched before heading for my car. "It would be more of an exciting adventure if Paul was sleeping in the same room with me, rather than Rita and Wendy."

Jules laughed. "I'm sure it would be." He held the door open for me as I climbed into my car. "Try to have some fun. And remember to stop by Phantastic Candies if you get stuck! I'd love to be able to help you solve one of these things, especially since the stakes are so low."

I laughed. "I'll do that."

"I'll check on Misfit first thing in the morning, and then I'll be at the shop until about six if you need to pick up your key. After that, I'll be at home. If you need me to check on him again, just let me know."

"Thanks. I appreciate it."

Jules closed the door for me and stepped back with a wave. I returned it, and with a sigh, I was on my way back to Ted and Bettfast.

Much of the activity had ceased by the time I got back to the bed-and-breakfast. Rita and Wendy had retired for the night, as had the entirety of the Cherry Valley team. Only a handful of people remained downstairs, chatting. They glanced my way as I entered, with some giving me a suspicious look, as if they thought I'd cheated during my trip home, even though I was back before the actual lockdown had begun.

Lydia and Richie stood apart from the group, watching. Richie saw me enter, shot a look toward the closed office door, and gave me a subtle nod. Apparently, my escape had avoided Oliver's notice.

"Hey, Krissy," Carl called out, motioning me over. "How have you been lately?"

I crossed the room and joined him as he stepped apart from the others. "Great. How about you? How's the doctoring?"

"It's been good. I haven't seen you around the office lately. I assume that's a good thing."

I'd earned my fair share of bumps and bruises over the years, thanks to my many adventures chasing killers around town. Too often, I ended up paying the doctor's office a visit afterward, though, thankfully, for nothing major.

I crossed my fingers, which caused him to laugh.

The rest of the small group, which included Austin, Shari, and the two remaining members of the Levington teams, whose names I had yet to learn, stood nearby, talking quietly, while shooting glances toward Oliver's watchful assistants.

"Has there been any more excitement since the argument between Scott and Drew?" I asked.

"Nah," Carl said. "Just talk."

"I thought it might come to blows, earlier," I said.

Carl sighed. "Tell me about it. Drew can be . . . difficult."

"You know him?"

Carl nodded. "Not well, but yeah, I know him. He's a nurse at Levington Memorial Hospital. I've come across him a few times in passing." Like his friend and practice partner, Darrin Crenshaw, Carl split his time between the local Pine Hills practice and the hospital in Levington.

"He seems intense."

"He can be," Carl said. "He's been reprimanded at

the hospital a few times for his behavior with patients. Can't tell you what exactly he did, just that it happened. You know how people talk."

Boy, did I ever.

Just then, the small group moved closer to us, with Austin shooting a thumb over his shoulder, toward Lydia and Richie.

"I swear those two think we're going to somehow ruin this whole thing," he said. "They haven't stopped watching us."

"It's no wonder," one of the men I didn't know said. He had light brown skin and a pierced eyebrow. "After what Scott said, they're probably making sure we don't talk about them."

"It's not like any of it is true," Austin said.

"So, you're saying you *didn't*—"

Austin cut him off. "No, I didn't, Tony. And I don't plan on it here or anywhere else."

Tony of the pierced eyebrow spread his hands, though his smile said he didn't quite believe him.

"Scott isn't trying to upset anyone," Shari said. "He just . . ." She shrugged. "I guess he craves the attention, and it's the only way he knows how to get it."

The other man, who was short and plump, spoke up, surprising me with a soft, whispery voice. "I wish he wouldn't."

"What did he say about you, Curtis?" Tony asked. "Are there scandalous photos of you and the neighbor floating around."

Curtis grinned. "You wish, Mr. Yates." He turned to me. "Hi, we haven't met. I'm Curtis Rittenberg." He held out a hand.

I shook. "Krissy Hancock."

"I'm Austin Helms."

"Nice to meet you," I said, turning to Shari. "And you're Shari, right?"

She nodded. "Shari Carter. You're from here in town, right?"

"I live in Pine Hills, yeah," I said. "But I'm originally from California."

"Really?" Curtis said. "What part?"

Before I could answer, Richie and Lydia approached, and Richie was the one to speak up. "It's time to head to your rooms," he said. "Lockdown begins in five."

"We start at eight a.m. sharp," Lydia said. "Be sure to be down here fifteen minutes early. Oliver doesn't want to have to wait for anyone."

Curtis saluted. "Yes, ma'am. Will breakfast be served?"

"You're on your own for that," Richie said, glancing toward the office door. He looked terrified that Oliver might come through it and scream at him for not having everyone in their rooms already. "Get a good night's sleep."

The group headed for the stairs together in silence. Lydia and Richie didn't follow us all the way to our rooms, but they watched us filter up the stairs. "Good nights" were said as we parted, with Austin and Shari heading to the room they were sharing with Scott, and Curtis and Tony heading down the hall for the door to the room they shared with Drew. Carl vanished into the room across the hall with a wave. I caught a glimpse of my doctor, Paige Lipmon, standing with Darrin Crenshaw inside, and then the door closed, leaving me alone in the hall.

I considered knocking on the door to the room I shared with Wendy and Rita, but decided against it, just in case they were already asleep. I opened the door and stepped into the room to find Rita was indeed already tucked into bed, snoring. Wendy was sitting at a small desk, staring intently at her open laptop. She didn't look up until I closed the door.

"Oh!" she said as she snapped her laptop closed. "You're here."

I nodded and looked pointedly toward Rita.

"She passed out not long after we came into the room," Wendy said. "She wants to make sure she's rested for tomorrow." A pause. "She's really out, so we can talk. My phone went off like five minutes ago, and she didn't so much as twitch."

Sure enough, despite Wendy talking at normal volume, Rita didn't budge.

"I think I might call it a night soon, too," I said, frowning at the bed. Rita was sprawled across it, taking up the whole thing. There were two small, inflatable mattresses on the floor that looked less than comfortable. They would have to do.

"Yeah, you're probably right." Wendy looked longingly at the top of her laptop before setting it aside. I wondered if she was writing a story, since she was a member of the writer's group, or if she'd simply been checking her email before I'd come in. "This is going to be fun, isn't it?" She sounded uncertain.

"I'm sure it will be."

Wendy didn't appear convinced as we chose our

mattresses and settled in next to one another. As soon as the lights were off and I lay my head on the pillow, I knew sleep wasn't going to come easily. The mattress wasn't as uncomfortable as I thought it would be, but it wasn't ideal either. I was too close to the floor, with the Rita-occupied bed towering above me on one side, and Wendy lying on the near edge of her own mattress on the other. Claustrophobic was the word.

An hour passed with me doing my best not to toss and turn. Wendy had fallen asleep soundlessly and barely moved from her initial position. I could hear Rita rolling around above me between her snores. Every time I shifted, the floorboards creaked, causing me to freeze, half-afraid I'd wake up the entire bed-and-breakfast.

After the first hour had passed, I found myself lying on my back, phone in hand, browsing the internet. I was curious about Oliver Quick, so I Googled him. He'd run a theatre in Levington that had some success a few years ago but eventually started struggling, like so many places dedicated to the arts. People wanted their entertainment cheap or for free and had publicly complained about his theatre's pricing until he'd been forced to close.

I found an article written about Oliver and the production he was putting on in Pine Hills, but it told me little outside what I already knew. It was a play and a game all in one. It was big. Oliver expected it to bring him—and the town—a ton of attention. He'd given an interview in which he made it sound like Hollywood would come knocking the moment it was over, though he didn't say how anyone in Hollywood would know about it in the first place. It wasn't like there would be cameras following us around.

And, besides, wouldn't someone involved with the stage want Broadway to take notice, rather than Hollywood? Oliver's interview gave me mixed signals that made me feel as if the man wasn't quite sure what it was he actually wanted.

I put away my phone with a sigh. I don't know why I was having such a hard time enjoying myself. Like the article said, it was a game, a mystery. I liked mysteries. I was with friends. I could have fun if I allowed myself to. I shouldn't worry about Scott and his gossiping, or Oliver and his arrogant pride.

A series of creaks sounded in the hall.

The movements were slow, measured. You know, like someone who didn't want to be caught was creeping down the hall, toward the stairs, from one of the upstairs rooms.

I sat up and listened, more intrigued by the sound than I should have been.

The creaks reached the stairs and soon went down them. A moment later, a second round of creaks followed.

"What's that?" Wendy whispered from her mattress, causing me to jump. I hadn't even heard her sit up.

"I'm not sure." I worked my way to my feet. My mind was working overtime, imagining all sorts of things. Sure, it could be nothing, but what if it wasn't? What if someone was planning on sabotaging the event? What if it was a pair of lovers, secretly sneaking off to have a few quiet moments alone without their teammates watching?

Honestly, if it was, it was none of my business, but I was already hooked. I crept toward the door, with Wendy close on my heels. Rita continued to snore on the bed, oblivious. I paused at the door as the second set of creaking footfalls worked their way down the stairs. Once they were gone, I opened the door a crack, peeked out, and, seeing no one, stepped into the hall.

Dim night-lights lit up the hallway, which meant I didn't need to use my phone to see. No light came from beneath any of the upstairs doors, telling me everyone else was likely asleep or close to it. Wendy clutched at my arm until she found my hand. I didn't know her all that well, but I let her hold on as we headed for the stairs.

We'd just reached the first stair when there was a shout.

"What do you think you're doing!"

It was followed by a meaty thump and a crash.

Abandoning any secrecy, I hurried down the stairs, Wendy right behind me, still clutching at my hand. Doors flew open upstairs and downstairs alike.

I reached the main floor in time to see Drew rear back, fist balled tight. He held Scott with his other hand, half-lifting the man from the floor where he'd crashed moments before. Scott already had a welt forming on his cheek, and if no one stepped in, another would soon join it.

"Hey!" I shouted, regretting it immediately when Drew turned his angry glare on me. "Leave him alone."

Footfalls pounded down the stairs as more people filtered into the room. The office opened, and Oliver appeared, his two assistants right behind him. "What is going on in here?" he demanded.

Drew took in the spectators and then dropped Scott to the floor. "He snuck up on me."

Scott scooted away, rubbing at his cheek. "He was cheating."

Drew spun on him, eyes going hard. "I was doing no such thing, you little runt."

The evidence from earlier was scattered across the room. Scott was sitting where it had once lain.

"You hit him?" Shari, still wearing her clothes, sans shoes, hurried across the room and helped Scott to his feet. "Really, Drew? You had to hit him?"

"He attacked me first!" Drew said. "Came up right behind me and laid his hands on me."

"I was trying to stop him from messing with the stuff." Scott motioned toward the scattered evidence. "He was going to go through it."

"I . . ." Drew clenched both of his fists as he looked around the room. "It was lying right here." He shrugged. "I couldn't sleep, and since it was quiet, I figured it was okay to look at it. I wasn't going to touch anything."

Scott opened his mouth as if he might contradict him, but a glare from Drew silenced him.

Oliver took two steps forward as if he might start yelling, but instead he abruptly spun on his assistants. "Clean up this mess," he said. "It should have been done earlier. The evidence shouldn't have been left out overnight where something like this might happen. I don't know what you were thinking."

He glared at them a moment and then marched back

into the office, where I assumed he'd set up a mattress to sleep, slamming the door behind him.

"But you told us to leave it," Richie muttered when he was gone.

Richie and Lydia headed over to pick up the evidence. As she passed, Lydia laid a comforting hand on Scott's arm. He stiffened and allowed himself to be led to the downstairs bathroom by Shari.

"Let's get you cleaned up," she said.

For some reason, that angered Drew even more.

"That's right. Go ahead," he shouted after them. "Baby him. He needs someone to watch out for him lest he get himself into a situation he doesn't come back from."

And then Drew marched toward the stairs, making sure to slam into my shoulder as he passed.

"Big man, that one," Austin said with a shake of his head. "I guess the excitement's over."

Near the office where Oliver had retreated, Vivian Flowers muttered under her breath and went back into her room. The rest of the Cherry Valley team hadn't come out to investigate the commotion.

"It's just a game," I said, watching as everyone started filtering back to their rooms as if nothing had happened. I mean, shouldn't Drew have been reprimanded, if not outright sent home for striking Scott?

Wendy muttered something about getting some sleep, and she too headed for the stairs.

Across the room, Detective Buchannan caught my eye. I walked over, half-mad about the whole situation.

"You should have stepped in," I told him.

He shrugged, and yawned. "I'm off duty." And then

he turned and headed down a short hall, to the room he was sharing with Becca and Lena.

I blinked after him. *Off duty*? Someone could have been hurt!

Lydia and Richie had finished gathering the evidence and had taken it back to wherever they were staying, leaving me alone in the big front room. I had a brief moment in which I wondered if I should do something about Drew and his temper, and decided it didn't matter. I just had to get through tomorrow, and all of this would be over. I could go back to my boring, normal life.

Yeah, I should have known better.

3

The body was laid out exactly as it had been the night before, as were the clues scattered around him. Oliver Quick, flanked by both Lydia and Richie, stood near the body, a grim expression on his face. He didn't move or react until everyone had shuffled into place around the scene.

"A murder has taken place upon my property!" he said with a wail that caused me—along with half the room—to jump. "I don't know the man, yet he's here, in my den!"

Behind me, I heard Vivian Flowers mutter, "Oh boy," and had to stifle a laugh.

"Detectives," Oliver went on as he paced back and forth near the body, handkerchief in hand as he blotted his dry forehead. "I implore you to get to the bottom of this most heinous crime. My reputation counts on it."

Some shuffling of feet followed, and someone cleared their throat.

Oliver's pained expression faltered as he tried not to

scowl. Behind him, Lydia made a motion with her hand, like a duck quacking.

"What can you tell us about what happened?" Becca Garrison asked. She shot Buchannan a dirty look and rubbed at her side, telling me he'd likely elbowed her into speaking.

Oliver recoiled as if she'd slapped him. "Why, nothing. Nothing at all. I wasn't here until but an hour before you arrived. I just returned from Hollywood, where I was directing my latest blockbuster feature."

A snort from someone in the group earned all of us a glare.

Oliver took a moment to compose himself before going on. "I came directly here from the airport. You can check with my driver. When I got home, I didn't enter the den right away, but when I did, I found this man just like this."

"Do you know him?" This from Austin.

"I've never seen him in my life," Oliver said, before giving us a sly smile. "Though I do recall overhearing a tale about a missing golden comb while I was enjoying a hot beverage after my flight. And look!" He pointed at the golden comb, as if we hadn't already seen it the night before, "There it is! Could this man be the thief? Or a victim of the real culprit?"

I opened my mouth to ask Oliver how he managed to have a drink after his flight when he'd just said he'd come straight home, but decided against it. It wasn't worth the glare I knew I'd receive.

Oliver paced twice more before his entire demeanor changed. He took a deep breath, closed his eyes, and made a hand gesture that I assumed meant he was now the ghost he'd spoken of last night. The scene was over. He stepped back, away from the body. Lydia stepped forward to take his place.

"Good morning, everyone," she said. "Think of this area here as part of the scene, the story, but the rest of the building is considered home base. You'll find nothing else pertaining to the mystery on the property. Once you've had a look at poor Link here, you may leave and start your search."

"You've all been given a number to text when you believe you've solved the mystery," Richie said. "A simple 'we know what happened' will suffice."

"After you do that, return here, and Mr. Quick will hear your solution," Lydia added. "Please do so in character."

"If a team is successful," Richie added, "the game ends, and the other competitors will be notified through text."

"Game?" Oliver's head snapped up, eyes blazing as he turned them on his assistant. "Did you just call my production a *game*?"

Richie paled. "I'm sorry, Mr. Quick. I misspoke."

Oliver was just about quivering in anger. "Do you realize the magnitude of your misspeak? There should be cameras here! News crews. This is the production of the century. It's nothing like anything this little Podunk town has ever seen!"

Rita made a displeased sound but, like the rest of us, didn't otherwise interrupt.

Oliver took a step toward Richie. "Do not belittle what I've accomplished here by calling it a game. These people"—he flung a hand toward us—"are a part of something that will be with them for the rest of their lives. They are honored, as you should be."

"I am!" Richie said. "I'm sorry, Mr. Quick, I wasn't thinking."

Oliver took a deep breath, made one of those hand gestures he was fond of, and closed his eyes, as if he were centering himself. He took a breath and said, "You are forgiven this time," before he stepped back into his role as ghost.

There was a beat of silence, in which Richie kept his head down and no one spoke. Then, into the silence, Lydia clapped her hands and said, "You may begin!"

The room erupted with motion. Teams huddled together, mostly around Link, the poor actor who was still playing dead in the middle of the room, though Drew, Tony, and Curtis headed straight for the door, apparently having seen all they needed from the scene.

Most of the evidence was snatched from the floor as teams started pawing over it. Buchannan immediately scoffed, and I heard him mutter, "This isn't how a proper investigation is conducted," before he knelt and picked up the empty cloth sack. He sniffed it, made a face, and dropped it back onto the floor.

"Where do we start?" Rita asked. She was practically dancing in her excitement. "I'm not sure what to make of our evidence. It doesn't seem to go together, if you know what I mean?"

"What about a hair salon?" Wendy asked, pointing at the comb, which Sara Huffington had picked up and hastily put down with a disgusted expression that made me wonder if she'd found a stray hair on it.

"It's a good thought," Rita said. "If a golden comb

was stolen, it was likely from a place like that. There's Fern's Perms. And what's the name of that place on the other side of town? Krissy?"

I jerked at the sound of my name. "What?"

Rita heaved a sigh. "Weren't you listening?"

"I was," I said. "But I was thinking."

Rita's eyes lit up as she eased closer. "What were you thinking, dear? You have a sixth sense when it comes to this sort of thing."

I didn't know about that, but I did have an idea.

And maybe a smidge of an ulterior motive.

"Oliver mentioned something about drinking a hot beverage when he heard about the comb, right?" I asked, to two nods. I left out the bit where it didn't fit with his original premise since I was pretty sure it was an oversight on his part, not a clue. "Doesn't that seem like a good place to start?"

As I spoke, the Cherry Valley team headed for the door, along with Buchannan's team, leaving three teams behind: Scott's, the team of doctors, and mine.

Rita's eyes sparkled as she smiled. "You're thinking we might find a clue there, that what Oliver said was a clue in itself."

Wendy glanced from Rita to me. "Where are you talking about?"

"Someplace I'm *very* familiar with," I said.

And then, before we could waste any more time, we headed for the door.

I'm not sure what I expected, but Death by Coffee looked just like it always did. A handful of customers were seated at the downstairs tables, drinking coffee or enjoying a freshly baked pastry. Up the short flight of stairs, a pair of women were browsing the bookshelves, looking for their next read. Jeff Braun stood behind the upstairs counter, watching them as he waited to see if he would need to ring up a sale.

I also noted we were the only team that was there.

I led the way to the counter, where Claire "Pooky" Cooper was busy wiping down the coffee machines. They were all due for a full teardown and deep clean, but that would have to wait until after closing one day soon, preferably when my best friend and co-owner of the bookstore café, Vicki Lawyer, was around so we could catch up on the latest in each of our lives. It was strange how we ran a business together and yet saw each other so little these days.

"Hi, Pooky," I said. "How did opening go?"

"Good," she said. A petite blonde, Pooky stood no more than five feet tall, and that's with her shoes on. "It was busy, like always, but nothing we couldn't han-dle. Beth's in the back cleaning up." She leaned for-ward, propping her elbows on the counter. "How's the game-thing you're doing going?"

I made a face of mock horror. "Don't call it a game! The guy running it will freak out if he hears you say it." I glanced behind me. Rita and Wendy were scanning the room, as if looking for whatever clue had been hid-den inside. I turned back to Pooky. "You don't happen to know anything about it, do you?"

She smiled, shrugged. "If I did, I'm not supposed to say anything." She lowered her voice. "Though there is a man seated at the table near the window who has been all but itching to talk to someone. I bet you might learn a thing or two from him."

"Thanks," I said, turning and immediately spotting the man. I should have noticed him the moment I'd entered. He was wearing a pink, button-up shirt with a light blue sweater tied around his neck by the arms. White pants and black loafers without socks completed the outfit.

He looked about as out of place as a man could get.

I joined Rita and Wendy. "There," I said, subtly pointing at the man. "I think that's our clue."

"Him?" Rita asked. "Well, I'm not so sure about that. There could be something else. We should check the bottom of the tables and see if anything has been stuck there."

Having seen the underside of the tables, and knowing kids' penchant for sticking gum and other sticky substances under there, I didn't think that was such a good idea. "Let's talk to him first and see if he has anything to say," I said. "If he doesn't, we can consider checking under the tables."

"I agree," Wendy said. From her expression, she must have dealt with table gum at some point too.

Before we could make our way across the room, the door opened, and Scott entered with his team. He jerked to a stop, as if surprised to see us. Shari very nearly collided with him.

"Get your coffee if it's so important to you, so we can get moving," Austin said, pushing past them both. I noted he stuck out his elbow so that he bumped into Scott as he passed, nearly knocking the other man off his feet. No apologies before Austin's gaze landed on the guy with the sweater. "Over there." He started toward the man.

"Hurry," Shari told Scott, squeezing his arm. "Don't take it to heart. He'll get over it." She followed Austin over to the table.

"We'd best get over there," Rita said. "I don't want to miss anything."

Scott headed for the counter, and I made a snap decision. "I'll be there in a second. Go ahead and join the others."

"But what about the clue?" Wendy asked.

"You and Rita can fill me in on anything I miss."

"Come on, dear," Rita said, patting Wendy's arm. "She knows what she's doing." The implied, "She'd better," was as loud as a shout.

I wasn't positive it would amount to anything, but I did get the feeling that Scott might have some sort of inside knowledge on Oliver and this little production of his. Rumors are one thing, and from what I'd heard, Scott told some pretty tall tales.

But most rumors *did* contain some element of truth to them. Maybe Oliver didn't wear a blood-mask for superpowers or whatever it was Scott claimed it was for, but perhaps he *did* use some sort of seemingly mystical remedies for the same result. How that would help me with this little mystery production, I had no idea, but I'd learned over the years that sometimes simply talking to people had a way of revealing clues in the unlikeliest of places.

I hurried over to the counter, just as Scott ordered.

"I'll take a caramel macchiato," he said. "Hot. And put it in this mug, please." He handed over a metal to-go mug. "But microwave it first. The coffee, I mean. Not the mug."

"The coffee is already pretty hot," Pooky said, ringing him up.

"I don't doubt that. I just like it *really* hot, and I plan on sipping from it all day. It's a pretty good mug."

Pooky glanced at me as if to make sure it was okay. I nodded and sidled up to Scott. "It's nice to be out of the bed-and-breakfast," I said as casually as I could manage. "It was getting pretty tense in there."

Scott cleared his throat, glanced away. "Uh, yeah."

"What do you think about all of this?" I asked. "Oliver's production, I mean. Do you think it's going to be as big as he expects?"

"He sure thinks it will be," Scott said as the door opened and Lydia slipped inside. She glanced around the room, saw the two of us speaking, and stepped aside to wait. "He tends to believe everything he touches will turn to gold, especially his shows."

"Has he done something like this before?" I asked as Pooky finished making the macchiato. She considered the caramel drizzle, and like I hoped she would, she decided to wait until after she microwaved the coffee before adding it.

Scott eased a step away, shrugged a shoulder. "Not really, I suppose." He swallowed. "You're Krissy Hancock, right?"

My eyes widened in surprise. "I am. You've heard of me?"

His nod was jerky. He had to push his glasses back up on his nose when he spoke. "You're the murder-lady, the one who causes"—he cut off, as if realizing what he was saying, and that I might "murder-lady" him for mentioning it.

I tried not to take offense. "I've helped the police on murder investigations, yes." Though the police wished I wouldn't. Heck, even *I* wished dead bodies would stop dropping into my lap.

Not literally, of course. If that ever happened, I'd be done with this murder-lady stuff for good.

Pooky finished pouring the now–scalding hot macchiato into the mug, added the caramel drizzle, and sealed it all up. "Here you go," she said, handing it over to Scott.

"Keep the change." He dropped a ten on the counter, and without so much as a "goodbye" to me, he hurried toward the rest of his team. Before he reached them, Lydia stepped forward, whispered something into his ear, and handed him a folded piece of blue paper. He took it, stuffed it into his pocket without looking at it, and then joined everyone at the table with the pink-shirt guy, who, at this point, was animatedly telling a story that had Rita enraptured with her hands clasped before her face.

Lydia watched the group a moment, as if making sure everything was going to plan, before she slipped back out the door, affording me only the briefest of glances as she went.

"You should get back to it," Pooky said. "We've got everything handled here."

"You're probably right." Though it appeared as if the story was winding down. Pink-shirt's enthusiasm had waned, and he was leaning back in his chair so that it rocked on two legs.

I crossed the room in time to hear him say, "He had a crystal eye." His voice was so gruff, he sounded more like a TV kid's show pirate than a guy sitting in a coffee shop wearing a pink shirt and blue sweater tied around his neck. "And that's all I saw."

"Oh my Lordy Lou," Rita said as Scott and his team bolted for the door, as if hot on the heels of the next clue. "That was some story. It's a shame you missed it, Krissy. I'm not sure I've ever heard a better-told tale."

Pink-shirt grinned as he settled his chair back on all four feet.

"You can tell me all about it on the way," I said, before asking, "Do you think I cause the murders that happen around here? Like they're somehow my fault?"

"Now, who would put an idea like that into your head?" Rita asked. "Of course, you don't, dear."

"No," Wendy said before pausing. "What murders?"

I didn't know if I should be alarmed or relieved that Wendy didn't know about the murders—or my involvement in them—that had happened around Pine Hills over the last few years. Either she was oblivious, which didn't bode well for her deductive skills, or she was focusing less on the horrors of the world and more on the good things. I'd like to think it was the latter.

"We should get moving," Rita said, taking me by the arm. "I don't want the others to get too much of a head start."

We left Death by Coffee. Rita gave me the rundown on Pink-shirt's story as we climbed into my car and headed for our next destination.

4

You could say one thing for Oliver Quick's production: if nothing else, it was convoluted.

Rita, Wendy, and I left Death by Coffee and promptly spent the next two hours running around town, chasing leads that led to more leads, which led to even more. It was always obvious when our clue was one of his actors since they were usually lounging around, dressed oddly. It was like Oliver thought Pine Hills was a town full of self-absorbed yuppies. I supposed that was a good thing because it made those particular clues much easier to spot.

Sometimes, the objects we found were as obvious as the actors, but not always. A lollipop had been left in a shoe store of all places. If I hadn't noticed the blue-green color matched Link the Corpse's lips, we would have been at a loss. That led us to Phantastic Candies, where an amused Jules pointed us to a forty-year-old woman playing a candy-loving teen, who sent us to

Scream for Ice Cream, where we found a wig. That led us to Fern's Perms, where a blonde straight out of Barbie-land told us of rumors of something valuable being left near a tree that smelled of grease. That led us to the Banyon Tree just in time to run into Detective John Buchannan and his team.

"Following me, are you?" Buchannan asked, blocking the entrance to the diner, which, despite it being the next location for our clue, was okay by me. Judith Banyon, who owned the Banyon Tree, did not like me one bit and would chase me right out the door if she saw me. "I figured that was always the case."

Behind him, Lena gave a dramatic roll of her eyes, which caused me to smile. Buchannan wasn't amused.

"Laugh all you want, but I'm beating you at this thing," he said, leveling a finger at me. "Officer Dalton isn't around to help you. We'll see how you fare without his assistance."

I wanted to point out that my boyfriend, Officer Paul Dalton, never helped me. In fact, he often told me to stay out of police business and would hold things back from me, just to keep me from running around town chasing leads better left to him and the rest of the department.

Better sense prevailed, and I held my tongue. Rita, however, wasn't so inclined.

"We'll see about that," she said. "The way I see it, without Krissy here, we'd still have murderers running all over town. None of us would be safe."

Buchannan's lips thinned as he pressed them together, though he kept his glare on me instead of Rita.

The stare-down lasted a good couple of seconds before he stomped past me, to his car, with a barked "Let's go" to his team.

"He's going to rant about you all the way to our next stop," Lena said as she passed. "Which, admittedly, he's been doing since we started." She grinned. "I'll fill you in about it later."

Becca merely chuckled as the two women followed Buchannan to his car. Once they were all safely strapped in, he gunned the engine and shot out of the parking lot like he was chasing a real criminal, and not just the next clue in Oliver's production.

"Should you really talk to him like that?" Wendy asked when he was gone. "I mean, he's an authority figure."

"That's something you can learn for your writing, dear," Rita said, patting her on the arm. "The police are people just like everyone else. Some are bad. Some are good. And some of them need to be knocked down a peg or two lest their heads grow too big for their hats."

With that iota of wisdom, we went inside the Banyon Tree.

The diner wasn't too busy since it was just before the lunch rush, which would make our jobs easier. One quick look around the room told me there were no actors inside, but one of the other teams was. They were being served by one of my friends, Shannon Pardue, who looked haggard, as a single woman with a young baby to take care of on her own often does. She saw me enter, waved, and trudged her way to the back.

"Where should we start?" Rita asked, planting her

hands on her hips while she scoured the diner. "I don't see anything valuable. And I sure don't see anyone who might know a thing or two about what's going on."

"Outside?" Wendy asked, sounding uncertain. "We were told that it was *near* the tree. Not inside."

Rita nodded. "You know, that sounds right." She turned back to the door, then paused when I didn't follow. "Coming?"

"In a minute," I said. "I need to make a pit stop."

It took her a moment to get it, and when she did, she made a face. "Well, make it quick. I don't want to fall any further behind the others. If Detective Buchannan was already here and found what he was looking for, that puts him ahead of us." She tsked. "Come on, Wendy. Let's find this valuable object."

As they exited, I crossed the room toward the restrooms, which put me in line to pass by the table in which the Cherry Valley team were seated. Vivian and the others looked as relaxed as could be and in no hurry to continue with the search for clues. As I approached, Albert Elmore said something, which caused Vivian to laugh. Sara Huffington, the youngest of the trio, didn't look all that amused, though she did smile when Albert looked her way.

"Hey," I said, stopping at their table. "How's the hunt going?"

Vivian grunted. "I've had just about enough of this foolishness," she said. "All this running around, and for what?"

"It is kind of silly," Albert added. "Even for me." He ran a hand over his short hair. It was a new hairstyle for him, and honestly, it looked far better than when he'd tried to conceal his receding hairline with a horrible part that only pointed out that he was balding.

Sara made a face. She was dressed like a million bucks, which, from what I understood, she *was* worth. "We should have stayed home."

"I hope you win it," Vivian said, pointing at me. "But I'm not going to count on it. I heard the team run by that guy who was trying to cheat last night is flying right through without hardly stopping to look for clues. Makes you wonder if he has inside information."

"He might just be good at this sort of thing," Albert said, though it sounded like he didn't quite believe it.

"I'm pretty sure I saw him secretly talking to one of the assistants last night before we all went to bed," Sara said.

"Oh?" I asked. "Which one?"

"The guy, I think." She shrugged. "Though I suppose it might have been one of the other competitors. It was dark, and they were outside, so I didn't get a good look at either of them. I saw them through the window."

I assumed it must have happened while I was feeding Misfit, since she'd said it was before everyone went to bed.

"Either way, it made one of the other guys pretty upset," Vivian said.

"Which other guy?" I asked.

"The rude one who likes to talk about everyone." Vivian looked to Albert, who spread his hands and shook his head: he didn't know.

Sara was the one who answered. "Scott what's-his-face. His team was here when we got here. He was having an argument with one of his teammates. Dustin?"

"Austin," I supplied, before asking. "Was it about Drew?"

A trio of blank stares met me.

"The guy who tried to cheat."

"A little," Vivian said. "Scott what's-his-face was insisting he needed to go somewhere that the others didn't want to go. Dustin-Austin kept saying that the Drew fellow was headed to the nameless inn, which is obviously that hotel on the edge of town, in case you need the clue. Scott said he wasn't going there, that he had to go to this other place first, and he needed to do it without the others. He claimed that with the other guy—Drew, I suppose his name was—cheating, it didn't matter anyway. The woman just stood by, looking helpless, before the Scott character stomped off into the restrooms. That's when the other two left."

"Left? As in left him?" I asked.

Vivian shrugged, while Sara answered. "I think so. I'm pretty sure I saw them drive off as we were being seated."

I looked outside to see Rita standing in the parking lot, tapping her foot. Wendy was pacing at her side. "Actually, I need to use the restroom myself. If I take much longer, my team might leave *me*."

"You do that," Vivian said, taking a sip of iced tea. "I'm going to enjoy a nice meal and perhaps go back to our room to take a nap. Oliver Stick-Up-His-Butt can whine about it all he wants, but I think I'm done."

"I'm with you there," Albert said, shooting a side-eyed glance at Sara. "A nap sounds fantastic, actually."

"I'm glad I ran into you all," I said. "We need to get together soon and catch up."

"That we do," Vivian said.

I started to turn away, but Sara stopped me with, "You'll have to use the men's room. The women's is out of order."

Sure enough, a yellow sign hung on the door, which was propped open with one of those big yellow cones. "Thanks," I said, already dreading it as I headed for the men's restroom. I've seen what a men's room could look like, especially around the urinals, but here, the floors were dry and as clean as a restroom floor could get. I was also glad to see there was no one inside, which meant no awkward eye contact on my way to a stall.

I quickly did my business, and as I went to flush, I noticed something on the floor, poking out from behind the toilet.

I have a rule about not touching anything left in a public restroom, especially something tossed onto the floor. It's gross, and you didn't know where that item had been or what it was used for before being discarded.

But this wasn't just any random piece of paper. It was blue. I didn't see blue paper all that often.

Yet, earlier that day, I had.

Before I could change my mind, I snatched up the paper and smoothed it out, thankful it was dry and unsmudged. Scott, who, according to Vivian, had entered the restroom earlier, must have dropped it. Either he'd tried to flush it and missed, or he'd dropped it accidentally. The note was handwritten and short, written in a tight, clipped hand that looked nothing like what I imagined Lydia's handwriting would look like.

1308 Hazelwood. 10 a.m. Emergency.

It wasn't signed, but since Lydia had been the one who'd handed it to Scott, I assumed it was from her. I supposed it could have been from Oliver, but why would he want to talk to Scott during the investigation when Oliver was supposed to be an uninvolved ghost?

Unless this whole thing is fixed.

The more I heard, the more I was starting to think that it very well might be.

I stuffed the page into my pocket and hurried out of the Banyon Tree to the waiting Rita and Wendy.

"Well, it's about time!" Rita said as soon as she saw me. "I was about to send Wendy in to make sure you hadn't fallen in. We've got to go to—"

"1308 Hazelwood Lane," I cut in. "I'll explain on the way."

"It's kind of out of the way, isn't it?" Rita asked as we pulled up to 1308 Hazelwood Lane, which was tucked away in a heavily wooded portion of town. Abandoned machinery sat next to a stack of logs. Stumps were still poking out of the ground nearby, though at this point, the area was looking overgrown. A small, abandoned trailer sat in a clearing.

"I signed the petition to get this to stop," Wendy said, scowling at the ugly yellow machines. "They planned on cutting down every last tree."

"Looks like it worked," I said, shutting off the engine. Silence settled on the area, giving it something of an eerie vibe, despite it being bright and sunny. No other houses could be seen, just the yawning, sightless eyes of the empty trailer, which I assumed had been converted into an office for the logging company before it had been shut down.

"The company is still fighting us about it," Wendy said. "But we're not going to give up. There's no reason for them to come in and clear-cut. If they'd done it right—taken a little, replanted for what they took—it wouldn't have been a problem. It's not like they planned on building anything out here after they cleared it out."

We piled out of my vehicle. The drive had been longer than I'd expected, so if this didn't pan out, I'd just ended any chance of us finishing first. My gut said that this was important, that Lydia wouldn't have pulled Scott away from his team—by Oliver's say or otherwise—without a good reason.

"Where should we start?" Rita asked, rubbing at her arms. "It's a smidge cold out here, isn't it?"

That it was. "I'm not sure," I said. "All the note gave was an address and that it was an emergency."

"That doesn't sound like a clue," Wendy asked. "I mean, couldn't the note have been about something else?"

"It might have been," I admitted. "But why send Scott out here, taking him away from the investigation, if it wasn't important? Why not wait until afterward or talk to him privately in town where he could get right back to it once they were done?"

"You're thinking that this place might hold a clue?" Rita asked. "Like an important one that would allow him to solve the case before anyone else?"

"I wish I knew," I said. "There's only one way to find out." My eyes fell on the trailer. "And one place to look."

There weren't any signs that anyone had been there, at least obvious ones. There were a few scattered pieces of trash, but it looked like leftovers from when the tree-cutters were here, not remnants of kids come to party or campers looking for an out-of-the-way place to relax.

"Well, it's unlocked," Rita said, tugging on the door. It swung open with a faint creak. Inside, a small office space had been set up. The desk was cheap and wooden. The office chair was one of those small, wheeled ones that often felt like they were about to tip over the moment you tried to roll backward. A filing cabinet sat in the corner, the drawers open and seemingly empty. There were a series of pegs screwed into the wall, with only one of them holding a hard hat. A pair of closed doors down a short hallway appeared to lead to the only other rooms in the place.

We entered, and Rita immediately started waving a hand in front of her face.

"Whew. It smells in here."

I sniffed and regretted it. It *did* smell, but not in a musty, unused building sort of way. The scent was familiar, but sour. Like someone had left an open drink out for too long.

"Let's make this quick," I said. No one was here now, and I was beginning to worry that no one had been there at all. There was a chance that Scott had met with Lydia, or whoever the note was really from, outside, spoken for a few minutes, and driven off. That would mean we'd find no clues. No actors. Nothing.

"I'll check down there," Wendy said, indicating the hall and one of the closed doors beyond.

"I've got the filing cabinet," Rita said. "Maybe something's taped inside one of the drawers."

I settled on the hard hat and the desk, which had a single drawer. The hard hat had nothing tucked inside it, only a single long red hair caught in the adjustable band. The desk was likewise empty of everything but a small, startled spider that scurried for the dark corner in the back of the drawer when I opened it.

"Nothing," Rita said, after a quick look into the filing cabinet.

Wendy hadn't returned from the room down the hall, so Rita and I headed that way with a cursory peek inside what amounted to a tiny bathroom that held a lone, lost paper-towel roll and nothing else. We found Wendy crouching over something—or should I say, *someone*—on the floor that had my heart doing a series of rapid hiccups.

"What did you find?" Rita asked.

"I'm not sure," Wendy said. "He's pretty good." She lifted the man's hand and opened it, but he wasn't holding anything. She let his arm fall to the floor with a heavy thump. "He hasn't moved since I came in."

"Are there any clues?" Rita asked, joining her. "I can't believe they tried to cheat like this. I bet the solution to the whole mystery is here." She paused. "What *is* that?"

"Coffee, I think."

I swallowed a lump the size of my fist. I could place the smell now. Coffee and caramel and milk. "Who is it?" I asked. My feet were rooted in place, and no matter how hard I tried, I couldn't make myself step into the room to see past Wendy and Rita.

"One of the actors." Wendy paused. "I think it is, anyway?"

"Is there anything in his pockets?" Rita asked. "I hope another team didn't take the clue. We're not supposed to, though I suppose if they tried, our dead man here would have stopped them."

"Ew. I don't want to stick my hands in his pockets," Wendy said, before adding to the downed man, "No offense."

"Do you think we're supposed to put all the clues together?" Rita asked, patting the man's shirt pocket. "So far, it doesn't really make sense, does it? Just leads us from one place to the next. Maybe if we set them all out, we'll see a pattern."

Finally, my legs started working again. I crept into the room and moved so I could look down on the man they were busy frisking.

As soon as I did, my heart sank.

"Don't touch him," I said, my voice coming out as a whisper.

"What was that?" Rita asked, glancing up from her crouch at me. "Did you say something, dear?"

"Don't touch him," I repeated, this time louder. "That's not an actor." The man's head was turned to the side, and a coffee-wet towel had been draped over his face so you couldn't see his features, but I knew who it was. The empty to-go coffee mug lying next to his hand told me everything I needed to know. "It's Scott. And I'm pretty sure this isn't part of the game."

5

I stood on a stump a few yards away from the trailer-turned-office-turned-murder scene, phone raised high into the air.

Zero bars. No amount of waving my phone around or repositioning changed that fact.

Only five minutes had passed since I'd realized the body in the room was Scott Flanagan and not part of Oliver's production. I'd spent nearly the entirety of the time since then trying to get a signal so I could call the police, but to no avail.

As I hopped from the stump, Rita approached. "Anything?"

"No." I pocketed my phone and nodded toward my car, where Wendy was huddled in the back seat. "How is she?"

"Still freaking out," Rita said. "But calmer. She emptied an entire bottle of hand sanitizer and still wants more."

I could only imagine. "Finding a body is never easy."

I shivered and looked around. Nothing but trees, though my mind supplied killers behind each and every one of them. "We're going to have to leave so we can contact the police. We're not calling them from here."

"Should we really leave that poor man in there alone?" Rita asked. "What if someone else shows up looking for clues? Or what if the killer comes back to hide evidence? I couldn't in good conscience leave and let something like that happen."

I frowned. She was right. If we left, who knew what would happen while we were gone. It wasn't like there were cameras or neighbors to keep watch. But if we stayed, no one would know about the murder—and I was positive it was a murder. There hadn't been much in the way of blood, at least visible, but there were indicators that said this wasn't an accident.

"One of us needs to stay behind," I said.

Rita's eyes widened. "Well, I don't know about that. It's bad enough the three of us were tromping around in there with who knows who watching." Like me, Rita looked to the trees as if they were hiding a killer or two. "What chance would one of us have against a killer?"

"Then two of us stay," I said. "The other just needs to drive far enough down the road to get a cell signal so they can call the police. Then—"

Before I could finish the thought, a car pulled in behind my Escape, drawing our attention. Three doors opened and Detective Buchannan, Officer Garrison, and Lena stepped out.

Relief washed through me as I all but ran over to them. Rita followed behind at a more leisurely pace.

"I'm glad you're here," I said. "Did Wendy manage to get a call to go through to you?"

Buchannan's brow furrowed. "No one called me." He tucked his thumbs into his belt as he looked around. "Seems a bit out of the way, doesn't it?"

"No one called you?" I asked. "Then how did you know about the body?"

"What body?" Becca asked at the same time Buchannan said, "I followed the trail."

My hand went to my front pants pocket, and sure enough, the crumpled blue note was still there where I'd tucked it. If Buchannan was simply following the trail, did that mean this location was part of Oliver's production? If that was the case, it appeared more and more likely that Lydia had been helping Scott cheat.

But if so, why was he now dead? Seemed like a pretty crummy way of helping someone.

"Scott Flanagan's body," I said. "He's in there." I pointed to the trailer. "Someone killed him and left him inside."

Lena's hand went to her mouth, and she took a step back, while Officer Garrison's eyes went hard as she shifted into cop mode.

Buchannan, on the other hand, looked skeptical. "Are you trying to mislead me, Ms. Hancock?"

"Mislead you?" I was confused for a second before I realized what he was thinking. "This isn't part of the game. Someone's really dead in there!"

"Uh-huh." He started for the trailer, moving slowly, unconcerned. "We'll see about that."

"Tell me what happened," Becca said, as Buchannan headed inside.

I took a centering breath before I explained as best I could. I told her about seeing Lydia hand Scott the note, about finding it in the Banyon Tree men's room later and following the address to here, where Wendy found Scott's body. As I spoke, Wendy's pale face appeared in the window of my Escape, eyes wide, unfocused, before she slipped back down into her seat.

"You touched the body?" Becca asked, frowning.

"Only a little," Rita said from next to me. "Wendy didn't know it was a real live corpse." She paused. "Well, not live, I suppose. She thought it was part of the mystery and was looking for clues on him. I helped her search a little bit, and let me tell you, I knew something wasn't right the moment I stepped into the room. I just couldn't put my finger on it until Krissy pointed it out to us. She has a sixth sense about these things, don't you, dear?"

"I guess." I shuddered, trying vainly to get the image of poor Scott lying motionless on the floor, Wendy and Rita kneeling above him, out of my head. "He wasn't moved much. Wendy checked his hand, and Rita looked in his pockets. That's about it."

Becca looked at Rita. "Did you find anything?"

"In his pockets? Not a thing. Not even a wallet. Do you think it could have been a robbery?" She frowned. "Well, that doesn't make much sense, does it? Who would come all the way out here just to steal a man's wallet?"

The trailer door banged open, and Buchannan stormed out. "There's a dead man in there."

"That's what I tried to tell you!"

He scowled at me as he strode over to us. "And you didn't think to call anyone?"

From behind Becca, Lena said, "There's no service here." She pocketed her phone with a sigh. "I tried to call it in, but I can't get a signal."

"We were about to send someone down the road so they could call," I said. "But you showed up, so . . ."

"Did you see anyone else?" Becca asked. "Another car leaving the scene, perhaps?"

"No one." I glanced at Rita, who shook her head. "But since Lydia was the one who gave Scott the note, I assume she was here at some point." Before or after the murder? That was the question.

"Unless someone else gave her the note to pass along to that poor man," Rita said. "She doesn't seem like the type to kill anyone."

I agreed with her to a point, but if there was one thing I've learned over the last few years, it was you didn't count anyone out just because they didn't seem the type to commit murder. Push someone far enough, and, well . . .

Buchannan huffed and then marched past us. "Wait here. I'll make the call." He paused, hand on his car door. "No one is to leave or go in to look at or mess with the body. Understand? That goes double for you, Ms. Hancock." He glared at me long enough for it to sink in, and then he slid into the driver's seat, slammed the door, and sped off.

"Looks like we're waiting," Becca said, scowling after him. Once he was gone, she motioned to my vehicle. "Let's wait in there, where it's warm. I'll take everyone's statement so John doesn't have to do it when he gets back."

We piled into my Escape. Rita and Lena slid in on either side of Wendy, which made it a little cramped, but Wendy appeared to appreciate their nearness. I took the driver's seat, while Becca sat in the passenger's seat beside me. I didn't start the car, but it was warmer inside without the cool breeze.

"All right," Becca said with a heavy sigh, "we're going to do this one at a time. Only jump in if you have something significant to say. Otherwise, I'll get to each of you in turn."

"Shouldn't you take us somewhere separately?" Rita asked. "To make sure our stories match up."

"I don't think that will be necessary," Becca said with a faint smile. "Now, who wants to start?"

I went first, but didn't have much to contribute outside of what I'd already said. I'd seen no clues that Scott or anyone else had been there before us. I'd seen no cars, no tracks, no footprints. It was as if he'd dropped out of the sky, directly into that back room.

Rita, likewise, didn't have much to say, though she took her time in telling it. I had to speak up and clarify some of her embellishments and make sure Officer Garrison understood that much of what Rita had to say was speculation, rather than fact. Having dealt with Rita before, she got it.

Then it was Wendy's turn to talk. It came out slowly, haltingly. She was clearly in shock, and likely would be until she'd had a chance to get away from all of this. Lena had taken her hand, and from the way she sucked in a breath, Wendy was squeezing it with everything she had.

"I touched him," Wendy said as her story wound down. "I can still feel his hand." She squeezed harder, which caused Lena to wince.

"It's all right, dear." Rita patted her shoulder. "You couldn't have known. None of us did."

"What if I ruined evidence? Like it rubbed off on me somehow?"

"I'm sure that didn't happen," Rita said, looking to Becca, as if for confirmation.

"But what if it did?" Wendy started breathing faster. "The killer might get away because of *me*. I don't know if I could live with myself if I contaminated the evidence."

Buchannan returned then. He parked beside us, flew out of his car, steam practically shooting out of his ears. He took an angry step toward the trailer and about jumped out of his shoes when Becca knocked on the passenger-side window before she opened the door and stepped out to confer with him.

"I guess I should join them," Lena said, extracting her hand from Wendy's. She rubbed at it before reaching for the door "I wanted to get some experience, but not like this."

"You'll be fine, dear," Rita said.

Lena climbed out and walked over to join Buchannan and Becca, who'd moved to stand at the trailer door, as if guarding it from further intrusion. Her step was hesitant, but as she neared, Buchannan waved her over and barked something at her. She nodded and jogged back toward my car. She got in next to me.

"Detective Buchannan wants us to go back to the bed-and-breakfast and tell Mr. Quick to have everyone gather there and wait for him. That includes all the actors, along with the investigators and Oliver's assistants."

"I'm not sure he's going to listen to us," I said, though I did start the car.

"Probably not," Lena said. "But if he doesn't, he'll have an angry Detective Buchannan to deal with."

And that's something none of us wanted.

"This is an outrage!" Oliver paced the room, his face a deep shade of crimson. "This is a concerted attempt at ruining my vision. I demand that we be released immediately!"

No one contradicted him or tried to placate him. When I'd come in and asked him to text everyone and have them gather at Ted and Bettfast, he'd flat out refused. Even when I'd told him—with Lena's assistance—that Scott was dead, he didn't want to do it, claiming I was attempting to ruin him, like I'd killed Scott myself just to spite him.

Thankfully, someone else had taken it upon themself to contact the other teams and actors. Before long, everyone was packed into the bed-and-breakfast, muttering to one another. A quick head count told me the only people missing were Officer Garrison and Detective Buchannan. And Scott, of course.

"Who do you think did it?" Rita asked, as Oliver continued to rant about the injustice of it all. "Someone here?"

I'd been watching everyone arrive, hoping to catch someone acting guilty, but so far, no one had. "I'm not sure." Vivian and the Cherry Valley team looked distressed, but I doubted they had anything to do with the murder. The same went for the local doctors and my own team. There was no way Wendy had killed Scott while Rita and I had been searching the office area, though I'm sure Buchannan would ask her, just to be certain.

But the Levington teams? Austin looked angry, while Shari was as pale and appeared as distraught as Wendy. Drew and his team looked annoyed more than anything. The actors, many of whom I knew only by sight, were scattered around the room in small groups, talking among themselves in a way that felt too casual considering a murder had taken place. I knew none of their names, only the made-up ones they'd given us during their performances.

That left Lydia and Richie. Neither were in the main room now, having both gone to the back once the news about Scott had broken. I assumed one of them had texted the groups behind Oliver's back, but which one, I couldn't be certain.

Near the office, Robert was chewing on a thumbnail, frowning. He was annoying, but not a killer, so he wasn't a suspect in my book. At the other end of the room, Lena was comforting a still distraught Wendy. The young woman might be interested in writing mysteries, often with murders in them, but a real-life murder was too much for her.

Honestly, I couldn't blame her for that.

"When are the police going to get here?" Oliver shouted. "We've been waiting a half an hour."

"Would you shut up, Oliver?" Shari snapped. "Scott's dead. Think about someone other than yourself for once."

"And why should that matter?" Oliver flung his arms wide. "Is the sky falling? Will we be safer in here, rather than out there, moving forward with our lives? Do you think Scott would want us to stop on his account?"

Shari took a step toward him. "You know what, Oliver"—her voice seethed with unabated anger and hatred—"I've had just about enough of you. You've always been an a—"

Austin popped up from where he'd been sitting against the wall. "All right, Shari. Let's not make things worse." He put an arm around her shoulder and led her away before she could finish what she'd been about to say.

"He got what was coming to him," Drew said, which earned him a smack on the arm from Tony. "What? He did. The guy was always running his mouth."

"Yeah, but to kill him for it?" Curtis shook his head. "It's not right."

The door opened, and Detective Buchannan finally entered, expression grim. He took in the gathering, nodded once to himself, and headed for the center of the room.

"You need to let us continue with the production," Oliver said before Buchannan could speak. "You can't allow this inconvenience to ruin my hard work. Not after everything I've put into it." He paused. "Everything we've done to make this event a success."

"I think I'm going to have to agree with that woman," Rita whispered to me. "He's not a very nice man at all."

"Everyone," Buchannan said, raising his hands, ignoring Oliver. "I need everyone's attention."

The room fell silent, and that included Oliver, though he made sure everyone saw how offended he was at being ignored. He crossed his arms, blinked his eyes rapidly, as if moments from tears, and stepped back, away from Buchannan.

"My name is Detective John Buchannan. I'm going to be conducting interviews in private." He motioned toward the closed office door. "We're going to go one by one, and then I'll release you to your rooms." His eyes fell on Oliver. "This little play-murder mystery is over."

"Now wait one minute—" Oliver started, but a glare from Buchannan silenced him.

"I don't know why you're going to make us suffer through this," Drew said. "Everyone knows who did it."

"Really?" Vivian said, planting her hands on her hips. "And why don't you tell us and save the good policeman here the trouble?"

"He couldn't stop blabbing about everyone," Drew said. "Think about what he said last night. Oliver doesn't like it when anyone talks about him, and Scott did just that. Now look at what happened to him! It's not hard to put two and two together here."

"I had nothing to do with that young man's death," Oliver said, hand going to his chest, over his heart, as if wounded. "I've been here the entire time. I couldn't have done it." He looked around the room, as if searching for someone to corroborate his story. "You! You were here." He pointed at Robert, who flushed when half the room's eyes fell on him.

"I wasn't really watching," he said. "I mean, I guess he could have been here. I never saw him leave or anything."

Not exactly the ringing endorsement Oliver was hoping for.

"Let's not discuss it out here," Buchannan snapped. "I don't want any speculation or any wild guesses. I'm here for facts, and I expect you to give them to me clearly and concisely." He glared around the room. *"Privately."*

A general murmuring followed, a lot of it consisting of everything Buchannan didn't want to hear. He let it go on for a few moments before he cleared his throat and spoke up again.

"Those I've already spoken to are free to leave." Buchannan's gaze landed on me. "As in, go home, Ms. Hancock. Ms. Jablonski." His voice softened. "Ms. Wilcox. From what I understand, Officer Garrison has already taken your statements." He looked to where Lena was still consoling Wendy. "I could use your assistance, Ms. Allison." He paused. *"Deputy* Allison."

Lena's eyes widened as she stood. "I, uh, should I? I mean, this is a real crime."

"I need someone to keep the peace while I'm conducting interviews," Buchannan said. "At least until other officers arrive." He looked at me, frowned. "You're still here? Go."

"It had to have been them!" one of the actors shouted, pointing at Shari and Austin. "They were his team-mates."

"I saw them arguing." This from another actor. "They got rid of him because of it."

The room erupted as everyone started shouting at once. I took it as my cue to leave.

Rita followed me from the bed-and-breakfast, arm around Wendy, who looked lost and scared, as Lena's voice rose above the crowd in a vain attempt to get everyone to quiet down. She was going to have her hands full, but I did think it would be good experience for her.

"What are you going to do?" Rita asked when we were in the parking lot, standing beside our cars. I could still hear the commotion from inside, but at least out here it was muffled.

"Me?" I asked. "I'm going to go home, call Paul, and let the police take care of everything."

Wendy climbed into her car and put her head into her hands. She looked so vulnerable, I found myself taking a step toward her, but Rita waved me off.

"Go," she said. "Call that policeman boyfriend of yours. Maybe the two of you will come up with some-thing that will end this thing before it gets worse. I'll sit with her for a little while."

I hesitated, and then nodded. Rita might be a gossip who often poked her nose into everyone's business, but she was also a good friend. She knew Wendy better than I did and might know what to say to her that would break her out of her funk.

Not that I thought it would be that easy. You didn't just shake off finding a body, no matter how mentally strong you were.

"Thanks, Rita," I said. "I'll check in with her tomorrow."

"You do that, dear." She made for Wendy's passenger-side door. Her last words were spoken quietly, but I heard them nonetheless. "I have a feeling she'll be needing it."

6

"Someone's been murdered?"

I'd just walked through the door to Phantastic Candies when Jules rounded the counter to take my hands. Word about Scott's murder had spread quickly, as news usually does in Pine Hills.

"It appears that way," I said.

He clucked his tongue as he squeezed and released my hands. "This sort of thing seems to be happening more and more around here as of late."

"It does." And I was beginning to wonder if I were somehow responsible. Maybe Scott had been right and I was the murder-lady.

Jules sighed and reached into his bright red slacks for his keys. He removed my house key and dropped it into my hand without having to be asked. "I hope this one is solved quickly. There's more than enough drama going on around town right now without adding a prolonged murder investigation to it."

Despite myself, my interest was piqued. "What kind of drama?"

"You haven't heard?" Jules sounded genuinely surprised. "There was some sort of hubbub down at the community theatre earlier today. From what I gather, the police had to be called to keep it from getting out of hand." He paused. "Though I did hear this from Georgina McCully when she stopped in for her weekly licorice supply, so take that last bit with a grain of salt. You know how she can be."

I knew all right. Georgina was one of Rita's gossip buddies, and while they didn't outright lie, they did love to talk. That meant they often spread unsubstantiated rumors without bothering to check on their validity. "Really?" I'd gone past the theatre multiple times as I ran all over town with Rita and Wendy, and we hadn't seen or heard anything. "Do you know what it was about?"

Jules shook his head. "I only know what Georgina told me. She said that it got loud, but didn't say if that meant people were shouting or if it was just one guy banging on trash cans. I don't know if anyone was arrested or if, once the police had showed up, it calmed down. Georgina says she left as soon as the first badge appeared, as if she was worried they might arrest *her*." He laughed.

I managed to smile, but I was concerned. My best friend and co-owner of Death by Coffee, Vicki Lawyer, was a member of the community theatre. She hadn't dedicated her life to acting, like her parents had, but she did enjoy it. If something were to cause the theatre to shut down, like the last one had, I'm not sure what she would do.

I made a mental note to call Vicki as soon as I was able.

"I'd better get home and check on Misfit," I said, returning my key to its rightful place on my key ring. "He's probably torn the house apart by now."

"It was still in one piece when I checked in on him this morning. Mostly." He smiled. "There might have been an accident involving a stack of puzzle books and a bag of treats, but I cleaned it up."

"Thanks." A bag of treats and a few puzzle books were nothing. Misfit had a tendency to get into *everything* if left on his own for too long, especially overnight. "I'll have to find a way to pay you back. Are you sure you won't let me pay you?"

Jules waved me off. "Don't even think about it. It was my pleasure. And besides, I owe *you* for the missing key. I still haven't figured out where I put it."

"It'll turn up." Though if it didn't, I'd need to make sure to get a copy made. And maybe change the locks. I didn't think Jules or Lance would break into my house, but with how my luck usually went, someone had stolen the key and was planning on raiding my place. "I'll talk to you later."

"Tell Misfit I said hello."

"I'll do that."

I left Phantastic Candies and returned to my car. I hadn't lied when I said I wanted to get home to Misfit, but at the same time, I was curious about what had happened at the theatre. I couldn't help but wonder if it had something to do with Oliver's production. He *had* replaced the local actors with those from Levington, so there could have been a protest. I doubted Oliver would have sat back and done nothing if that was the case. I could see him standing on the sidewalk, screaming at everyone who passed to boycott the local theatre and to come see him in whatever production he planned next instead.

Okay, maybe I was exaggerating a bit, but I didn't think by much.

Not sure what I expected to find so long after the fact, I drove over to the community theatre and parked in the side parking lot. There were no others cars there, and the doors to the theatre itself were closed. There were no signs that anything had happened either: no graffiti or trash on the ground. No busted windows or crime-scene tape.

I drummed my fingers on the wheel, thinking. No, nothing appeared to be out of place, but that didn't mean everything was okay. If the police had been called, someone was in trouble. Someone from the theatre? Oliver himself?

There was one easy way to find out.

I used my car's touchscreen, which was connected to my phone, to make a call. It made me feel like I was living in the far future. Considering I could still remember what it was like to live without a cellphone, this seemed high-tech. The phone rang just long enough that I was afraid that maybe someone *had* been arrested when Vicki answered.

"Hey, Krissy." Even though my car's speakers made her sound far away and tinny, she sounded distracted. "What's up?"

"Hey, Vicki. Not much." I hesitated, then just bar-reled ahead. "I heard something happened down at the theatre today. Do you know anything about that, by chance?"

There was a long pause before she sighed and said, "Yeah, a little."

I waited a heartbeat for her to go on, and when she didn't, I pressed. "A little?"

Another long pause followed. In the background, I could hear rustling. Finally, she said, "I know what it was about, but that's it. Where are you?"

I looked at the theatre, and for a reason I couldn't quite fathom, I decided against telling her that I was sitting in the lot. "In my car. Why?"

"Would you mind stopping by? I'm at home and could use a break."

"Sure." A break from what? I had no idea. "Is Mason there?"

She snorted. "I wish." There was a pause, accompa-nied by more rustling. "I'll tell you all about the drama in the drama department when you get here."

"All right." My mind started to ease. If she was able to joke, whatever it was couldn't be all that bad. "I should be there in fifteen minutes."

"Great. I'll see you then."

"See ya."

We clicked off, and with one last lingering look at the theatre, I was on my way.

Vicki led me into the living room when I arrived. There was a domestic feel to the room, but I don't mean that in a bad way. There was a happy, lived-in vibe that made the house feel like a home, and not a set piece. There was a small cabinet of old knickknacks that once had belonged to Vicki's late mother-in-law and that were of the do-not-touch variety. A book with a torn cover that had been taped back on sat on a stand next to the recliner. A blanket that had been balled up and tossed to the end of the couch looked well-loved and was, as expected, covered in black and white cat hair. A cat tower sat near the window. Its wound-rope post was shredded to the point that it was sagging from the wood.

"Sorry about the mess," Vicki said, dropping onto the couch next to the blanket. She had a streak of dust across her forehead, which did little to mar her actress-quality good looks. "We've been going through the closets upstairs in the hope of getting rid of a few things. I swear, Mason is a pack rat. I kicked him out of the house for a few hours so I could work on it by myself, because if he was here, he'd find a reason to keep *everything*."

I laughed. "This is nothing," I said, motioning toward the fur-coated blanket. "You've seen my house."

Vicki smiled. "Life with cats."

That was all that was needed to be said.

"Where is Trouble anyway?" I asked, looking around for the black-and-white cat, who could often be found upstairs, prowling the books at Death by Coffee. Because of Oliver's production and the extra traffic the bookstore café might have seen, Vicki had decided it was best to keep him at home. Trouble had never tried to escape before, but it was best not to risk it.

"He's upstairs," she said, jerking a thumb toward the stairwell behind her. "When you called, I was trying to drag a couple of old suitcases out to the trash, but he decided they worked better as cat beds. He's managed to sprawl himself across the two of them, and I didn't have the heart to move him just yet."

I chuckled. "Cats."

"Tell me about it." She was smiling as she said it before her expression faltered. "So, you heard about the drama at the theatre?"

"Vaguely. Jules heard it from Georgina, and he passed word on to me. Georgina said that it got noisy and the police had to be called. That's about all I know. Were you there?"

Vicki shook her head. "No, but I know what it was about." She paused as she considered what to say next. "Do you remember Kenneth Purdy?"

I blinked in surprise. That wasn't the name I expected to hear. "I think so. He's the guy who ran the old community theatre, right?"

"That's the one. He owned the building, but refused to put any money into it. That's why Lawrence decided to open the new theatre."

Lawrence Jackson was the director of an ill-fated Christmas play I'd taken part in. The old theatre was halfway to falling down, though it was still functional. After the play, Lawrence had opened the new theatre, thanks to donations, primarily from Rita. I remembered that it had caused quite the stir back when it had happened, but from what I'd heard, things had been going great for the local actors since they'd moved. At least, I thought they were. "Has Kenneth been causing problems?"

"Not at first. He wasn't happy about us moving theatres, of course, but there wasn't anything he could do about it. It wasn't like we were making him a ton of money or anything, so I assumed he'd put it behind him and moved on to more lucrative endeavors."

"But?"

"But, apparently, he hadn't." Vicki sighed. "It started when Oliver came to us about acting in the production he was putting on in town. Everything seemed to be going fine." A pause. "Well, as fine as an Oliver Quick production can go. He's demanding and extremely particular about every aspect of his plays. He thinks he's God's gift to the theatre world and isn't afraid to tell everyone about it."

I lowered my voice and tried to match Oliver's tone. "You are about to experience a movie-quality thrill ride of a production that Hollywood could only dream of!"

Vicki laughed. "Yeah, just like that." She sobered. "We'd barely gotten started on learning our roles when Oliver up and canceled on us. All he'd tell us was that he'd chosen to go in another direction."

"He didn't say why?"

"He didn't, but it was obvious. Hector Kravitz—he's one of the old hands at the theatre—said he saw Oliver talking to Kenneth the night before we were dropped. He swears up and down that Kenneth paid Oliver to remove us as payback for moving theatres on him."

"Did he hear him say that?"

Vicki shrugged. "Who knows? Hector can be excitable and likes to embellish, which is fine when you're acting, but it doesn't make you a very trustworthy source. I believe that he saw Oliver and Kenneth together, but beyond that . . ." She spread her hands.

"That's what the excitement at the theatre was about?" I asked. "Kenneth and Oliver?"

"It was. I was asked to go, but decided I wanted nothing to do with whatever Hector was planning. He thought we should try to sabotage Oliver's production—go around town and interfere with the Levington actors and whatnot. A few others were on his side, but a majority of us simply wanted to move on. It's not worth the headache."

My mind churned, and not in a good way. If this Hector Kravitz was angry at Oliver and Kenneth, and he wanted to sabotage the production, killing someone would be a fantastic way to do just that.

But why Scott Flanagan and not Oliver or one of his actors? Convenience? Opportunity?

Or was I missing a connection here?

"I'm guessing you haven't heard what happened," I said.

"Uh-oh." Vicki sat up straighter. "That doesn't sound good. Does it have something to do with Hector? Please tell me he didn't do anything stupid."

"I . . . I don't know if he's involved or not." I spent the next ten minutes telling her about everything that led up to Scott's murder. "And now, hearing about Hector's grievance against Oliver, it makes me wonder . . ."

"If Hector could go as far as to kill someone in order to mess up Oliver's production?"

"Yeah." I made a face. "It sounds kind of silly when you say it out loud like that."

I expected Vicki to agree, but instead she only grew more serious. "Hector has gotten into trouble before," she said. "Like police trouble. He busted someone's car window when they stole a parking spot he was eyeing at the grocery store last May. He waited until they'd gone inside to do it, so it wasn't a direct confrontation, but still."

Breaking a car window was a long way away from murder, but it did indicate someone with anger issues. "Did you know the victim?" I asked. "The murder victim, not the parking spot stealer. Scott Flanagan. He was from Levington."

"I don't, thank goodness. I know a few of the Levington actors, and Oliver, of course, but not well. None of the ones I've met seemed capable of murder, but who knows these days? The stress of working under Oliver Quick could easily cause the nicest person to break."

But to break and kill someone? I was still having a hard time seeing it. And if Hector Kravitz was somehow involved, did that mean Lydia had been helping him? Why else give Scott the note if not to lure him to his death?

Vicki didn't know, nor did I expect her to. We chatted for another twenty minutes—thankfully about nicer topics than murder—before she needed to get back to work upstairs. I wished her luck and was just climbing back into my car when my phone rang. A look at the screen and my heart did that little pitter-patter thing it always did whenever I heard from my boyfriend.

I took a moment to wipe the stupid grin off my face before I answered with, "Hi, Paul. I'm glad you called."

"Krissy." There was concern in his voice. "How are you holding up?"

I was about to ask him why he'd ask, before I realized, *duh, because of the murder*. "I'm all right. Wendy found the body. Do you know Wendy Wilcox?"

"She's one of the younger writer girls, right? College-aged or close to it?"

"That's the one. She's pretty distraught after finding him like that. She keeps blaming herself."

"I can only imagine. She knows it's not her fault, right?"

"That's what we keep telling her. It might take some time before it sinks in." If it ever did. "I plan on stopping by her place tomorrow to check in on her."

"You do that." He paused. "Are you at home now?"

"No. I'm just leaving Vicki's, but I'm planning on heading that way next." Despite how crummy my day had been, I found myself smiling. "Why do you ask?"

"Well, I have a little free time," Paul said, likely meaning he'd been told to take an hour or two to eat because he was going to be busy with the murder investigation over the next few days. "I thought I might stop by and check on you, but if you're out—"

"I can be home in fifteen minutes." Less if I sped there, but that wasn't something you said to a cop, even one you were in a relationship with. Paul had been known to bend the rules for me in the past, but he wouldn't be happy if I put other lives at risk, just so I could make it home a few minutes faster.

"I won't be able to stay," he said, confirming my earlier thought.

"That's okay. I could use the company. It's been a long day." And if I could pick his brain about the murder, all the better. And, hey, I *did* have a little bit of information for him, so it wasn't like I planned on prying without giving him something in return.

"All right, I'll see you in fifteen, twenty minutes."

"I'll see you then."

We clicked off, and I took a moment to bask in the joy of having someone in my life who cared about me. The good feeling ebbed quickly as thoughts of Scott invaded. Did he have someone who cared for him like I had Paul? Were they hurting right now, alone, wishing they could have done something to save him?

I didn't know, but for their sake, I planned on doing my best to make sure the mystery of Scott's death didn't go unsolved.

7

Angry yellow eyes stared at me from across the room. Every so often, an orange tail would flip from one side to the other, landing with a solid *thump* against the floor.

"It was only one night," I said from my place on the couch. I'd tried to coax Misfit over to me with treats, but he wasn't having it. "You didn't starve. Jules fed you this morning. There's nothing to be angry about!"

Still unmoved, Misfit's tail thumped to his other side.

"Paul's going to be here soon," I said. "Can you play nice with him?"

As if on cue, a car pulled into my driveway. A quick peek out the window confirmed it to be Paul.

The second I rose to my feet, Misfit bolted down the hall, toward the bedroom, where he'd likely hide under the bed until he'd forgiven me. I assumed that would be around dinnertime.

I opened the front door just as Paul reached it. He was wearing his police uniform, minus the hat he normally wore while on duty. The lay of his near-blond brown hair told me that he'd just taken it off when he'd pulled up. I had to fight down the urge to reach out and tousle it.

"Hey, Krissy, sorry it took me so long." He gave me a quick peck on the lips before I stepped aside to let him in. "Just as I was about to head this way, Chief pulled me into her office for a word."

Chief was his mom, Patricia Dalton. I always found it cute that he called her "Chief."

"That's all right. Misfit is pouting because I left him alone overnight, so I spent the time trying to make friends again. So far, it hasn't worked."

Paul led the way to the island counter, where he groaned his way onto a stool. He looked like he'd spent the last hour crouched over a crime scene, which he likely had. He rubbed at his lower back with a grimace.

"Coffee?" I asked him.

"Water would be good. I think I've overcaffeinated today."

As I poured, I asked. "Are there any updates on Scott's death? I don't need secret police info or anything. I'm just hoping you might have a lead or two that will help ease my mind."

"Not really. Thank you." Paul took the glass of water when I handed it to him. "We have the information you gave us, but there wasn't much at the scene to go on. John's still talking with everyone at Ted and Bettfast, so hopefully he'll learn something there."

"I can still smell the caramel macchiato." I shuddered. "He bought it at Death by Coffee, asked for it to be put in a mug he'd brought with him."

"Neither the coffee—nor the mug—was the murder weapon, if that's what concerns you," Paul said. "Right now, we're working on the assumption that there was an argument and the coffee got thrown at him."

A small knot released in the back of my mind. I hadn't even realized I was worried about whether my store's coffee was used in the murder or not.

"How did he die?" I asked, almost dreading the answer.

Paul gave me an "Are you sure you want to know?" look before saying, "Blunt force. Once again, it looks like a heat-of-the-moment thing. The killer took the weapon with them because it wasn't at the scene."

I slid onto a stool across from him. "I bet the murder has to do with that note Lydia gave him. I was thinking about it on the way home. I didn't find any clues there that would make me think that it was part of Oliver's production. I think she led Scott there on purpose. Or someone else did, and they used her to deliver the message."

"It's something to go on," Paul said, though he sounded doubtful. "But why give him the note in front of so many people if she was going to kill him? The same would go for anyone who'd given it to her. It seems like something you'd want to do in private."

"Maybe they didn't go there planning to kill him. Like you said: heat of the moment. There could have been an argument. Things got heated. Escalated . . ."

Paul nodded. "It's possible. If so, John will find out."

He took a long drink of his water. "How are you holding up now that you're home? I know how these things can weigh on you."

"I'm fine," I said. "Still a little shaken, I guess, but at this point, murder hardly bothers me anymore." I paused, not liking how that sounded. "I mean, it bothers me, and I don't like it and hope I never find another dead person again, but I guess I'm starting to feel kind of numb to it."

"I know what you mean." Paul reached across the counter to pat my hand. "You never get used to it, while, at the same time, you get used to it."

"Exactly."

The pat turned into a soft caress that had me shuddering again, this time for another reason entirely. "Just lie low this time, all right?" he said. "I know you can't help yourself and you'll be out there asking questions the moment I leave you alone, but I figured I'd at least ask."

I smiled. "I'll try." My smile turned chagrined. "About that . . ."

"Oh boy." There was amusement in Paul's voice. "What did you do?"

"I didn't do anything. When I went to pick up my house key from Jules, he told me about a disturbance at the theatre. I talked to Vicki about it, and she said that a man named Hector Kravitz was upset with Oliver Quick."

"And you think this Hector fellow might have something to do with the murder?"

I shrugged. "No clue. But I figured you might want to know."

Paul rubbed at his face, then nodded. "Yeah, you're right. I'll let Buchannan know." He polished off his water and stood. "I wish I could stay, but I really do need to be getting back. I have a feeling this is going to be another long week."

"Keep me updated?" I asked.

"As much as I can. And if you hear anything else that we should know . . ."

"I'll call you right away."

I walked Paul to the door, where we had a semi-long goodbye kiss. It made me wish that he didn't have to leave, or that when he was done for the day, he could come back here, rather than go home.

But I knew asking would be pointless. Not only did he have unpredictable hours during a murder investigation, he also had a pair of dogs to get back home to. Unlike Misfit, who would just glare and pout for a few hours, his huskies, Kefka and Ziggy, needed him a whole lot more. Sure, Paul had a dog-sitter, but Susie could only watch them for so long.

"I'll call you tomorrow," Paul said once we came up for air. His cheeks were slightly flushed. I imagined mine were as well. "Maybe we can have dinner."

"Sounds great."

Another kiss, this one far shorter than the last, and he was out the door. I watched his backside until he was ensconced within his car. He waved and then backed out.

Alone—and feeling somewhat melancholy now that I was—I closed the door and headed to the bedroom to try to coax Misfit out from under my bed. After a dozen tail thumps and a stare that warned me not to even try to touch him, I gave up. He'd come around, as he always did.

While I waited for him to stop pouting, I grabbed my laptop and sat down on the couch to do a little research. Yes, the police were the ones investigating, and, yes, I was supposed to stay out of it, but that didn't mean I couldn't look into the people who might be involved. I mean, what could it hurt, especially if something in their history led to the killer?

And why not start with my current best suspect?

Hector Kravitz loved social media. He had a blog and links to a half dozen social media accounts from there. His profile picture was different on all of them, but was of the same, professional photographer quality, though no credits for the shots were given. He looked to be in his mid-thirties, fit, with almond-colored eyes accentuated by eyeliner. Precisely trimmed stubble decorated his face, cut to a fine, smooth edge. He looked like a movie star.

I'm pretty sure that was the point.

I perused his posts—blog and social media ones alike—and quickly surmised that he used them as a professional device, rather than a place to rant about his personal life. He didn't bring up Kenneth Purdy or Oliver Quick or anyone else he knew, for that matter. He talked of acting, of other stars in both television and stage. He discussed his plans for the future, how he was looking to make it big someday but, for now, was content lighting up the local theatre's stage.

Honestly, going by his social media, I'd have said he

was a nice guy, but after talking to Vicki, I wondered if it was all an act. Considering he was an actor, I found it a pretty good bet.

I moved on from Hector to Scott Flanagan. I figured knowing the victim better might help me (no, no, help the police) figure out who might want to kill him.

Scott, unlike Hector, only had one profile I could find. He barely posted, but a quick look at the comments on what little he did say told me why.

"People really didn't like him," I muttered as I read. I didn't recognize any of the names, but the comments were an awful lot like what Drew had said to him at Ted and Bettfast. He needed to stop running his mouth. He needed to stop lying. He needed to stop airing other people's dirty laundry. He couldn't so much as post about having a nice day without some snarky comment lambasting him.

I made a mental note to tell Paul about the online posts, just in case someone from there had tracked him down and killed him. It didn't seem likely, but at this point, anything could be important.

Curious, I checked to see if he had anyone on his contacts list that I recognized, someone who might not have posted, but was watching everything he said. I was disappointed to find the list of names was set to private.

So much for online research.

Misfit eased into the room then, looking miffed, but less irritated than before. He sat down, facing me, eyes flickering to the bag of treats on the coffee table in front of me.

I closed my laptop and set it aside. "Am I forgiven?"

His ear twitch felt like him saying, "Not yet," though the way his eyes kept going to the treats told me how I could get there.

I picked up the bag and shook it once, which caused him to stand, interest piqued. I poured treats into my hand and was about to use them to lure him over to me when my phone went off.

Misfit, startled, bolted back toward the bedroom in a scrabbling of claws.

"Wait!" But it was already too late.

With a sigh, I set the pile of treats on the coffee table and answered the phone.

"Well, Wendy is all settled in back at her place, but I'm worried about her," Rita said before I could utter a word. "She kept saying that she feels responsible for that man's death, that if she had realized he wasn't acting faster, perhaps she could have done something and saved him. I told her that she did everything right, but she just wouldn't listen to a word I said. I think I'm going to stop over at her place in the morning to check on her, in case you want to come along. I know you already said you'd do it, but I want to make sure you haven't reconsidered. I'm sure a pair of friendly faces would be better than one."

"I'm going to be at Death by Coffee for the morning rush, but I can stop by afterward," I said. "Though I don't have her address."

"I'll send it to you as soon as we hang up. Do you think the police are going to be able to figure this thing out on their own, or should we help? I'm not sure I have much for them quite yet. I was so focused on finding clues for our little mystery, I wasn't paying much mind to anything else. And then, with Wendy, I plum haven't had time to even think about it! What about you?"

Thoughts of Hector and Lydia and Kenneth and Oliver swirled through my head, but I didn't utter them. Knowing Rita, she'd call her gossip buddies, and rumors about all four of them would start making the rounds, and somehow, it would all come back and bite me on the butt.

"I talked to Paul a little while ago and told him everything I knew, which wasn't much," I said. "I'm pretty much in the same boat as you."

"I see." Rita sounded disappointed. "Well, if you do come up with anything, be sure to let me know. If I could ease Wendy's mind by telling her who really is responsible for that man's death, it would go a long way to easing *my* mind. I can't believe someone would take advantage of our little mystery hunt like that. It has to be someone involved in it, don't you think? Like that team who was in the lead, perhaps?"

"Why do you think that?" I asked.

"It's all about that note you found."

"The one Lydia gave Scott."

"That's the one. I have a feeling that the young lady was giving him a clue, just like you said. He jumped the line, so to speak, but the other team, the one from Levington, was ahead of everyone else. Or, at least, that's what I've heard. If they were already there when Scott showed up alone, they might have realized he was cheating and gotten angry about it. It wasn't like they were friends."

I wanted to believe it was possible because it would make solving the case that much easier, but to kill someone over a game? Whether Oliver wanted to call it that or not, that's exactly what it was. "I'm not convinced the logging camp was part of the game," I said.

"Really? Why not?"

"Scott went there because of the note from Lydia," I said, thinking it through as I spoke. "We went because I found the note in the Banyon Tree bathroom. If the note was a lure for Scott so someone could kill him, the camp wasn't part of the game. If he was cheating, why go alone and not bring his team? And why wait for so long? Why not go there right away? I saw no evidence that Drew and his team were ever there either. And can you imagine all three of them as being in on it?" I shook my head, even though she couldn't see me. "There has to be another explanation."

"But we already know evidence led to that camp, don't we?" Rita said. "I mean, we weren't the only team to show up there."

I was about to ask her what she meant, when it dawned on me. "Buchannan's team."

"Exactly! If the note was just a lure and the camp wasn't the location of one of the clues, how was it that John Buchannan and his team showed up after us? I'm almost positive that Scott fellow was cheating and that someone caught him doing it."

8

*B*uchannan *found a clue that led him to the murder scene.*

The thought followed me around the house as I passed the time by doing mindless cleaning. He couldn't have seen the note in the Banyon Tree restroom or he would have beat me and my team there. I suppose it was possible he'd found the note, but hadn't put two and two together until after he'd followed up on the hotel clue. He hadn't seen Lydia give it to Scott, so how would he know who or what it was for?

But if he'd found it, why hadn't he taken it with him? And why would Scott go to the logging camp on his own, rather than take his team if it was part of the game?

And, perhaps most important, why did the note say it was an emergency and then have him meet nearly two hours after giving it to him?

"I need to talk to Detective Buchannan."

Misfit looked up from his spot on the couch as I

made for the door, keys in hand. His tail swished once, in clear disapproval, before he lowered his head and went back to sleep. I'd give him more treats when I got back home; otherwise, bedtime would be a cold, cat-less affair.

As I drove, I kept going over what I knew, trying to come up with answers. Lydia gave Scott a note. Why? He wanted to go alone. Why? Buchannan arrived after me, but likely hadn't seen the note on the bathroom floor. How? Was the note from Lydia? From Oliver? From someone else? Did it tie back to Oliver's production? Or was it about something else? Scott had a tendency to talk about people. Could he have said something about Lydia that she wanted to clear up? And failing that, was she willing to kill him to silence him?

I had no answers, but I hoped to get some soon.

I pulled into the Ted and Bettfast lot and was immediately disappointed by what I found. Quite a few of the cars were gone, including Buchannan's own. There were still vehicles remaining, and a quick count told me that most, if not all, of the Levington people were still there. I might not get the chance to talk to Buchannan, but Lydia might still be around. She seemed like the best person to talk to about the note.

And if nothing else, there's always Oliver. The director would be able to tell me definitively whether the logging camp was part of his production, or if was merely a good place to murder someone.

With that happy thought in mind, I got out my car and headed for the front door.

"I know the police were here, but I had nothing to

do with it." Robert's voice met me the moment I was through the doors. "They're not shutting us down or anything like that. It didn't happen here, so there's nothing to worry about."

Bett Bunford, one of the owners of Ted and Bettfast, was leaning on a cane, her face haggard. She looked like a woman who'd led a long, fruitful life, but was at the point where she just wanted to sit by the window and read. Behind her, her husband, Ted, was frowning. He had one hand on her shoulder and, every so often, would squeeze it.

"Unless the killer is hiding under our roof," Bett said, her voice quavering ever so slightly. "That is something we should all be concerned about." She caught sight of me and joined Ted in frowning. "She should know."

Robert glanced back at me, and for a moment, I was struck by how stricken he looked. "Kris had nothing to do with it either," he said, turning back to the Bunfords. "The murdered guy was staying here, sure, but he died elsewhere. I bet no one here had anything to do with it. They could have killed him in his room if they wanted him dead. In fact, it was probably an accident. Not a murder at all."

Bett heaved a sigh that seemed to deflate her even more. "I need to sit down. Ted?"

Ted sprang into action, taking his wife by the elbow and leading her away, back toward the office, where Oliver had set up command earlier.

"I'll set everything to rights!" Robert called as the door closed. As soon as they were gone, his shoulders sagged, and he turned to me. "This is a disaster."

"Someone *was* murdered, Robert. It wasn't an accident."

"Shh!" He rushed over, finger to his lips. "They don't know that for sure. Bett fears another murder is going to shut this place down for good. She's even reconsidering selling! She said that it might just be better if the place falls to ruin." He just about wailed it. "If she doesn't sell, I don't know what I'm going to do. I've sunk everything into this."

"I'm sure she's just upset," I said. "This isn't the first time something like this has happened here." Like when someone was murdered in one of the rooms upstairs. Bett still hadn't forgiven me for that one, even though I didn't have anything to do with it.

"I know," Robert said. "It's just . . ." He looked around the room, at the old wood, the windows in need of repair. "I want to bring this place back to life, you know? Turn it into somewhere people want to go. Don't get me wrong, it's pretty awesome as it is now, but imagine it fixed up and teeming with guests."

I had to admit, the thought of Ted and Bettfast returning to its former glory was a nice one. With how rundown it had gotten over the years, it was hard to imagine how it must have looked when it was new. The way the hedge animals out front were now mostly just shapeless masses of dead sticks never failed to give me a sense of loss as I drove past them.

"You should take a break," I said. "Go home to Trisha and R.J. You've been here all day. They'll both be thrilled to see you."

Robert was staring over my shoulder at the wall. I didn't think he'd heard me at first, but then he nodded.

"I suppose you're right. It's not like there's much I can do around here right now anyway. The police finished up about twenty minutes ago, which is why the Bunfords are here. They want to make sure everything is secure, like I wouldn't do my best to do that on my own."

"I'm sure they mean well," I said, before shifting gears. "Is Oliver still around? Or Lydia?"

Robert pouted a moment longer before answering. "Yeah. Well, Mr. Quick is. I don't know about Lyds."

Lyds? I somehow doubted Robert knew Lydia well enough to call her by a shortened version of her name. Not that he'd care.

"Where is Oliver?" I asked.

Robert jerked a thumb over his shoulder. "Employees-only room back there. He offered to move once the Bunfords got here."

"Thank you," I said. And then, because, despite our differences over the years, I was starting to think of Robert as a friend, I rested a hand on his arm and squeezed. "Everything will work out for the best, okay? Have faith."

"Yeah, thanks, Kris."

I squeezed harder, clenched my teeth, and walked away.

Behind me, Robert muttered, "Ow. What was that for?"

I ignored him as I made my way toward the closed door he'd indicated. The door was old and pitted, like someone had repeatedly nailed signs and decorations to it, permanently marring the wood. There were no

decorations now, just metal lettering that said, EMPLOY-
EES ONLY.

I raised my fist to knock, but Oliver's raised voice
stopped my hand. He didn't sound angry or worried or
anything you'd expect out of someone whose production had just been ruined because one of the participants, a man he knew, had been murdered.

In fact, he sounded excited.

"No, I'm telling you, it's great," he was saying,
voice only slightly muffled by the door. "Do you
know what kind of attention something like this will
bring me?"

There was a stretch of silence. Whoever he was talking to was either a quiet speaker or he was talking on
the phone. I was guessing the latter.

"Yes, yes, I know. It's terrible. But why not capital-
ize on it?" Another pause. "Haven't you been listening? The media will be all over this. The *media*, India.
I couldn't get them interested in my event before, but
now they'll have no choice but to cover it. There'll be
far more articles on it than just a tiny little blurb in a
newspaper that no one will read. It might make national news!"

I leaned closer to the door in the hope of catching
what India said. The floor betrayed me, however, by
creaking loud enough that everyone in all of Ted and
Bettfast had to have heard it.

"Hold that thought, India," Oliver snapped. "I think
someone's here." More floorboards creaked as he approached.

Not wanting to appear as if I was eavesdropping—

which I was, of course—I hurriedly knocked on the door, adding a "Mr. Quick? Are you in there?" for good measure.

"I'll call you back. Yeah, yeah, I hear you." The door opened a moment later, revealing a scowling Oliver as he tucked his cell phone into his pocket with enough force it was a wonder it didn't pull his pants down. "What do you want?"

"Hi, Mr. Quick. I'm Krissy—" I cut off as he waved a disinterested hand in my face.

"I don't care. What do you want? And make it quick. I'm rather busy at the moment."

I bristled at his tone, but kept my emotions in check. "It's about the clues hidden around Pine Hills," I said. "I was curious as to what it was that was supposed to lead everyone to the logging camp where Scott was found, and if there was supposed to be a clue there that we were expected to find."

Oliver's already unhappy expression hardened. "I'm not going to divulge information that will ruin the surprise. You'll have to continue your investigation to find out which clues are and aren't pertinent to the mystery."

I blinked at him. *Continue my investigation? He couldn't mean* . . . "You're thinking of continuing with the production?"

"Why not?" he said. "Once the media catches wind of this, they'll all but insist we continue. We can do it in Scott's honor! We can show the world that we have the will, the strength, to press on, despite the tragedy."

With the way he'd started grinning as he spoke and with the excitement in his voice, I didn't think he thought Scott's death was much of a tragedy. In fact, he sounded as if he was happy Scott had died.

"Don't you see?" he went on, despite my stupefied expression. "Scott's murder proves how important my production is. It caused someone to *kill* in order to win, to be the first to solve the mystery. They understand how important this is for us all. We can't walk away from that." He was all but salivating in anticipation of the attention it would bring him.

I, on the other hand, felt as if I might be sick. "Scott's dead. He's not coming back from that."

Oliver did his best to look mournful for about two seconds before reverting back to his usual self. Let's just say his acting wouldn't be winning him any awards.

"Yes, yes, what happened is terrible. Look, I need to make another call. I have your information. I'll contact you as soon as we begin again and you can get with your team and reevaluate what you think you know. Thank you for your time and concern."

And then he stepped back and closed the door in my face.

The urge to shout, "Jerk!" at him was so strong, I'd pursed my lips before I caught myself. I didn't care about how Oliver had treated me, but to use Scott's death for his own personal advancement? It didn't cast Oliver Quick in a very good light. In fact, it made me wonder if *he* might have been the one to give Lydia the note to deliver to Scott. Could he really have killed a man, just so the media would pay attention to him?

I turned and started for the door just as the "dead" actor, Link, entered wearing a jogging outfit that was just this side of too tight. His face was beaded in sweat, and his lips were a normal color, if not slightly flushed from his run. His step faltered when he saw me, but he didn't flee when I approached him.

"Hi, Link. I'm Krissy, one of the participants in Oliver's mystery."

He nodded, wiped his forehead with the back of his sweaty arm. "Yeah, I remember seeing you. And it's Lincoln. Friends call me Link."

I ignored the implied *and you're not my friend*. "I was wondering if you could tell me anything about Oliver?" I made it a question. "Like what kind of man is he?"

Lincoln's nervous gaze flickered toward the office door where Ted and Bett had gone and Oliver no longer resided, but I got the idea. He was nervous about being overheard. "There's nothing to say. He's driven. He knows what he wants and will push to make sure it happens."

"How driven?" I pressed. "He doesn't seem too upset about Scott's death."

Another eye flicker before he took a step away from me. "Look, I just finished a run. I need to shower and get cleaned up. I don't have anything to say about Mr. Quick or what's happened. I'd suggest you drop it. No one will talk about him or Scott's death—no one who wants to have a career afterward."

"Why's that?" I asked, but to no avail.

Lincoln shook his head as he hurried away, toward a downstairs hallway. He didn't look back as he vanished down it.

Well, that was weird.

A man was dead, and all anyone seemed to care about was how it affected them and their careers. I mean, we were talking about community-theatre people. Not big Broadway stars, but actors who put on shows for only a handful of people at a time. Yes, I respected what they did, but I also knew they weren't going to be making money doing it. It was also unlikely their work here would draw the attention of anyone who *could* make them money.

That is, unless Oliver publicizes it to the point where it does *make national news.*

I felt as if I'd wasted my time in coming here as I made for the doors. I could still go looking for Detective Buchannan, but if he was out chasing leads, that wouldn't be as easy as it sounded. I wasn't about to go knocking on doors in the hopes of finding Lydia to ask her about why she'd given Scott the note to meet either. Even if I did find her, she was apt to slam the door in my face, rather than tell me anything. I wasn't a cop. No one had to talk to me.

"Psst."

I jerked to a stop, hand on the door leading outside. It took me a moment to find who had made the noise. He was kneeling beside a nearby chair, head lowered as if hiding his face, though I knew who it was the instant I saw him.

"Richie?" I asked, but snapped my lips closed when he waved a panicked hand in front of his face.

He glanced around to make sure no one was listening before he whispered, "We should talk. But not here."

He wanted to talk? To me?

"Death by Coffee?" I whispered, glancing toward Oliver's door. Richie's agitation was making me nervous. "It's downtown."

Richie nodded. "Twenty minutes. Come alone."

He peeked around the chair and, seeing no one, popped to his feet and speed walked his way to the back door, which lead outside and to the pool, which was closed this time of year. He didn't glance back as he slid the door open and stepped outside.

Okay, I took back what I'd thought about Lincoln being weird. Richie Husted and his secretive whispers were the epitome of strange. They made everyone else seem close to normal.

But I could deal with oddball behavior, especially if it led to discovering who killed Scott Flanagan and why.

9

Business was slow at Death by Coffee, which was standard any time after the lunch rush. There were only two people in the dining area and another pair meandering through the bookshelves. Sitting around the coffee table upstairs were Yolanda Barton, Avery Mills, and three boys who'd once pranked the store with fake cockroaches. They were bent over a board game, looking serious, as if they were afraid that making the wrong move might end civilization as we knew it.

Pooky Cooper looked up from where she was lounging behind the counter as I entered. She didn't spring into action like so many employees did when their bosses appeared. Instead, she gave me a lazy wave and smile before crossing her ankles. "Back already?"

"Couldn't stay away." I rounded the counter, dropped a cookie into a cup, and poured my own coffee. Perks of ownership. "I'm sorry about the long day. I could always take over for you if you want to go home."

Pooky waved me off. "I want the hours," she said. "Beth and Jeff offered to hang around after Eugene got here, but we're slow, and I don't mind sticking it out. There's not much left to do, so I can take it relatively easy." She paused. "Not that I'm slacking off. I've kept everything clean and fresh."

Upstairs, Eugene Dohmer, a lanky employee whose heavily lidded eyes always made him look as if he was seconds from falling asleep, was busy ringing up a book sale for the couple who'd been browsing when I'd come in. He glanced down at me, waved, and took their card.

"Did anything happen around here after I left earlier?" I asked. "Like did one of the actors or someone from one of the other teams act strangely by chance?"

Pooky shook her head. "That one guy in the weird outfit took off like someone had lit him on fire, but otherwise, that's it. A few people were in and out throughout the day, but nothing dramatic happened."

Not surprising. I doubted the killer would have come to Death by Coffee to brag about the murder to his friends, but sometimes, it was best to ask, just in case.

I took a sip from my coffee, savoring the bitterness. While a cookie added a little sweetness, it was the gooey mess it left at the bottom once the coffee was gone that was the real treat. Not everyone liked—let alone understood—my habit. That was okay. It just meant more coffee and cookies for me.

I glanced toward the door, but Richie had yet to arrive. I was starting to wonder if he'd changed his mind and had bailed on me. With how everyone seemed to be afraid of upsetting Oliver, it wouldn't surprise me.

"How are things going with Donnie?" I asked, turning back to Pooky, who was watching me with mild concern. She knew as well as anyone that when something happened around Pine Hills, I aways seemed to be at the center of it.

"He's been a challenge, but we're doing okay." Her brother had fallen on hard times a few months back and had moved in with her for a little while. He'd gotten too comfortable and had started bossing Pooky around and acting like he owned her apartment.

So, with my help—and urging—she kicked him out.

"Has he found a place of his own yet?" I asked.

"Not yet. He's living with a couple of his friends right now." She made a face that told me all I needed to know about his friends. "That's going about as well as expected." Which meant not well at all. "He's still trying to get me to change my mind about letting him move back in, but I'm not going to do it. He's burned that bridge, and it's going to take more than a little begging to get me to relent."

The door opened, and Richie finally entered. He had a ballcap pulled low on his brow, though it did little to conceal his features. He scanned the dining area, frowned, and spotted me behind the counter with Pooky. He hurried over.

"Can I have a caramel macchiato?" he asked. "Hot, with extra caramel." He noted my surprised expression and added, face flushing, "It's in honor of Scott."

As Pooky jumped to fill the order, I said, "I didn't know you knew him that well."

Richie shrugged, wouldn't meet my eye. He looked like a kid too embarrassed to talk to a teacher about his bullies. "I don't, not really. But every time we did run into one another, he had something caramel in hand. He loves"—he closed his eyes, took a sharp breath, and amended his wording to, "*loved* caramel. Drinks, candy, whatever. I swear he lived on the stuff."

My stomach clenched as I thought about how *my* caramel macchiato had been at the scene, how it appeared as if it had been thrown into Scott's face, likely before he'd died. It might not have been the murder weapon, but it was a part of what happened to him. It made me feel connected to it, like I had an obligation to help solve his murder.

Of course, I always felt that way, no matter the circumstances.

"Here you go." Pooky placed the drink on the counter. "Caramel macchiato, hot, with extra caramel."

Richie paid with exact change and looked uncertainly around the room as he scooped up his drink.

"Let's sit down," I said, rounding the counter to join him. I motioned toward the table by the window where the actor with the pink shirt and blue sweater had sat earlier. It seemed fitting. "We can talk privately over there."

We crossed the room and took our seats. Richie immediately started staring out the window, hands wrapped around his coffee. He didn't just seem nervous; he seemed terrified. Of Oliver? Of the killer? Of being caught? I had no idea, but hoped our conversation would clear it up.

I let him stare for a couple of minutes more before asking, "What was it you wanted to talk to me about, Richie?"

He jumped and took a long, slow drink of his macchiato. When he lowered his hands and set the cup down, he did so just as slowly. "It's about Scott."

Well, duh, went through my head, but I didn't voice it. I nodded for him to go on.

"He told me you're like the lady in that old show." His eyes flickered my way before returning to what lay beyond the window. "The one who solves murders and writes books about them or something like that."

"*Murder, She Wrote*?"

He flashed me an awkward smile. "That's the one. He told me about it, but I've never seen it. It was before my time."

Honestly, it was before my time as well, but I didn't point that out. "You two talked about me?" I asked instead.

"We didn't really talk, as in hold important conversations or anything. Scott didn't have a lot of friends, though we kind of ran in the same circles, so we knew each other. He was doing the Scott thing and talking about people, and I just kind of sat back and listened to him. It's not like it hurt anything to let him have his say, you know? He said a lot of crazy stuff, but . . . that was Scott. You got used to it."

Upstairs, Yolanda hooted, which caused the three boys to laugh. Apparently, the board game was going well.

"Scott said you're always involved in the murders that happen around here," Richie went on. "He thought it gave you an advantage over the rest of us since you had practice. It's why I wanted to talk to you. I mean, if you're used to this sort of thing . . ." He shrugged.

"I wouldn't say I'm used to it," I said. "And if you know something, you should talk to the police."

Richie paled. "I told that detective everything I knew. I'm not sure he thinks much of what I had to say."

Knowing Buchannan, he'd probably scoffed at half of what anyone said, even when it was important info.

Richie fidgeted with his macchiato before going on. "Scott was the kind of person who got into everyone's business. I swear he was researching everyone until the wee hours of the morning. Stalking them, I guess. I think that's why he was so sure Drew was planning on cheating."

I leaned forward. "He knew about Drew before they got into the argument last night?"

Richie took a quick, gulping drink, as if to calm his nerves. "Even before their fight, Scott knew Drew was going to do whatever he could to win. He didn't want to call him out on it because that wasn't Scott's style. He liked to talk, but rarely ever did anything about it. Does that make sense?"

I nodded. "He was a gossip, not a meddler."

"That's right. I tried to talk to Mr. Quick about it, but he swore up and down there was no way Drew or anyone else could cheat the system. I don't think he thought anyone would dare, which is why he was so angry when Drew tried to sneak an extra peek at the evidence while everyone was supposed to be locked away and asleep."

I still didn't get that. Why set everything up and leave it lying out if you didn't want anyone to look at it? It was almost as if Oliver was daring us to defy him.

"Scott knew what Drew was planning to do," Richie went on. "So when he followed him, it wasn't by chance. Austin told me that Scott had waited by their room door until Drew made his move. It's why I was pretty sure that when Scott snuck outside, it had to do with Drew."

"Wait," I said. "Back up. Scott snuck out? Of Ted and Bettfast? When?"

Richie took another drink. He still wouldn't meet my eye. I got the impression that was just the way he was, not that he was afraid of me. "I guess it wasn't really sneaking as much as slipping out. It happened after Oliver's prologue, but before everyone was supposed to go to bed."

Which was when I was at home, feeding Misfit.

And when Sara claimed to have seen Drew talking to someone she'd thought might have been Richie outside her window.

Could she have been wrong and it was Scott who'd talked to Drew, not Richie? How did that make sense, considering how they'd fought before *and* after this little meeting supposedly had taken place?

Could their spats have been for show? A production in itself?

"Scott met with Drew?" I asked, voicing my thought out loud.

Richie made a face like it was the most ridiculous thing he'd ever heard. "What? No. He met with Lydia."

A big *ta-da* rang in my head, so loud it was a wonder

no one else heard it. If Scott had secretly met with Lydia, it confirmed that Scott and Lydia were . . . what? Conspiring? Or could Scott have been trying to tell Lydia about Drew and his plans to cheat since Oliver wouldn't listen to anyone else? If that was the case, why slip away to do it? Why not call him out in front of everyone?

No, it had to be that they were conspiring with one another somehow. Why else give him the note?

But if Lydia and Scott were working together, why had he ended up dead?

"Do you know what they met about?" I asked.

"No, sorry, I don't. My orders were to watch the investigators and make sure no one did anything that would ruin Oliver's plans." His face reddened. "I know I let you leave and that Scott and Lydia slipped outside, but it wasn't like you all were hurting anything. And I guess I kind of wasn't paying much attention. It was only by chance that I saw him go, and that was because Lydia said she needed a little air just before that and I was watching her."

Something in his tone made me wonder if he was watching her not because he was bored and had nothing to else to look at, but because he was interested in her. Lydia was a good-looking woman, and Richie seemed lonely. It made sense, even if it was a little creepy.

"Did you happen see Drew around then?" I asked, thinking back to what Sara had told me. "Was he still in the room when Lydia and Richie went outside? Did he follow them by chance?"

"Drew?" Richie thought it over. "I'm not sure. Why?"

"He was seen talking to someone outside around the same time you said Lydia was with Scott." And then, because I was curious to see what he'd say, "They thought it was you."

Richie had just started to take a drink. He sucked in a breath, which caused him to suck his macchiato down the wrong tube. He choked, spraying caramel and coffee onto the table—and me—as he started hacking.

I rose, intent on rushing around the table to, I don't know, beat him on the back until he stopped choking, but he waved me off.

"I'm fine," he gasped. "Wrong tube. That *burns*." He rose to grab a handful of napkins, hacking and coughing all the way.

Every eye in the house was on us, including those of Yolanda and the board gamers, who were peering at us over the railing separating the upstairs bookshop from the dining room.

"He's okay," I said, wiping macchiato from my arms. "Everything's okay."

There was a moment when everyone continued to stare, and then, as if someone had flipped a switch, they returned to what they'd been doing, though Yolanda watched me a moment longer before going back to her board game.

"Sorry," Richie said, as he returned to wipe up the mess. His coughs had mostly subsided, though every once in a while he'd let loose with a couple he tried to suppress. "You caught me by surprise."

"Does that mean you met with Drew?" I asked.

"Me? Gosh, no. I was surprised because of how crazy it sounded."

Crazy? "Why's that? You're one of Oliver's assistants, and as you said, Drew was determined to win. I can think of half a dozen reasons why he'd want to pick your brain." Especially if he planned on cheating.

Richie's expression darkened. "No way. Drew and I don't get along. He doesn't really get along with anyone, to be honest. I can't imagine anyone would want to talk to him on purpose." He paused. "Well, there is one person . . ."

I waited for him to tell me who that one person was, but all he did was clear his throat and grimace. He considered his macchiato a moment and pushed it away.

"Richie?" I pressed. "Who would Drew have met with? Someone from his team? Oliver?"

There was a buzzing sound. Richie jumped, smacking his knees against the bottom of the table, and pulled out his phone. He glanced at the screen and paled. "I have to take this. It's Mr. Quick." He stood, but didn't walk away. He acted like he didn't know where to go or what to do. "Hello?" A short pause. "Yes, I know."

I could just barely hear Oliver's voice on the other end of the line, but couldn't make out what he was saying. His tone sounded anything but happy.

"Really?" Richie's voice rose in pitch. "When? All right. I'll be there right away."

He clicked off.

"Something important happen?" I asked. In my mind's eye, I saw Oliver standing over yet another corpse, already planning on how best to use it to his advantage. Why he'd need Richie for that, I had no idea, but I couldn't shake the thought.

Richie tucked his phone away and patted his pockets, as if to make sure he hadn't missed. "I'm needed back at the bed-and-breakfast. It's nothing." He took a step away and stopped. "You wanted to know who Drew had a history with that might have led to them meeting?"

"I do."

"Talk to Austin Helms. If anyone met with Drew outside that night, it would have been Austin."

10

A loud whistle filled the house, causing Misfit to bolt for the bedroom. I rose, unalarmed, cracked my back, and headed for the kitchen to make my tea.

I'd been sitting at the table since I'd gotten home, browsing as many websites tied to people involved with the production as I could. I wanted more information on Oliver Quick, but it just wasn't there. Or, at least, I didn't know where to look. I didn't know the names of his actors, other than Lincoln, so they were dead ends as well.

On the Pine Hills side of things, there were countless articles referencing Kenneth Purdy, but none of them painted him as a hateful, vindictive man. That didn't mean he wasn't one, of course. It just meant that he was good at showing others what he wanted them to see.

I'd been about to begin looking up the other contestants, starting with Drew MacDonald, when my tea water had started boiling.

As soon as I poured water into the mug with the spiced chai tea bag, I leaned against the counter and rubbed my temples. Staring at a computer screen for hours on end wasn't my idea of a good time, but I didn't know what else to do. Someone was dead, and I wasn't the type of person who could sit around and do nothing. I was trying hard not to go running around town, talking to everyone involved, but it wasn't easy. I was getting nowhere online. When I talked to someone directly, they often let something slip, especially because I wasn't a police officer, which made them feel more comfortable.

This is still the job of the police, not yours.

"I know, I know," I muttered, hoping that talking to myself wasn't a sign of a declining mental state. Sometimes I—and half the town, to be honest—wondered.

Misfit peeked into the kitchen from the hallway. When no loud sounds followed, he eased back into the living room, hopped up onto the couch, and curled back into an orange ball so he could resume his nap.

Actually, a nap sounded pretty good right about then. Perhaps after I'd had my tea, I could join him.

I yawned as I carefully carried my mug, which was perilously filled to the brim, back to the table. It wasn't all that late, but it had been a long day. And that's not even considering the poor rest I'd gotten the previous night when I'd attempt to sleep on the inflatable mattress at Ted and Bettfast. When this was over, I was going to crash *hard*.

I sat down and glanced at my phone, willing it to ring. I hadn't heard from Paul since he'd left earlier that day. I knew he'd said he'd call tomorrow, but I was hoping he might decide to check in on me before it got too late. You know, call, see how I'm doing, and come over to give me some relaxing Paul-time.

I raised my mug to my lips, mentally planning everything I'd say—and do—to him, when my phone went off.

I didn't jump much, but it was enough. Hot tea sloshed over the lip of the mug, onto my hand, which caused me to jerk again, spilling even more tea. But instead of landing on my hand, this time it splashed across on my laptop's keyboard.

"Crap!" I shot to my feet, pushing the chair back, and spilling even *more* tea onto my hand and the table. Out of the corner of my eye, I saw an orange streak shoot from the room, back down the hall, as I finally set down my mug, though, at this point, it hardly mattered.

There was a moment when my mind blanked and I could only stare at the tea seeping around the keys of the keyboard and the spreading puddle on the table that was slowly inching toward my phone, which had stopped ringing. There was a flicker from my light-up keys, and my keyboard went dark. That somehow triggered rational thought again, and I snatched up my phone, just before the tea could reach it.

"No, no, no." I rushed into the kitchen, ripped a handful of paper towels free of the roll, and ran back to the table. I blotted at my keyboard, knowing it was already too late. The screen went black and the little ON light flickered off. I wasn't sure if it was the tea I'd spilled on the keyboard itself or the puddle that had spread underneath it, but my laptop was dead.

Sighing, I dropped into my chair and stared at the black screen, rubbing at my scorched hand as I did. I didn't have anything important saved on the hard drive, which, I supposed, still might be salvageable, but still. I'd had the laptop seemingly forever. And while my phone could do pretty much everything my laptop did, and was far more portable, it was still *mine*.

I picked up the laptop and tipped it over the table. Droplets of spiced chai pattered onto the wood from the underside. It wasn't a steady rain, but there was enough to tell me that quite a lot of tea had gotten inside.

Maybe if I put it in rice, it'll somehow save it. That was supposed to work, wasn't it?

Figuring I might as well give it a try, I rose to do just that.

I carried my laptop into the kitchen, put it into the only thing big enough to hold it—an extra large skillet Dad had given me back when I'd first moved out of the house—and dumped an entire box of white rice on top of it. I left it on the counter as I went back to the table to mop up the rest of the tea.

I was just dumping the damp paper towels into the trash when headlights lit up the front of my house and then died. My heart leapt, thinking that perhaps it was indeed Paul coming to check on me. And, boy, could I use his comfort right then.

I quickly rinsed off my sticky fingers and rushed to the door, just as there was a tentative, decidedly *not-*Paul-style knock. I opened the door, still mildly hopeful, but it was still a surprise when I saw who was standing on my doorstep.

"Lena?" I asked, gaze flickering to the minivan in my driveway. "What are you doing here?"

"I'm sorry to stop by so late," she said. "I tried to call, but you didn't answer, so I thought that, since I was in the area, I'd stop by and see if you were still up."

"You called?" Duh, as if I hadn't just been cleaning up the results of that attempted call. "Come on in." I stepped aside. "I had an accident with my laptop and was cleaning it up. It's why I missed your call."

"Ah." Lena entered and immediately burst into a grin. "Is that my big boy?"

Misfit, who'd once again returned from down the hall, saw Lena, and instead of running away, like he did with most people, he fluffed himself up as big and floofy as he could make himself. He turned sideways, pranced in place, and waited for her to come over and pet him.

I shot him a glare as I closed the door. He never acted like that around me. Then again, I was willing to pet him whenever he wanted, so why should he bother making himself cuter than he already was for my bene-fit?

Lena ran a hand over him and scratched him under his chin and behind his ears. "I miss having a cat. Mom was never big on them, but Dad likes them. You've met her. She gets what she wants, so"—a shrug—"no cat." She sighed and pushed her way to her feet. "I'm hop-ing to get a place of my own soon, so maybe I'll get one then. I just need life to stabilize first."

"How's the training going?" I paused. "Has Scott's murder interrupted that?"

"Actually, it's been going pretty good." She frowned. "Well, not good. It's never good when someone dies."

"I know what you meant."

She ran her fingers through her hair. I was once again struck by how strange it was to see so little color in it. Purple fit her, was almost a character trait of hers. Like, without her colorful hair, it wasn't really Lena Allison, but someone else.

"Detective Buchannan isn't letting me full-on investigate," she said, "but he's letting me help out on the little things. I've been allowed to watch some interviews, but only if the person being interviewed permits it. It's a real crime, so they're being careful. Since I'm technically training with him and Becca, it's good experience for me. I just wish someone didn't have to die for me to get that experience."

"No, it's not ideal, but that's life as a cop." I watched as Misfit rolled onto his side, begging for more petting. "Was that why you called? Has Buchannan sent you to ask me more questions?"

Lena paced away from Misfit, much to his disappointment. "Nah, he doesn't want me talking to you about it at all." She grinned. "But Becca said I could, just as long as I'm not telling you anything that might compromise the investigation."

"I wouldn't want you to do that." Though if they had a clue as to who killed Scott, I wouldn't mind a heads-up.

"Like I said, Detective Buchannan let me hang around while he worked, and I learned a few things, mostly about how to function as a police officer, and less about who did what and why. Does that make sense?"

I nodded.

"It's just . . ." She paused, considered what to say next. "Everyone he talked to seemed to be hiding something. At least, those interviews I sat in on did. Like I kept wondering if they could be the killer because of how they were acting. It got to the point where I was beginning to believe everyone was in on it. I'm not sure who to believe, if anyone."

"It's like that a lot," I said. "Even when someone doesn't have anything to hide when it comes to the murder, they often have secrets they don't want to get out, and talking to the police makes them feel insecure about those secrets, no matter how unrelated they may be."

"I don't know how anyone can sort through what's real and what's made up," Lena said. "I mean, we were there, and I found myself wondering if I was misremembering things. Even when stories were consistent, they felt off somehow. Two people talk to the same person, hear the same thing, yet come away thinking different things about the interaction. Stuff like that."

I understood, but wasn't sure how I could help her. "I tend to go with my gut feeling," I said. "Which isn't always right, but it gives me somewhere to start."

"Yeah, well, I'm trying to become a police officer, so I'm not sure gut feelings will work for me. There're all these rules you have to follow, even when you know the rules are preventing you from getting to the truth. It seems unfair to let a bad guy get away just because regulations say you can't question them or look into the trunk of their car without reason." She shook her head. "Though, I suppose I wouldn't want anyone to go through my stuff if I didn't do anything wrong."

Which was why I figured I was able to help solve so many cases before the police. I could sometimes go where the police couldn't. It didn't mean I could go around breaking the law, but as I noted before, sometimes people were more willing to talk to me rather than a police officer because they thought they could pull one over on me more easily.

"Anyway," Lena said, "it got me thinking. While we were trying to solve Oliver Quick's mystery, Detective Buchannan was being secretive about the clues. He wanted to solve it on his own. You know, beat you." She grinned.

"I'm honored." I mirrored her grin. It was good to know Buchannan thought so highly of my deduction skills.

"It means I don't really know what we were running around doing half of the time. Neither does Becca. We just followed him around and tried to have fun with it."

A mental lightbulb went on in my head. "You were wondering if I might have seen something in the clues that would help solve the murder."

Lena nodded. "I know it's a long shot, but it seemed like a logical move. I know about the note you found and that it led you to the scene, but what about other clues? There were some sitting around that were obviously tied to the production."

"Like the wig," I said, thinking of how it had sat on the table at Scream for Ice Cream like a beacon.

"Yeah, like that." She paced away and back again, brow furrowed. "But no matter how hard I think about it, I can't, for the life of me, figure out why we went to that defunct logging camp. Like I said, I know you found that note, but I sure don't recall seeing one. And no one else mentioned seeing it, either."

"The only reason I knew what it was was that I saw Lydia give it to Scott at Death by Coffee."

"Right. And no one else has admitted to seeing it," Lena said. "Detective Buchannan checked his phone a few times while we were at that hotel at the edge of town, and the next thing I knew, he was yelling at us to get in the car. He sped all the way to the camp, where we found you. I don't recall him finding a single thing that made me think he'd found a clue. And I know he never found a note because he would have acted on it right away. So . . ."

"What led Buchannan to the camp?" I asked, finishing the thought.

"Exactly."

I considered it, but had no answer. "He checked his phone? Like he was getting texts?"

"I don't know. I was kind of hoping you might."

I shook my head slowly. Could Buchannan have been the one cheating, and not Drew? Could he have had someone from the inside feeding him clues? Someone like Richie or Lydia?

No, that didn't make sense. As far as I knew, he didn't know either of them. But he could have had someone like his wife, Elsie, checking for clues around town for him. Or maybe other cops filled him in on whatever they found as they cruised the town.

Lena jumped and tugged her phone from her back pocket. She glanced at the screen and gave a massive roll of her eyes. "It's Mom wondering where I am. I swear, she still treats me like I'm twelve."

"That's what moms do," I said. There was a faint twinge in my chest, thinking about how my own mom had been taken from me far too soon. Yeah, I still had Dad, but what I wouldn't give to have Mom around to treat me like a child every now and again. It's probably why I felt so protective over my younger employees; I wanted to "Mom" them.

"Yay for me." Lena smiled as she said it. "I'd better go before she explodes. We should compare notes sometime, see if we can figure out what it was Detective Buchannan saw that led him to the camp. There had to be a clue somewhere, right? He wouldn't have just rushed off and randomly shown up where you found the body without a good reason."

No, he wouldn't have. But if there *was* a clue, how come no one else seemed to have found it? The idea that another cop might have helped him was stuck in my head and wouldn't shake loose. I'd have to ask Paul if he knew anything about it when I talked to him next.

"I'll ask around," I said. "Maybe Rita or Wendy saw something I missed. If so, I'll let you know."

"Thanks. Wouldn't it be amazing if I somehow came up with the murderer on my own? Buchannan would die."

"It would be something," I said, following her to the door. "Good luck with your mom. Say hi to her for me."

She laughed. "Thanks, I'll do that. She's probably more worried about the car than me."

Doubtful, but I didn't say it out loud. Sometimes, it was better to let your kids think that way, just a little bit, so that they didn't feel smothered.

Lena left, and I closed the door with a smile that was

just a smidge sad. She might have passed years ago, but I hoped Mom was still keeping an eye on me. She'd probably act like Janice Allison and pretend she didn't care nearly as much as she really did, all while finding a way to keep me safe.

Like I said, it's what moms do.

11

Caramel oozed from the bottle in a slow drizzle that seemed to have no end. The world around me had vanished. All I could see was the caramel, the coffee, the red, burnt hands, and a towel-covered face. My throat started to close as my mind tried to conjure another face lurking on the edges of my vision, one I was sure I'd seen before. But which one?

Austin, Drew, Oliver, Lydia. Each face morphed into the next. Robert, Link, Richie. Me.

"Uh . . . Ms. Hancock? I think that's enough."

I jumped, squirting caramel across the counter. The caramel macchiato I was supposed to have been making now consisted of mostly caramel.

"Sorry about that," I said. "I'll make another one. I spaced out there for a second."

Jeff stared at me with concern before turning to the customer, who, thankfully, looked more amused by my brain freeze than annoyed.

We were at the tail end of the morning rush, and the

customer whose macchiato I'd ruined was the last in line. We'd have a few more morning stragglers come in throughout the next ten minutes or so, but it was nothing Jeff and Beth couldn't handle on their own until lunchtime, when Vicki was going to stop in. With Lena spending more and more time with the police, especially now with the murder, we were feeling a smidge shorthanded. Enough so that I was starting to believe we were going to need to hire another person or two.

I finished the new macchiato with the appropriate amount of drizzle and handed it over to the customer, who thanked me before whistling his way out the door. I sagged back against the counter and closed my eyes. I was in desperate need of a breather—both physical and mental.

"Are you okay?" Jeff asked.

I cracked open an eye to see him wiping up my mess with a rag that was already in need of changing, thanks to other messes I'd made throughout the morning. "I am. I'm just tired."

"I've been there." He set the rag aside, produced another. He gave me a side-eyed glance, but was too nice to comment on how many times I'd messed up orders. I'd likely made his job far more difficult than if he'd been trying to handle the morning rush alone.

"It was a long night," I said, forcing myself upright. I grabbed a rag of my own and began the process of wiping everything down in preparation for the lunch rush.

"Is it because of the murder?"

"Yeah. I hate that I wasn't able to help the police." And that my mind refused to let it go, even when we were so busy, there was hardly time to think. "I was there. I should have seen *something*."

"I wish I could help," Jeff said in an aw-shucks tone. "I don't like feeling like I never contribute."

"You contribute," I told him. "I don't know what I'd do without you here. And I'm glad you haven't had to deal with a murderer yet. It's not a lot of fun."

He shrugged, seemingly unconvinced.

We fell silent as we continued cleaning. Jeff wasn't much of a talker, which was okay normally, but today I needed the distraction. Beth was busy running around upstairs, dealing with the books, which were often left sitting out after the rush. People would buy their coffee, then go upstairs to browse, often pulling books off shelves and setting them aside when they were done. I never quite understood why they couldn't just put them back where they found them, but I guess not everyone was like me when it came to books.

I finished with the coffee machines and glanced out into the dining area. There were still customers sitting at a couple of the tables, but for the most part, they were empty.

"I'm going to start working on the tables," I said, itching to be out from behind the counter. I was starting to feel boxed in and hoped the open dining space would dampen my building anxiety.

"I've got it here," Jeff said before vanishing to the back with his caramel-loaded rags.

I rounded the counter and started with the nearest table. I tried to focus solely on my cleaning, and I did a decent job of it at first. I sprayed cleaner on the table, wiped it down, and did the same to each of the chairs.

There was a rhythm to it that you could easily get lost in. The first two tables went quickly. Spritz, wipe. Spritz, wipe.

And then I approached an empty table sitting next to an occupied one.

"I heard he was planning a bank heist," a young man said to his companions. "His partner offed him before it went down because he was afraid of getting caught."

"A bank heist?" the only female of the group said. "Come on, Theo. You can't really believe that."

The young man leaned back in his chair, hands raised. "Hey, that's just what I heard."

"I heard it was because of that game they were playing," another man said. This one was so pale, I was afraid the sunlight streaming in through the plate-glass window might burn him. "He was keeping secrets from his teammates, and when they found out, they killed him for it."

I caught myself spraying the same spot over and over, only occasionally remembering to wipe off the cleaner, as I strained to listen. It was obvious they were talking about Scott and his murder.

"What kind of secrets do you think he was holding back, Clay?" the woman asked.

"I don't know, Karla, what kind of secrets?" Clay shot back with a grin.

"How am I supposed to know? It's your rumor," Karla said. "I'm just glad it's over. People were in and out of Fern's all day, and none of them wanted a haircut. I hated it."

"You just wanted the tips," said Theo.

"I don't think it had to do with the game," Clay said. "The way I heard it, he was talking about everyone and knew something about a member of his team that made them nervous."

"What? That they were going to rob a bank?" Theo chuckled.

"Stop it with the bank!" There was a smack as Karla whacked Theo on the arm.

"I bet they were lovers," Clay said. "Think about it. He catches them together, and if they were both already married or seeing someone, he could use it as blackmail. Maybe he tried, and they decided to do away with him instead of paying up."

"You watch too many movies," Karla said.

"I'm just telling you what I heard. You can always—" Theo looked up then and saw me openly staring. "Let's go, guys."

Chairs screeched as they were pushed back from the table. Theo muttered something to his friends, who all proceeded to look my way, before whispering to one another on their way out the door.

Great, they'll probably go somewhere to talk about me *next.*

I went back to cleaning the now-drenched table, though my mind wasn't on it any longer.

Everyone who knew him knew that Scott Flanagan loved to gossip. Drew claimed Scott had said something about Austin sleeping around with his neighbors. True or not, it had to bother Austin that everyone was at least *thinking* that he might have. When I'd seen them at Death by Coffee later that morning, Austin had given Scott the cold shoulder, though Shari didn't seem to be upset with Scott, but rather was somewhat supportive. Then, later, Vivian had said Scott had argued with Austin, and that both Shari and Austin had left him behind.

Could Clay have been right and Scott had caught Austin and Shari together? Scott didn't seem like the kind of guy who would blackmail someone, but perhaps he'd tried. And if he had, how did the note Lydia had given him fit in?

The door opened as I moved toward the table the gossiping trio had recently vacated. A small, extremely pretty Black woman entered. She paused just inside the door, and upon seeing me, she burst into a wide smile that instantly lit up the room.

"There you are!" she said, striding my way.

"Cassie!" I gave her a quick, careful hug. Considering I was covered in spilled caramel, I didn't want to ruin her clothing. "I've been meaning to call you."

Cassie Wise and I had recently become friends after an ill-fated summer marathon. We were mostly exercise buddies, despite how my body hated the word *exercise*, let alone actually performing it.

"I know you've been busy," she said. She was wearing a form-fitting runner's outfit that I wouldn't even dare to attempt. She, however, made it look good. "But I was out on my morning run and saw that the new gym is finally open! I figured I'd stop in here and see if you'd be interested in checking it out tomorrow?"

"Tomorrow?" I did a quick mental schedule check. "I could do that. What time?"

"I was thinking nine, if that's all right with you? I have a doctor's appointment in the afternoon, so I'd like to get an hour or two in before running home to shower."

"Nine works." Though my legs and back were already screaming at me to cancel. "Meet you there?"

"Sounds good." She checked her Fitbit. "I wish I could stick around and chat, but I have to run. I'll see you tomorrow."

"See you then."

Cassie gave me another quick hug, making sure to keep her body from pressing against mine, and she power walked out the door. As soon as her feet hit the sidewalk, she started to run.

Already feeling the burn, I finished up with the tables and returned to behind the counter, where I deposited the spray bottle and rag. A quick look around showed me that Jeff had done a good job with his own cleaning and that there was little else for me to do.

"I think I'm going to head out," I said as Jeff exited the back room, a stack of clean washrags in hand. "Unless you need me to stick around so you can snag a quick break?"

"I'm okay," Jeff said. He deposited the rags under the counter and checked the time on the coffee before allowing himself a moment to relax.

Upstairs, Beth had just finished tidying up the bookshelves and had brought out the broom to sweep. It appeared as if everything was under control.

"If it picks up again and you need help, just call," I said, though I knew they wouldn't.

"Sure thing, Ms. Hancock."

I almost corrected him, but didn't. I was going to be Ms. Hancock to him until the day I died.

I grabbed my things from the tiny office in the back, already planning my first stop. Cassie mentioning a doctor's appointment got me thinking about the team of doctors who'd taken part in Oliver's production. Perhaps one of them saw something, or if not, I hoped Carl's relationship with Drew would yield some sort of information that would help bring the killer to justice.

I opened the door, mind already working on what I was going to say to the doctors when I saw them, and just about walked into a scowling Detective Buchannan.

"Oh!" I said, caught by surprise. "What are you doing here?"

Buchannan's scowl deepened. "What do you think I'm doing?"

I backed up, letting him enter Death by Coffee. "You're here for your morning cup of joe?"

His stare could have melted steel.

My shoulders sagged as I sighed. "I take it you want to talk to me."

"If you have time." His tone seemed to add, *You'd better*. "It won't take long."

I didn't bother to argue. I walked over to the nearest table and sat down. Buchannan nodded to himself and, instead of joining me right away, headed for the counter to order that cup of joe.

I fidgeted in my seat while I waited for him. Buchannan only ever wanted to talk to me when he thought I knew something and was keeping it from him. It wouldn't be a pleasant conversation, especially since I didn't have anything for him but speculation.

Buchannan *hated* speculation.

Jeff handed over Detective Buchannan's coffee with a nervous glance my way. Buchannan sampled the coffee and smiled before he headed my way. He'd never admit it, but I'm pretty sure John Buchannan was becoming a Death by Coffee regular.

Another sip, and he sat, wiping a hand across the top of the recently cleaned table before setting his coffee down. "I want you to walk me through how you ended up at the logging camp once more," he said, folding his hands in front of him.

I suppressed a sigh and did as he asked, starting from the moment my team had left Ted and Bettfast and all the way up until the moment I'd tried to call the police after Wendy had found Scott's body. I tried not to leave anything out, but it wasn't easy considering how long of a day it had been and how much running around we'd done. By the time I was done, my brain was fried from working so hard.

"And you're absolutely certain you saw no one?" Buchannan asked. "You didn't talk to your team about the note anywhere anyone else could hear?"

I shook my head. "I saw no one, and no one else knew about the note. Even if they did, there's no way they could have beaten us to the logging camp to kill Scott and get away before we arrived."

"You're certain?" he pressed. "You didn't make any stops along the way? You didn't take an indirect route?"

"No. We went straight there." I paused. "How did you know about the camp?"

Buchannan's face went stony. "I followed the clues."

"What clues? No one else showed up after we found the body. You couldn't have been the only one to find the clue. And if a team was there before us, wouldn't it be easy to prove?" A new thought. "What if one of the actors was stationed at the logging camp and they killed Scott when he showed up alone?"

"Why would they do that?"

I opened my mouth to answer, but snapped it closed again without saying a word. I had no answer for him.

Buchannan nodded to himself. "And do you have any evidence that someone was stationed there? Or that any other team arrived before you?"

"Well, no," I said. "But Oliver Quick would know, wouldn't he? Have you talked to him?"

That earned me another one of Buchannan's patented flat looks.

"Of course, you have," I said. "Did he say anything about why Scott might have been at the camp? If it *wasn't* part of his production, perhaps he would know . . ." I trailed off, uncertain what it could mean.

"Ms. Hancock, you know I'm not going to discuss details of the case with you. Suffice it to say, I've talked to those deemed important to the investigation."

"I'm just confused," I said. "Lydia gives Scott a note. Scott, according to Vivian Flowers, tells his team that he needs to go to the logging camp alone, though I don't think he said exactly where he needed to go, so I don't believe the Cherry Valley team, nor Scott's team, knew anything about his plans."

Buchannan pulled out a notepad, jotted something down, and nodded for me to go on.

"Scott leaves the Banyon Tree alone, ends up at the logging camp, where he's killed. I found the note Lydia had given him in the bathroom at the Banyon Tree not too terribly long after he'd discarded it or accidentally dropped it. The Cherry Valley team was still at the Banyon Tree to see him leave, so it had to be, at most, twenty minutes? Thirty?"

"You said his team abandoned him?" Buchannan asked.

"Yeah. Vivian and the others said he argued with Austin before Scott went into the bathroom. They said that Austin and Shari had left while Scott was still inside."

"And then Scott leaves, heads to the camp, and is murdered."

"Exactly."

"How did he get there?"

I stared at him, stunned. How *did* Scott get to the camp? If his team had left, he wouldn't have had a ride. I doubted they would have taken separate cars to the Banyon Tree. Every team had a designated driver, and that included Scott's own.

"See, that's what's been bothering me," Buchannan said. "Mr. Flanagan couldn't have walked to the logging camp in time to get murdered before you arrived."

"Someone gave him a ride," I said, mind racing. *But who?*

"But who?" Buchannan said, echoing my silent question. "So far, no one I've talked to has copped to it. In fact, no one claims to have seen him after the Banyon Tree. Most say the last time they remember seeing him was at Ted and Bettfast. So who gave him a ride?"

I thought about it, but had no answer. Could Scott have called an Uber? Did Pine Hills even have Uber drivers? It wasn't like it was a big town where there'd be constant fares to be had.

"The Banyon Tree has security cameras," I said, thinking it through. "Did you check them to see if they showed who picked him up?"

The look Buchannan gave me would have killed a lesser woman. "Of course, I did," he said. "But he walks off screen. He never gets into a car. Never calls anyone, nor does he appear to talk to someone standing out of sight."

"Oh. It was just a thought."

Buchannan took a drink from his coffee and stood with a sigh. "Think about it," he said. "You might not have been the last person to see Scott Flanagan alive, but you were hot on his trail, meaning you might have seen something important without realizing you did. If you figure out what that might be, I want you to tell me immediately. Don't go running around town poking your nose into my investigation. Don't try to verify what you think you saw by talking to potential killers. Call me the *instant* you think of something. Do I make myself clear?"

"Crystal," I said, though I'd barely heard him. Someone drove Scott to the place where he'd been murdered. That someone was either a murderer, or might have seen something—or someone—that could lead to the real killer.

Buchannan stared at me for a long couple of seconds before he gave a curt nod. "Good. I'll contact you if I have further questions." And he turned and walked out of Death by Coffee. He paused on the sidewalk, checked his phone, and climbed into his car.

I watched him drive off, my mind still churning over the fact that someone out there had driven Scott to his death, and I didn't mean that figuratively. That someone could be the key witness in a murder, and I had no idea where to start to find them.

Not that I should be looking. But if my nosiness led to a killer, Buchannan couldn't truly be mad at me, could he?

I knew the answer to that, but pretended I didn't as I rose. Buchannan might not want me to talk to anyone, but I couldn't sit around and do nothing, not if I could help.

And while I doubted Carl knew anything about who drove Scott to the logging camp—or why Lydia had given Scott a note to meet there—he *did* know Drew MacDonald. If nothing else, it was a place to start.

12

The downtown doctors' office was the only Pine Hills medical practice I was aware of, though considering the number of people in town, I could have been wrong. I'd once dated one of the doctors, Will Foster, but he'd taken a job in Arizona, leaving the practice to his friends, Carl and Darrin, and my personal doctor, Paige Lipmon. Every time I entered the office, I thought of Will, and they weren't bad thoughts. We'd parted on good terms, friendly even, but I couldn't help the "what ifs" that swirled through my brain. I was more than happy with Paul, but Will was a good man as well.

An elderly receptionist sat behind the window across the room from the door. Bea had been the receptionist ever since I'd started coming here years ago, and she hadn't aged a day in that time. She was eighty if she was a day, and I was beginning to wonder if perhaps she'd found some sort of cure for aging, because while older, she still appeared as if she could whip me upside the head a good one if I stepped out of line.

There was only one other person in the waiting room when I entered. She glanced up at me, eyes wide and terrified. She had a hand pressed against her belly, and while it could simply be an upset stomach, I was betting she was there for another reason entirely.

I gave her a reassuring smile before I headed for the window. "Hi, Bea. How have you been?"

The older woman grunted, glanced at her monitor. She didn't click or type anything when she said, "I don't have you down for an appointment, Ms. Hancock. Doctor Lipmon is quite busy."

"I'm not injured," I said, giving her a big smile to prove the point. "But I do need to talk to one of the doctors. It doesn't need to be Paige. It's about what happened yesterday."

Bea glanced at me over the top of her bifocals. "The doctors cannot discuss the health of anyone, living or murdered."

"It's all right, Bea," Carl said, poking his head into the reception area from the back. "Go ahead and send her back."

Bea's jaw tightened, but she nodded toward the door that led to the exam rooms, which had just opened. A nurse was quietly talking to the scared young woman, who kept shaking her head as she eyed the door as if she was afraid to walk through it.

I slipped through while they were still talking. I felt for the woman. One of my friends, Shannon, had recently had a baby out of wedlock. She was getting by, and while it was often a struggle, Shannon was doing pretty well, thanks to her supportive friends. I hoped this young woman was just as lucky.

"Back here," Carl said, as I stepped into the back. He walked briskly past the exam rooms, to a small space that held a computer sitting atop a desk that was crammed into the corner. Files were stacked next to the monitor, and more were sitting in baskets hanging from the wall. One look made me wonder how the doctors ever found anything.

"I'm sorry to just drop in on you like this," I said, turning my attention to him.

Carl waved me off. "Actually, I expected a visit sooner or later." He sat down in the chair behind the desk and motioned me to the chair opposite him. "In fact, Detective Buchannan warned me against talking to you, so I was positive you'd be around eventually."

"Buchannan told you not to talk to me?" I almost laughed. Of course he had.

"He did, though it's not like there's anything I could tell you that would matter. I didn't witness anything that you didn't also see."

"Maybe not, but you do know Drew better than I do."

Carl considered that and nodded. "I suppose I do. Not all that well, as I told you before. Just in passing."

"If there's anything you can tell me about him that might help . . ."

Carl was shaking his head even before I finished. "Drew and I know each other by sight, and that's about it. I told you he was reprimanded at the hospital."

I nodded.

"Drew has an attitude, one he doesn't drop at work.

He can be abrasive, and as we all saw, he can get physical with people who upset him."

"Do you think he could kill someone?"

Carl thought about it before answering. "Physically, he's capable. But do I think he'd actually do it?" He shook his head. "No, I think Drew MacDonald is the kind of man who talks big, who will push someone around he knows he can dominate, but he will back down if pressed too hard. He's also in the medical field. I suppose I'm biased, but I can't imagine that someone who dedicates their lives to helping others would kill someone."

It was a nice thought, but thanks to a handful of Netflix documentaries I'd seen recently, I knew that Carl was being naïve.

"I'm sure Buchannan already asked you this, but did you see anything at all that might be important?" I asked. "Like did someone talk to Scott who shouldn't have? Did someone sneak off somewhere? Make a comment that seemed innocent at the time, but upon further reflection, could be construed as threatening?"

Carl's brow furrowed. "I don't recall anything like that. At least, nothing that we all didn't witness."

"Did you see Scott with Lydia, perhaps? Or perhaps Drew snuck off to talk to someone?"

Carl shook his head. "I'm sorry."

"What about the rest of your team? Could Paige or Darrin have seen something you missed?" I was taking a stab in the dark, but already felt as if I was going to get nowhere.

"I doubt it," Carl said, confirming my thought. "I mean, I suppose it's possible, but if one of them had seen anything, they would have told Detective Buchannan when he interviewed them." He leaned forward, looked me in the eye. "Should you be looking into this, Krissy? I know it's in your nature, but one of these times, it's going to come back and bite you."

I smiled. "You sound like Paul."

Carl chuckled and sat back. "I guess you probably hear that all the time from him, don't you? I'd forgotten you two were dating. I still think of you as being with Will, even though he's not here any longer."

There it was, that old pang. "Will and I still talk every now and again," I said. "And I see his sister and niece here and there." And every time I did, it made me miss the time we'd spent together.

"Jade and Gemma were here just yesterday for their yearlies. I'm always happy to see them." Carl sighed, expression shifting to thoughtful. He drummed his fingers on his desk and seemed to make his mind up about something. "I probably shouldn't be telling you this, but while Paige, Darrin, and I might not have much for you, Anne might."

"Anne?"

"Doctor Anne Logan, our newest partner. You haven't met her, I don't believe?"

I shook my head. "Not yet. She knew Drew?"

It was Carl's turn to shake his head. "Not Drew, but the victim. She . . ." He stood. "Actually, she's taking a break right now. She should tell you. Wait here." He quickly strode from the room.

I fidgeted as I waited, trying hard not to jump to conclusions. My mind was trying to make connections without having any solid facts to support those connections. Anne knew Scott. Scott needed a ride from the Banyon Tree. Could he have called her and she'd picked him up? And if so, could something have happened where she ended up getting into an argument with him and killing him?

I mean, it was possible, sure, but realistically? Unless there was some serious bad blood between the two, I couldn't see her killing him—not that I knew anything about Anne Logan. And if there *was* bad blood between them, why would Scott call her to pick him up in the first place?

He wouldn't have. Stop letting your imagination run away with you.

Still, the moment Anne Logan walked through the door, chewing on an apple slice, I was checking for any signs that she might have murdered Scott. There was nothing there, of course. It wasn't like she'd come strolling through the door with blood on her hands or wearing a shirt splattered with caramel macchiato.

"Hello. Krissy, right?" She wiped her fingers on a napkin she was carrying before reaching out to shake. "I'm Doctor Logan. Anne."

I rose long enough to shake her hand before sitting again. "Krissy, yes. Krissy Hancock."

Anne rounded the desk and sat in the chair Carl had recently vacated. She was a short, stocky woman with a no-nonsense attitude to her that leapt out the moment you saw her. That didn't mean she wasn't pleasant, because as she sat, her smile was warm, friendly, but I could tell that none of her patients would be able to pull one over on her. It was something in her eyes.

"What can I do for you, Krissy? Carl said you wanted

to talk about Scott Flanagan?" She made the last a question.

"You knew him?"

She tossed her napkin onto the desk and sat back in her chair. "I did. It's been something like two years since I last talked to him, but we were acquainted. We went to high school together." She smiled fondly, as if she had pleasant memories of those years. "That feels like a lifetime ago."

Considering she was younger than me, her comment made me feel ancient. "What was Scott like back then?" I asked.

Anne considered it before spreading her hands, palms upward. "Just your awkward teenager, really. Everyone knew him, but I don't think he had a ton of friends. He liked to talk."

I didn't have to ask to know that she meant he was a gossip, even back then. "Did he get into a lot of fights?"

"Not that I recall. I'm sure he was picked on, but you know how it is. I was focused on my own studies and friends. Scott was in most of my classes, so we interacted here and there, but weren't close or anything. He was book smart, but wasn't world smart, if you know what I mean?"

I did. There were some people who could do math in their head, could name all the world's capitals at a whim, yet when it came to simple stuff that normal people often knew, they were oblivious.

"You said you talked to him a few years ago," I said. "Did he reach out? Or was it a class reunion or something like that?"

Anne laughed. "Oh no, I'd never set foot near one of

those. I might not have hated my high school years, but I don't wish to go back and revisit them." She glanced at her watch, sobered. "It happened by chance. I was working at a clinic in Levington when he came in with a welt the size of a baseball on his face. He was worried his eye socket might be chipped or broken, but he was fine."

"What happened to him?"

Anne considered me. I didn't know if my question broke the doctor code or if she was simply hesitant to answer health questions about a dead man. It was probably some combination of the two.

She picked up her napkin and rose slowly. When she spoke, she didn't sound nervous exactly, but there was a hesitation to her voice. "Look, I need to get back. I have a ten o'clock."

I stood, disappointed, but I understood. "Thank you for talking to me," I said. "I really do appreciate it."

Anne nodded and walked over to the door, where she paused. There was a brief internal debate, and she said, "Scott Flanagan wasn't a bad person."

"No, he didn't seem like he was."

She glanced out into the hall, then back to me. "I can't tell you exactly what happened to him two years ago because I don't know for sure. Since he knew me from school, he kind of just started talking while I was looking him over. He told me a long, convoluted story that ended with what he called a misunderstanding that got out of hand."

A nurse appeared from down the hall. "Ms. Prince is waiting in room three," he said before hurrying away.

Anne took a step into the hall, but stopped once again.

Something told me that she wasn't quite done with our conversation, but wasn't sure she should continue.

I waited her out, hoping she would.

"I don't remember the whole story," she said after a moment. "But I do remember a name. I guess it stuck with me because I knew Scott, and it always bothered me that he'd been hurt. Like I said, he wasn't a bad person. He just didn't seem to understand how to deal with people, and it often got him into trouble."

"He deserves justice," I said, not sure if a name from two years ago would help now, but I wanted to know it anyway.

Anne pressed her lips together, checked down the hall once more, before she said, "I don't know if it will help with that, but I hope it does. The person who struck him and who very nearly broke Scott's eye socket over a 'misunderstanding'"—she made air quotes—"was a man named Lincoln Freel. That's all I know."

And with that, she walked down the hall, to her appointment.

Lincoln Freel. As in, Link the actor? I had a feeling it was.

I left the doctors' offices in a daze. If Scott knew Link and claimed that their fight two years ago was only a misunderstanding, it was possible he could have called the actor to pick him up from the Banyon Tree. Link's role consisted of playing a dead man at the beginning of Oliver's production and then . . . well, nothing as far as I could tell. That meant he might have been free to leave, unless Oliver had been using him behind the scenes, though I had no evidence that he was.

And what about that misunderstanding? Scott might have considered it to be nothing more than a spat, quickly forgotten, but to Link, it might have been more. It might have festered over the years, and then, when he saw Scott at Ted and Bettfast, it boiled over to the point where he decided to kill him.

My phone buzzed as I climbed into my Escape. I answered without even looking at the screen. I kept imagining Link, dressed in his dead man getup, killing Scott. The image had a definite horror-movie vibe to it.

"Hi, Krissy, I stopped in at Death by Coffee, but you weren't in."

"Paul?" My brain slammed into the here and now. "Yeah, sorry. I was there earlier, but left after morning rush." I paused, a smile finding my face, despite my recent less-than-pleasant thoughts. "You stopped in to see me?"

"I did. I bought candy from Phantastic Candies and planned on sharing, but since you weren't there, I went ahead and ate it myself."

"You wouldn't dare!"

"I guess you'll never know."

There was one of those brief silences that was full of warmth and comfort where no one needed to talk. I couldn't stop grinning like a fool. Paul and I had been dating off and on for years now, yet it often still felt like we were in those wonderful fledgling stages of our relationship where the smallest thing felt like winning the lottery. I hoped that feeling lasted until we were old and gray.

No, not just until then, but forever.

"I need to get back to work here myself, but thought I'd call and see if you might want to get dinner tonight. Geraldo's?"

My mouth was already watering. "Dinner would be great."

"Perfect. Pick you up at seven?"

"I'll be waiting."

We said our gooey goodbyes, and I spent the next couple of minutes in anticipatory bliss before reality started to seep back in.

Scott's murder. Link's possible involvement.

And then, in big, block letters, WENDY'S WELL-BEING!

"Crap!" I'd completely forgotten that I'd promised to stop in after work.

I slammed the car into gear and sped out of the doctor's office parking lot, hoping that I hadn't missed Rita, because her wrath is something that I'd rather avoid.

13

Rita's car was still in the lot when I pulled up to Wendy's small apartment complex. I double-checked the apartment number and hurried to the front door. The complex was tidy, clean, the sort of place college students might live if we had had a college in Pine Hills. I took a moment to calm my nerves and knocked on the door, just under the number 7.

The door opened, but it wasn't Rita or Wendy who answered.

"Haley?" I asked, surprised. I often saw Wendy and Haley together. They were of a similar age and were both members of the writers' group; as far as I knew, the two were good friends, yet I hadn't expected her to be here. She was wearing pajama bottoms and a thin T-shirt. Her hair was pulled up in a messy bun that looked as if she'd slept on it. "Do you live here?"

"Yeah. Wendy and I room." She stepped aside without me having to ask. "She's in the living room with Rita."

"Thank you." I entered the apartment.

Haley and Wendy might look like college kids, but their apartment showed they weren't the stereotype. The place smelled of warm cinnamon due to a candle burning in the tiny galley kitchen. All the surfaces were clean from both dust and clutter. A round table that could seat two or three people max was tucked in a space barely big enough for those two or three people. Two laptops rested atop it, both closed and, unlike mine, free from tea.

The living room was five steps from the doorway, blocked from view by a wall. Rita was standing by a well-worn rocking chair that looked to be an antique, while Wendy was seated on the couch, legs tucked under her and a blanket pooled in her lap. She gave me a wan smile as I entered.

"There you are!" Rita said, turning. "We've been waiting for two hours for you to show. I swore up and down to Wendy that you'd be here and was starting to question myself."

"I'm sorry. I got caught up at work." Not quite the full truth, but I didn't want to tell them that I'd gotten so wrapped up in looking for a killer, I'd nearly forgotten about my promise.

Rita sighed. "It's all right, dear. We've spent the time talking things through. Sometimes, talk can help, especially after such a traumatic event."

Haley slipped past me into the room. She eased down onto the couch next to Wendy, who immediately reached for her hand. I noted there was a faint tremble there, which was worrying. No, I didn't expect her to be over finding the body, but I had hoped she'd be better today.

"We've gone over everything at least a dozen times," Rita said. "Dissected every little thing we could remember."

"Are you sure that's a good idea?" I asked.

"Why wouldn't it be?" Rita's hands found her hips. It was a sure sign that she was annoyed with me. "We all want to get to the bottom of what happened, don't we? What better way to do it than to put our heads together? Good idea? Geesh!"

I let her tone wash over me without complaint. I deserved it after being late. "Did you come up with anything?" I asked.

"Not really," Wendy said. "I've wracked my brain, but . . ."

"It's the darndest thing," Rita said, cutting in. "I swear we've gone over it a thousand times, and nothing leapt out at either of us."

"I know I didn't see anything," Wendy said. "I've closed my eyes and thought about it as hard as I could, and nothing comes to me. I keep seeing him, seeing that coffee mug, but that's it."

"It's like whoever killed that man was a ghost," Rita added. "They left nothing behind. No clues, no evidence that they were there at all!"

"Other than Scott's body," Wendy said with a shudder.

"Other than that, of course," Rita agreed.

Everyone looked at me. I felt like I should say something profound, but what? I didn't have much in the way of evidence either. I'd been right there with Rita and Wendy the whole time, so what they saw was what I saw, maybe even less, considering Wendy and Rita were the first two in the room where Scott was found.

But that wasn't the only place of importance to the crime.

"Do either of you remember if anything strange happened at Ted and Bettfast?" I asked. "Other than the fights we all witnessed."

Wendy and Rita shared a look before Rita shook her head and answered. "Not that I recall. I went to bed early so I could get an early start and sure don't remember anything happening after I woke up."

"I . . ." Wendy frowned. "It might be nothing."

"What is it? Anything you saw could be important."

Wendy bit her lip, squeezed Haley's hand. When she spoke, she did so slowly, as if testing each word before saying it. "It was after the scuffle that happened downstairs after lights out."

"What scuffle?" Rita asked.

I waved her into silence.

"Like everyone else, I went back to bed once it was over," Wendy went on. "But before I got to our room, I saw a couple of people in the hallway. As soon as they saw me, they stopped talking and went to their rooms. I didn't think anything of it at first, but now . . ."

"Did you hear what they were talking about?" I asked. "And who was it?" There were only so many people it could have been. Richie and Lydia were cleaning up the evidence. Buchannan and the police officers, as well as the Cherry Valley team and Oliver, were stationed downstairs. Shari was helping Scott clean up. Rita was still snoring away in our room. That only left a handful of people it could have been.

"Not everything," Wendy said, answering the first question. "I think one of them said, 'You know what to do,' just as I reached the top of the stairs, but I can't be sure. It could have been something else."

"That sounds rather suspicious," Rita said.

Indeed, it did. "Do you remember who was speaking?" I asked.

Wendy looked to Haley, as if for support. "I'm not sure about their names," she said. "It's all such a blur."

"It's okay. Take your time." My heart was pounding. "Can you describe them?"

She considered it, and nodded. "I think so."

I leaned forward, anticipation making me want to crowd her. Could Wendy have overheard co-conspirators talking about killing Scott? Considering how things turned out, I found it likely.

"The first guy was the one who started the fight. Drew, right?"

I nodded. "Yeah, Drew MacDonald." I wasn't the least bit surprised he was involved.

"He's the one who was talking when I headed upstairs. I only heard him because he was talking louder than he intended. You know what I mean? He wanted to whisper, but was so angry, it came out almost like a shout."

"We've all been there," Rita said.

"What about the other person?" I asked.

Wendy's brow furrowed as she thought about it. "He

looked kind of tough, like he'd once been into sports but had let himself go over the years. Hair kind of shaggy. Dark blond. Or maybe it was brown?"

A thrum of excitement shot through me. I knew exactly who she was talking about. And not only that, but Link had mentioned the exact same person as having a history with Drew MacDonald.

"Austin Helms," I said. "Scott's teammate."

And, quite possibly, his murderer.

Austin and Drew had a history. If I didn't miss my guess, they were likely the two Sara had seen talking outside her window at Ted and Bettfast. Then, later, Drew says something extremely suspicious to Austin, who, the next day, appears to be angry with Scott. Then Scott goes off on his own, thanks to a note Lydia had given him, while Austin and Shari continue their investigation without him.

But what if Austin didn't actually leave, but instead followed Scott?

I was on my way to Ted and Bettfast to see if I could find out if he had. I still didn't know how Lydia's note played into Scott's death, nor did I know how Austin could have killed Scott with Shari in tow. It was possible that she was involved, but I was having a hard time seeing it. Out of everyone, she seemed to have liked—or at least tolerated—Scott the most.

And what about Anne's comment about Link and Scott having a history? Could Link have been in on the murder as well? Could he have driven Scott to his death, even offered to do it because he knew what was coming? And could Lydia have been an unwitting accomplice? If Link had given her the note, claiming, let's say, it was from Oliver, she might have delivered it, thinking she was helping her boss.

I felt I was getting closer to the truth. I just had to untangle the facts from the fiction and somehow put it all together with a neat bow on top for Detective Buchannan.

Because, yeah, I'm sure he'd be thrilled to learn I was poking around his investigation yet again.

I drove past what had once been hedge animals and parked in a lot that was still relatively full. I hoped that meant the Levington teams were still hanging around and hadn't headed back home.

I parked and hurried for the door. As soon as I was through it, I jerked to a stop, surprised by what I saw.

Oliver Quick was in the middle of the front room, watching as Richie rearranged furniture by the back door. Lydia, arms loaded with the props that had been surrounding Link when he'd been playing dead, stood by, waiting to be told what to do. Her cheeks were flushed, eyes puffy, yet she remained on standby. When she saw me enter, she flinched ever so slightly before relaxing, as if she'd expected it to be someone else.

Detective Buchannan, perhaps? If Scott's murder *was* one big conspiracy and she was involved, it would be no wonder. I'd be nervous too if I'd hand-delivered the note that had led someone to their death, even if I was just the messenger.

"No, no, no," Oliver said, clapping his hands with

every word. "Not like that. Think of where the sun will be, how it will cascade over the scene. You don't want me to be washed out, do you?"

"I'm sorry, Mr. Quick," Richie said, turning the chair a fraction to the left.

Oliver sighed. "Better, but still not right. Let me—" He must have sensed me watching because he cut off and spun around. There was a glint of excitement in his eye that died the moment he saw me. "Oh. It's you."

I tried not to be hurt by the disappointment in his voice. "I don't mean to interrupt," I said, stepping farther into the room. "I was hoping I could talk to Link for a few minutes. Or Austin. Are they still here?"

"Link?" Oliver scowled. "Why would you need to talk to one of my actors?"

Because I want to know if an encounter from two years ago caused him to kill Scott. "No reason, really." I raced to come up with an excuse I thought Oliver would buy. "He did such a good job playing the victim the other day, I was hoping I could talk to him so he could give me a few pointers on how he managed it."

Across the room, Richie paused in shifting the chairs around to stare at me in disbelief.

"He's not here right now." Lydia's voice was barely about a whisper. "I'm not sure where Austin is."

I faced her and was struck by how vulnerable she looked. When we'd first started, she appeared to be the mentally stronger assistant. Richie had been tentative— and, honestly, he still was—while Lydia had taken charge.

Now it appeared as if all she wanted to do was crawl into a hole and hide from the world until everything blew over.

Did that mean she was involved in the murder?

Or, remembering what Richie had said about them sneaking off together, was she somehow involved with Scott?

"Did they go home?" I asked her.

She shook her head, but it was Oliver who answered.

"Of course not. We still have work to do here." He sighed. "If you must know, Lincoln went out for a run on the grounds. He should be back sometime soon, but I'd appreciate it if you found somewhere else to be. We need this space." He spun. "Set those down, Lydia, and get me a water. Ice-cold. Not that lukewarm bilge you brought me before."

Lydia quickly set her armload down on a table and scurried toward the hallway. She glanced back once, almost pleadingly, as if she was begging me to somehow save her from Oliver and his demands, before she vanished down the hall.

"What about Austin?" I asked. I wanted to talk to him just as much as I did Link. Drew, I thought, could wait. I doubted the angry man would talk to me, much less admit to conspiring to murder.

Oliver glared at me before saying, "How am I supposed to know? He's around town somewhere, I'm sure. Now, if you would . . ." He fluttered his hands at me in a "go away" gesture.

Only slightly miffed at his dismissal, I turned and headed for the door. I paused outside it and scanned the grounds for Link. A run meant he could be anywhere from a few yards away to clear across the large Ted and Bettfast grounds. I wasn't too keen on searching for him, and thankfully, I didn't have to.

Link was standing across the front yard, near a small copse of trees, staring off into the distance. He was wearing all white, and he glistened in the sun. I assumed it was whatever lotion he'd put on, because no one shone like that naturally.

I crossed the large, barely tended yard to join him.

"Nice day out," I said, causing him to jump ever so slightly. "It's usually a lot colder this time of year."

He nodded, but didn't otherwise respond.

"I'm surprised you're still here now that Oliver's production has halted. Why haven't you gone home? Did the police ask you to stay?"

Link sighed, glanced at me out of the corner of his eye. "No. Oliver hopes to make something out of this disaster. He asked us to stick around, just in case we are able to resume. I think he's delusional, if I'm being honest." He glanced back toward the bed-and-breakfast, as if to make sure Oliver hadn't heard him. "I expect to be leaving by tomorrow, perhaps the day after."

I considered how to bring up what Anne had told me gently and decided, screw it, and just blurted it out. "I heard you and Scott got into it a couple years ago due to a misunderstanding."

Link's entire body went rigid. He didn't speak, didn't appear to so much as breathe.

"Link? What happened back then?" *And is it why you killed him?*

Seconds ticked by during which he remained so motionless, it was impressive. It was as if he was once again playing the corpse, and he thought that if he stayed quiet long enough, I'd go away.

Obviously, he didn't know how stubborn I could be.

"Scott's team left him at the Banyon Tree," I pressed. "I'm assuming he needed a ride to the abandoned logging camp. Did he call you?" *Did you kill him?*

Link let out a breath that caused his entire body to deflate. When he spoke, his voice was emotionless. "What happened between Scott and me back then has nothing to do with what happened to him here. I'm sorry, but I have to go."

And with that, he spun around and speed-walked his way back to Ted and Bettfast.

The determined part of me wanted to give chase and continue to pepper him with questions. Did Scott call him? Did he give Scott a ride? Had he given Lydia the fateful note to pass along?

But the chances of him answering me were so close to zero, it wasn't worth the hassle.

Still, his reluctance to talk about the past made me wonder. Why not clear things up if he was innocent? Sure, it was possible that whatever had happened back then was bad enough that it would implicate him for murder now, but merely admitting to it might help make him look less guilty now.

Alone, and slightly chilled, I decided to call it a day. I had a date to prepare for.

14

The middle of my back barked as I stretched up onto my tiptoes to reach the corner with the duster. I'd spent the last hour and a half cleaning every inch of my house, anticipating coming back here after my date with Paul. It wasn't like my house was a mess, but I wanted it to be perfect. While we'd recently decided to table whatever it was Paul had been wanting to talk to me about, I still held out hope that he'd finally open up and spit it out, and that it would be something life-changing, and in a good way.

I caught the stubborn corner cobweb, then sagged back down on my heels. Every surface was polished, the floors swept, the windows washed. And now, every cobweb and dust bunny had been found and vanquished. My house smelled of pine cleaner and chocolate, the latter thanks to the brownies I'd made earlier.

Misfit, who had been freshly brushed so that he wouldn't leave tufts of fur all over the house while I was at dinner with Paul, sat in the living room, watching me with interest. The duster was one of those long, feathery ones that kind of looked like a cat toy.

"Sorry, you can't play with this one," I said, tucking the duster away.

Misfit flipped his tail from one side to the other with a heavy thump, gave me one of his deadly kitty glares, and turned and hopped up onto the couch for his evening nap.

I pressed my palms against my lower back and leaned back. The crack was loud enough I was afraid the entire neighborhood had heard it. I winced, rubbing at the sore spot in my back, while worrying about the throb that had started to grow between my shoulder blades. The house might be cleaner than it had been in years, but now I was concerned I might be too sore to enjoy my evening out with Paul.

What I needed was a good hot shower. And perhaps a few minutes with a heating pad.

And maybe a nice long back rub after dinner.

I was about to head to the bathroom to take care of the first step of my relaxation plan when my gaze fell on my laptop. It was still sitting on the kitchen counter, buried in rice. I crossed the room, considered it, and then carefully, so as not to spill any rice onto my freshly swept floor, I removed the laptop, shaking off stray grains so that they fell back into the container. Once that was done, I set the laptop down, opened the lid, said a quick prayer, and pressed the power button.

Nothing. Not even a blip on the screen.

"I guess this is goodbye, then," I said, closing the lid with a snap that made me feel a smidge melancholy. I'd had the laptop for years now. Sure, it had been showing its age, but it had been a loyal companion, a research assistant. It was almost like losing a friend.

I dumped the ruined rice into the trash, put the container in the dishwasher, and hesitated with the laptop hovering over the trash can. Throw it away? Or see if I could salvage something?

I considered it a moment longer before placing the dead laptop onto the island counter, next to the cooling brownies. It might not work any longer, but I couldn't just pitch it. If nothing else, I could find someone who knew a thing or two about electronics, and perhaps they could save the hard drive or use any undamaged bits for parts. If I could transfer the data from the old laptop to a new one, it would save me a massive headache.

I turned to the hall so I could finally take my shower when my phone rang. Noting Rita's name on the screen, I almost ignored it, figuring I could call her back once I'd cleaned up, but on the off chance that it was an emergency, I went ahead and answered.

"Hi, Rita, I can't really talk—"

"Turn on channel four, quick!"

The excitement in her voice had me reaching for the remote without having to think about it.

"Why?" I asked as I turned on the television. An old black-and-white movie was playing on whatever channel I'd last left it on. I couldn't even remember the last time I'd sat down to watch something on live TV. With streaming services, where I could pause and resume whenever I pleased, it hardly seemed worth my time. It even took me a moment to figure out which button changed the channel.

"You'll see," Rita said. "Call me back when it's over."
She clicked off before I could respond.

Channel 4, which was based out of Levington, came on mid-segment. A banner across the bottom claimed it to be a special report. A female reporter took up the right side of the screen, almost out of the picture, while someone I recognized stood front and center.

"It was a direct assault on me and my production," Oliver Quick was saying. "That poor man, Scott Flanagan, was targeted not because he deserved to be harmed, but because he was an associate of mine and was a far easier target."

Oliver was standing just behind the chair Richie had been adjusting by the back door of Ted and Bettfast earlier that day. The props were sitting on a table next to him. Oliver looked stricken, like he'd lost his best friend and was using the back of the chair for support. The waning sun shone in through the glass behind him, illuminating him and giving him a glowing aura that made me think of an angel, which I was sure was the point.

The reporter was eating it up. Her eyes were wide, and she was looking at Oliver like he was the victim, not Scott. "You believe the attack was a way for the culprit to get at you?" she asked.

"I do," Oliver said, voice somber. "Ever since I started working on this project, there have been people moving against me. They want me to fail. They want *us* to fail. This isn't the first time they've tried to harm me and my production."

"They've attempted this before?"

A moment of uncertainty crossed Oliver's features,

but it quickly morphed into sadness. "They have." I could see the wheels turning behind his mask. "I'd hired local actors—*Pine Hills* actors—to take part in the production. It felt like the best way to get the community involved, to get them to buy in. And then someone came along and sabotaged our working relationship. I don't know who did it or why. All I know is, I was forced to bring in my own troupe to take on the roles, and now . . ."

Oliver turned away, seemingly overcome. And just as the scene cut away, back to the news desk, I saw a crocodile tear glimmering in his eye.

"Once again, a murder in Pine Hills, directed at a town-wide production, has taken place. We'll have more on this story, including a sit-down with the director, Oliver Quick, tonight at eight."

An overly cheery commercial began. I snapped off the television, stunned.

No, I wasn't surprised that Oliver was using Scott's murder for his own ends—I already expected that, thanks to the conversation I'd overheard. I was shocked that people seemed to be buying it. There had been murders in Pine Hills before, and sure, they'd been on the news, but never like this.

My phone buzzed in my hand. Rita.

"Can you believe what we just saw?" she said before I could say anything. "That man is claiming the murderer is after *him!* I thought it was preposterous at first, but then I started thinking about it. Could he be right? Could someone be out to ruin him, and that poor man, Scott, simply got in the way?"

I didn't know how to answer. Heck, I could barely think straight. I stared at the black screen of my TV, wishing I'd imagined the whole episode. To think Oliver would go so far as to go on television and claim the murderer was after *him*? I'd seen no evidence that it was even remotely possible that the killer was targeting his production. It was insulting.

"Krissy?" Rita's voice cut into my thoughts. "Are you still there?"

"Yeah, sorry. I'm here," I said. "I'm just a little stunned right now."

"Do you think he could be right? Could the killer be trying to ruin the production and Scott was a convenient victim? I mean, this whole production is a big deal for our little town. What if it's not an attack against Mr. Quick, but one against Pine Hills? Could someone be trying to ruin our town?"

I found it hard to believe—both that Oliver might be the target or that it was a grudge against Pine Hills— and said as much.

"Well, it's something to think about," Rita said, sounding put out that I hadn't agreed with her assessment. "I can't say I think too highly of how Oliver Quick went to the news to talk about it. He could have told the police his concerns and left it at that. If someone really *is* after him, they'll be far more careful now that he's blabbed to the news."

"I really don't think—" A knock at the door cut me off and sent the once-snoozing Misfit flying across the room and down the hall. "Sorry, Rita, someone is here. I've got to go."

"All right, dear," she said. "Just be careful. If a killer went after Scott to get at Oliver, who knows who could be next?"

With that comforting thought, I hung up and headed for the door, but didn't open it right away. Did I think someone killed Scott Flanagan to ruin Oliver's production? No. Was I going to be careful about who I opened my door to, just in case a crazed killer had decided to pay me a visit? You'd better believe it.

"Who is it?" I called, one hand on the doorknob, the other holding my phone, ready to call the police.

"Hey, Kris, it's Robert. Can we talk?"

I closed my eyes and pressed my forehead against the door with a groan.

"It's about what's going on at Ted and Bettfast."

I opened the door and stepped aside. "I can't talk long," I said as he entered. "I've got to get cleaned up." The words *for a date* were on the tip of my tongue, but oddly, I didn't want to say them to my ex, despite the fact he knew I was dating Paul and that Robert himself was married. There was zero chance we would ever get back together, yet it still felt odd. Go figure.

"Yeah, sure, sure." Robert crossed the room and made straight for the kitchen, where he started opening drawers.

"Robert? What are you doing?"

"Ah!" He removed a butter knife and carried it over to the island counter, where he cut into my freshly baked brownies. "Have you heard the news?" he asked, as he scooped out a brownie and took a big bite.

I stared at him, my mouth agape. He *so* didn't just do that.

Sure enough, he had, and was about to do it again when I walked over and snatched the knife out of his hand. "Are you talking about the report on channel four?" I asked, pushing the brownies away from him.

Robert chewed, swallowed. "Yeah. I haven't seen it, but I was there when they were setting up. It should bring a lot of attention to Ted and Bettfast."

"I don't think a murder investigation is the sort of attention anyone wants."

Robert shrugged, reached for the container of brownies. I pushed it farther away.

He glared briefly, but let it go. "It's been nuts there ever since this whole thing started," he said. "I don't know how you deal with it."

"Trust me, Robert, a murder isn't something I ever want to deal with."

"Yeah, I know, but still . . ." He sighed and walked away from the counter. "I've been trying to keep the peace, but, man, some of these people are high-strung."

"Oliver?"

"Him and a couple of others. I swear one of their petty arguments is going to eventually come to blows. I kind of wish everyone would go home so I can focus on the sale."

Interest piqued, I followed Robert, who had paced into the living room. "What petty arguments are you talking about?"

Robert picked up the remote, and for a moment, I thought he might turn on the TV and drop down onto the couch to watch it. He bounced the remote in his hand a few times and set it back down.

"So, like, there's this guy."

"What guy?"

"One of the actors. He played the dead man."

"Link?"

"Yeah, that's the one." Robert crossed the room, peeked down the hall. What was he looking for? "He's been acting kind of weird."

I followed Robert back to the island counter, where I stood guard over the brownies. "Weird how?"

Robert flopped down onto one of the stools. "Nervous, I guess. It made me think of you."

"You think I act nervous?"

Robert reached out, patted my hand. "Nah, Kris. I mean, you'd be checking the guy out, thinking he was looking to kill someone. Or that he already had."

Heart thumping, I sat down across from him, held his eye. "Robert, has Link done something suspicious?"

Robert's gaze moved to the brownies, then back to me. He pouted out his lower lip and didn't say a word.

I heaved a sigh. "Fine." I cut a brownie myself and handed it over. "Now, tell me what you know."

Grinning, Robert took a big bite from his brownie and spoke through it as he chewed. "So, you know I went home to hang with the fam, right? Well, it didn't last too long. Trisha and R.J. ended up taking a nap, so I headed back to Ted and Bettfast to see if I could help Oliver with anything. This was before the news people showed up."

I motioned for him to hurry. I wanted to know what he had to say, but I also wanted to get that shower before Paul arrived.

"When I got there, no one paid attention to me, so I headed back to the office to check to see if Ted or Bett were around, but on the way, I heard some people talking."

"Link and Oliver?" I guessed.

"Yeah. The actor guy was acting all panicked, said that *'she'* knows, by which I assume he meant you." He winked. "So, I think to myself, 'what does she know?' and so I listen in, right? Oliver is doing his best to calm the other dude down. He said that it doesn't matter what anyone knows, that everything will work out, and that the Link guy needed to keep his head down and not to say a thing. Oliver said he'd take care of everything."

"Take care of what, exactly?" I asked.

Robert shrugged, polished off his brownie, and stood. "Beats me. They got all whispery and stuff, and I went looking for Ted and Bett. I honestly forgot all about it until I was headed home. I decided I could spare the time and stop by here for a few minutes to let you know all about it before I picked Trisha up." His smile turned smarmy. "We've got a babysitter tonight, so we're going out for a little romantic evening, if you know what I mean?" He waggled his eyebrows.

Ugh, I so didn't want to think about anyone having any sort of romantic evening with Robert. "That's nice," I said, and then, because I was worried he'd somehow ruin my own romantic evening, I asked, "Where are you two going? Geraldo's?"

Robert snorted. "Heck no. If I'm buying Ted and Bettfast, I can't afford a place like that. We're going to go to the Banyon Tree for a bite to eat, then we'll probably head home for a little *us* time."

I sagged in relief. If I'd have had to look at Robert

while I was trying to enjoy my evening with Paul, I probably would have canceled. "You two have fun. Tell Trisha I said hello."

"Sure." Robert headed for the door. "This has been a real crazy week. I can't wait until it finally settles down and things gets back to normal."

"You and me both."

15

I paced the living room, glancing at the clock every couple of seconds. It was five after seven, and Paul had yet to arrive. My stomach was in knots, and it wasn't because I was hungry. I wanted to talk about the murder with Paul over dinner, but at the same time, that wasn't exactly the best way to spend what I hoped would be a romantic evening.

But Robert had gotten me thinking about Link and Oliver. Then there was what Richie said about Drew and Austin meeting privately. And what about Lydia and Scott and the note. And, of course, Link and Scott's seemingly violent history with one another? And Austin's annoyance at Scott during the hunt? And . . . and . . .

I took a deep, calming breath when headlights lit up the front of my house as Paul pulled into the driveway. I could do this. How hard could it be to simply enjoy dinner and save all the murder talk until morning?

"I'm sorry I'm late," Paul said as I opened the door.

"I stopped by at home for a quick shower after work, and Ziggy was being a terror." As Huskies could be.

"No need to apologize," I said. "Ready?"

"Ready." He cocked an elbow, which I promptly took. He gave me a quick peck on the cheek that had my heart racing, and we were headed for his car and then onward to Geraldo's.

The restaurant was located downtown and was rather inconspicuous from the outside. The exterior was simple brick, with a sign proclaiming it to be Geraldo's hanging from the wall. Nothing fancy. Nothing that would make you think it was the nicest restaurant in all of Pine Hills.

The inside, however, always made me feel underdressed. The wait staff wore black and white suits and dresses, the walls were painted, and the lighting was dim, yet colorful. The prices weren't heart-stopping, which was a plus, but the food was fantastic enough to be worth double what they were charging. There was no dress code, which, in Pine Hills, was a good thing. People came dressed casually, which made me wonder why the employees went to all the trouble to dress up for work.

We were led to a seat in the corner by a nervous teen who was swimming in what was clearly a hand-me-down suit. The table felt private, romantic even.

"This is nice," I said as I sat.

"It's no Banyon Tree."

I made a face. Paul loved the diner, but my history with the owner prevented us from eating there often.

Our waiter appeared and took our drinks order. She,

like the poor kid who'd seated us, looked uncomfortable in her dress. I hadn't seen either of them here before, which made me wonder if Geraldo's had recently gone on a hiring spree.

The waitress, Kelly, as per her name tag, thanked us and hurried off to fill the drinks order.

Paul watched her go with an amused smile. "You know, I really needed this. The murder has stressed us out at the department. It's really started to weigh on me."

He gave me an in! As much as I might have wanted to avoid murder talk over dinner, it was now inevitable. "Do you have any leads yet?"

Kelly returned with our drinks before Paul could answer—or reprimand me for prying. We took a moment to order our food without having to look at the menus, and I propped my chin on my hands to await Paul's response.

"Nothing that you likely don't already know," he said with a sigh. He'd learned long ago that telling me to butt out of police business would never work. Stubborn might as well be my middle name. "John has Becca and Lena talking to people, but that's getting us nowhere."

"Lena's still helping?"

Paul smiled fondly. "She is. She mostly stands back and watches Becca work, but every now and again she's allowed to take lead. Those interviews are usually with people who aren't suspects. Like a neighbor or business owner who might have crossed paths with the victim. It's mostly to get her a little experience without risking us missing something or causing some sort of legal issue." He paused. "Not that I think she's doing a bad job."

"I know what you meant." You didn't want your trainee talking to a major witness. You wanted someone with experience doing that, someone who might pick up on something that the inexperienced might miss.

"It's good for them both, I think. Lena's learning a lot, and it gets Becca away from John." He chuckled.

"Do you know if they've talked to Lincoln Freel?" I asked.

Paul's brow furrowed. "Lincoln?"

"He goes by Link. He's one of the actors Oliver brought along with him."

Paul considered it and shook his head. "I don't know. Why?"

"His name has come up." At Paul's stern look, I continued. "I was talking to Doctor Logan earlier today. She knew Link from high school."

"Do I want to know why you were talking to a doctor about somebody who might be a suspect in a murder?"

"I didn't plan on talking to her. I went in to see Carl, who knows Drew MacDonald, who got into a fight with the victim the night before the murder, and he's the one who said I should talk to Anne—Doctor Logan."

"Uh-huh." Paul didn't appear to be annoyed but, rather, amused. "And what did Doctor Logan have to say?"

"Just that Link and the victim, Scott, had a history. I

guess about two years ago, Scott came in with a few injuries sustained in what he called a 'misunderstanding' with Link. She didn't go into detail, but I imagine fists were involved."

"Does Link have a temper?"

"I haven't seen it if he does. But he has acted strangely whenever I've tried to talk to him."

That earned me another stern look. "Krissy . . ."

"I know, I know. It's just—"

"You can't help yourself."

Nope, I could not, even if my life depended on it. "That's not all. Apparently, Link was overheard talking to Oliver Quick—he's the guy running the production—and Link was afraid I knew something about him. Oliver said he'll take care of it."

"What's that supposed to mean?"

I shrugged. "No idea. But it has to be about the murder, doesn't it?"

Paul frowned. "Who did you hear this from?

I reddened, wouldn't meet his eye. "Robert."

"Robert? As in your ex, Robert?"

"He stopped by before you showed up. He's the one who brought it up." *Because I'm the murder-lady, according to Scott.* "What if Oliver and Link planned the murder together? Oliver's now using Scott's death to promote the production. He even thinks he'll be able to start it up again, but this time with the whole world watching. What if that was the plan from the start?"

"That seems a little far-fetched, doesn't it?"

"Maybe, but think about it. Scott and Link get into an argument years ago, one that becomes physical. Oliver plans to use the Pine Hills actors for his production, but suddenly fires them so he can use his own actors, which just so happens to include Link. He'd have known Scott was on one of the teams and might have known about the history between the two. He uses Link to go after Scott, allowing Link to get his revenge and Oliver to use the death to get eyeballs on his production."

"Revenge for what, exactly?" Paul asked.

"Does it matter?" I asked. "Whatever happened, it was serious enough that Link hit Scott, sending him to the hospital. There could have been a festering resentment between the two boiling ever since."

"I'm still not convinced," Paul said.

Honestly, neither was I, but I pressed on anyway. "Then there's Drew MacDonald, who got into it with Scott a couple of times the night before the murder. What if that was all for show? I was told Drew and Austin, who was one of Scott's teammates, met secretly. Then, on the day of the murder, Austin was upset with Scott."

Doubt was written all over Paul's face. "So you think Drew and Austin were in on it too?"

"And Lydia, Oliver's assistant, passed on a note to Scott, which led him to the logging camp where he was killed."

"That's what? Five people who you think might be involved?"

He was right; one or two co-conspirators, I could buy. But five? It seemed rather unlikely.

"There's probably a simpler answer." Paul reached across the table and took my hand. "I'm not saying you're wrong about Lincoln Freel or any of these people. They all could very well have had a part in Mr. Flanagan's murder. But I can't see them all working together on it. It would have been too much of a risk."

He was right, of course. And what about motive? Would Link have killed Scott over a misunderstanding? Would Oliver really have planned a murder, just to make his production stand out to the media? And would Drew kill him because he was upset with Scott's penchant for talking about people? And Austin because . . . I didn't even know *why* Austin was upset with Scott.

"I guess it would be hard for any of them to have committed the murder," I said, unable to keep the dejection out of my voice.

"What do you mean?"

"We were all teamed up. Austin was with Shari. Oliver and Link were back at Ted and Bettfast, as far as I know. Drew was with Tony and Curtis. It would have been hard for any of them to slip away and kill Scott without someone else noticing their absence."

Our food arrived then, and conversation fell away from the murder. We talked about our pets and about possibly planning a trip to California to visit my dad and his girlfriend, Laura.

Before long, I was able to relax and focus on Paul and my plans for the rest of the night. I was looking forward to an evening where I thought about nothing else. And since Paul's huskies, Ziggy and Kefka, were staying with their sitter, Susie, overnight, that meant he had nowhere to be until morning.

We finished our meals and rose from the table, full and in high spirits. I tucked my arm into Paul's as we headed for the door.

The good feeling lasted right up until we stepped outside.

"You could play him in the movie, Brian!" The man who'd spoken wasn't wearing his pink shirt or blue sweater, but I recognized him immediately. "You look just like him."

Another man—Brian, I assumed—stuck out his tongue and rolled his eyes back so only the whites were visible. As he did, he staggered sideways, into a woman I recognized as another Levington actor. "How'd I do?" he said, righting himself.

"Eh, it was okay," the first man said with a laugh. "A little too mobile for a dead man."

"I always thought Link played dead better than me," Brian said, nudging Link with an elbow.

Link was smiling and had just opened his mouth to say something when he noticed Paul and me. The smile vanished like smoke, and he suddenly appeared as if he wanted to be anywhere else.

"Link can't play Scott," the woman Brian had bumped into said. "He's got to play himself. You, on the other hand, don't have an important role in Oliver's gig. And, hey, you've always done annoying far better than any of us."

Brian pressed a hand to his chest. "Dear Claudia, you wound me." He was grinning as he said it.

A flare of anger shot through me. The smart thing to do would have been to ignore them and head home to have a pleasant evening with Paul, but the way they were talking about Scott . . . It was indecent.

"A man is dead," I said, as we drew even with the group. "It's not a joking matter."

Brian rolled his eyes. "So what? No one cared about that guy."

"We're just having a little fun," Claudia added. "Lighten up."

The anger turned into something akin to rage. It was Paul's hold on my arm that kept me from leaping at one of them. "He's *dead*." I almost felt the need to spell it out. "He's not coming back. Someone killed him. That means there's a murderer on the loose." My eyes landed on Link as I said the last.

He didn't so much as flinch.

"And?" Brian said. "That doesn't mean the rest of us shouldn't keep on living."

"With how he kept running his mouth, it's a wonder it took this long for someone to off him," Claudia added.

At that point, I was nearly apoplectic. I sputtered, but couldn't come up with anything to say. I mean, how could they act so dismissive of a murder? Who cares if Scott rubbed them the wrong way? Who cares that he spread unsubstantiated rumors? That didn't mean he deserved to die.

"Come on, Krissy." Paul gently tugged me away from the group and toward his car. Link said something under his breath that caused the others to laugh. It took all my self-control not to spin around and shout after them some more.

Not that it would do any good. They simply didn't care.

I seethed all the way back home. I'd started to think that Link and the others couldn't have killed Scott, but now I was almost hoping they had. Oliver, Link, Drew, all of them. Was there a decent human being among them?

"You okay?" Paul asked as we pulled up in front of my house. "You haven't spoken since we left Geraldo's."

I closed my eyes, forced my disdain to the back of my mind. "I'm fine. Those people . . ." I made a frustrated sound. "It just got to me with how they were talking about Scott. I'll get over it."

"They didn't do themselves any favors acting like that," Paul said. "I'll have to have a word with John about them."

We climbed out of his car, and I led the way into the house. Misfit, who normally tries to escape whenever I come home, was stretched across the couch, watching us with one eye open. He yawned and closed it, apparently too tired to bother to attempt an escape.

I took a deep breath and managed a smile as I closed the door behind us. "So, Officer Dalton. We're here. Alone. What do you have in mind for us to do?"

The smile that stretched across Paul's face was enough to make my toes curl.

He took a step toward me. His hand rose to cup my cheek. My entire body tingled with anticipation with what was to come next.

That's when my phone went off.

My first instinct was to throw it across the room or, better yet, out the window. In a movie, that's exactly what I would have done, and Paul would have swept me up and carried me to the bedroom, where the screen would fade to black, but everyone would know exactly what went on in the darkness that followed.

But this wasn't a movie. It wasn't even a low-budget, made-for-TV flick.

I made an *I'm sorry* face and took a quick peek at my phone's screen, thumb already poised to cancel the call and turn the phone off so it wouldn't interrupt us further.

Vicki.

"I should take this," I said, making the *I'm sorry* face again. "It'll only take a second."

Paul, to his credit, didn't act upset. His smile remained in place as he stepped aside to let me answer the call.

Vicki was speaking before I'd even brought the phone to my ear. "I really need to talk to you," she said. "I know it's getting late, but can you come over?"

The worry in her voice had me straightening. "What's going on?"

"It's . . ." She made a frustrated sound that echoed my own from earlier. "I can tell you all about it when you get here. I'm not sure what I'm going to do!"

I glanced over at Paul. I didn't know if he could hear Vicki's voice or if he was able to discern what was going on by my expression, but he nodded. It appeared as if our romantic evening together had ended before it even had begun.

"I'll be over in fifteen minutes."

"Thank you. I wouldn't have called unless . . ." She heaved a sigh. "I'll be here."

I clicked off. "It was Vicki. She wants me to stop over. There's some sort of emergency going on, and I—."

"Go," Paul said, cutting me off. "I can wait here if you want me to."

I almost told him that, yes, I wanted that very much.

But instead I found myself saying, "You should probably just go home. I don't know how long this is going to take."

I was crestfallen, but Paul handled it like a champ. He crossed the room and rubbed both of my arms as he kissed me on the forehead. "Friends are important," he said. "Go take care of your friend."

And, with his blessing, I did.

16

Nervous energy had me bouncing in the seat of my car as I drove to Vicki's. Visions of murderous actors floated through my head, to the point where I was almost positive I'd find a body in her front yard when I arrived.

But when I pulled up in front of her house, everything looked calm and quiet. The house was lit up, and as soon as I stepped out of my car, Vicki was at the door.

"I'm sorry about this," Vicki said as she stepped aside to let me in. "I shouldn't have called you out of the blue like that. As soon as I hung up, I realized how I must have sounded."

"It's fine," I said, entering the house. "What's wrong?"

Vicki led me into the living room, where her husband, Mason Lawyer, was seated on the couch. He looked just as worried as she did, which did little to calm my nerves.

"Hey, Krissy," he said. "Can I get you anything? Coffee? Water?"

"No, thank you, I'm good." I stopped in the middle of the room and turned to Vicki, who was pacing and wringing her hands together. "What's going on?"

She glanced at Mason, who nodded and rose. When he passed by her, he squeezed her arm, which seemed to calm her down slightly since she stopped her pacing. He gave me a pleading look I interpreted as saying, "Do something!" before he headed upstairs, leaving the two of us alone.

"It's Kenneth," she said as soon as he was gone.

My mind instantly jumped to the murder. "Kenneth Purdy killed Scott?"

"What?" Vicki made a face. "No. Well, not that I know of, he didn't. Though, with how he's acting, I kind of hope he did."

Color me confused. "Okay then, back up. What's going on?"

Vicki took a moment to compose herself. Her hair had come loose from her ponytail, and a strand fell into her face. She tucked it behind her ear before she spoke.

"Kenneth called me a little while ago. Why he chose me, I have no idea, but I was the one he picked to scream at."

"What did he want?"

"You know how I told you about Hector Kravitz and how he was looking to cause a stink?"

I nodded.

"Well, big shock, Kenneth heard about it and has decided that Hector, along with the rest of the community theatre actors, must be conspiring against him. He believes everything that's been going on recently is an extension of what happened when the other theatre closed. 'The next step' as he put it."

"He's upset that Hector saw him talking to Oliver?" I asked, still confused.

"That, and he thinks we killed that man, Scott. He swears up and down that he has evidence that we, as a troupe, killed him in order to ruin Oliver's production and somehow frame Kenneth for the crime."

My head was spinning. "Wait, he thinks *you* killed Scott?"

"Not me personally. I think that's why he called me, rather than going to Hector directly. Kenneth fears that he might be next and has demanded I do something to stop Hector. As if I have any sway on what anyone else does."

"If he's scared, why not go to the police?" I asked.

"That's the thing, he threatened that he would. Kenneth says he has proof of Hector's involvement and that if I don't do anything to stop him before he causes any more trouble, he's going to go to the press with it."

"What kind of proof?" I asked.

Vicki shrugged. "Beats me. I asked him, but Kenneth refused to say. All I know is that I'm supposed to contact Hector, get him to back off or turn himself in or something, or else Kenneth is going to sue me and the theatre for defamation and conspiracy. Can he even do that?" She threw her hands into the air and let them slap down onto her hips. "I don't know whether to laugh or cry at this point."

I stood there and tried to make sense of what I was hearing and somehow piece it all together with what I already knew about Scott's murder. I got that Kenneth was upset. The same went for Hector Kravitz. But to kill Scott Flanagan? I couldn't see either man going that far—not that I knew them well enough to know if they had it in them to kill someone. I supposed it was possible, considering people have killed for less.

But if Hector or Kenneth *were* involved, how did Lydia's note fit in? Or all the secret meetings between actors and competitors I'd been hearing about?

"What does Kenneth want?" I asked. "I'm assuming he called you for a reason."

"That's just it," Vicki said. "I have no idea. He didn't demand anything beyond telling me to talk to Hector. I mean, I don't know what he expects me to do. He wasn't getting threats, as far as I know. I'm supposed to get Hector to back off, but from what?" She shrugged. "I could talk to him, but all that'll do is make him angrier."

"Could it be about whatever happened at the theatre? Hector's protest?" Or whatever it was that had happened. I still wasn't clear on that.

"No clue," Vicki said. "But why not go to someone who has some sway with Hector? I barely know the guy." Vicki sighed and rubbed at her face before tucking that stray strand of hair back behind her ear again. "Honestly, I think Kenneth is trying to stir the pot and is using the murder because it is convenient."

"You don't think he actually has evidence?"

"If he did, why call me? Why not go to the police immediately? Honestly, I'm more concerned about his threat to sue. The theatre can't afford to hire a lawyer. We barely scrape by with ticket sales and donations as it is. If we have to fight a legal battle, no matter how bogus, it will ruin us. Kenneth wouldn't need to win in order for him to win, if you know what I mean?"

I did. Lawyers weren't cheap, even in a small town like Pine Hills. If Kenneth went through with suing, and if he had some sort of evidence of the theatre's wrongdoing, manufactured or not, it would suck their coffers dry, so to speak. Even if the theatre won, they'd have no money left to operate, unless they countered with a suit of their own.

The best way to stop Kenneth Purdy would be to solve Scott's murder and prove the Pine Hills actors had nothing to do with it.

But how?

"Do you know if Hector knew the victim?" I asked.

"I'm not sure," Vicki said. "If he did, he never said so to me. That's something you'd have to ask Hector himself."

I made a mental note to do just that. "I was at dinner with Paul earlier—"

"Oh no! Did I interrupt? You should have told me!"

I waved her off. "It's fine. We were done eating." I decided to leave out the fact that Paul and I were at my house planning to finish off the evening on a high note. "When we left Geraldo's, some of the Levington actors were heading in. They were talking about Scott, making fun of him."

Vicki's expression darkened. "That doesn't surprise me."

"They don't seem like very nice people," I said. "Can you tell me anything at all about them? If one of them killed Scott . . ."

"It would clear Hector and show that Kenneth's proof is manufactured."

"Exactly."

Vicki considered it and shook her head. "I wish I could help more, but I don't know any of them well enough to help. A few have attached themselves to Oliver to the point where I'm pretty sure that if he had told them to kill someone, they would have considered it."

"Do the names Brian and Claudia mean anything to you?"

"That's two of Oliver's pets. They are in everything he directs, but that's about all I know."

"What about Lincoln Freel? Link?"

"Sorry, no. I might have heard the name before—it's vaguely familiar—but I don't actually know him."

I wasn't sure what to do next. I could talk to Hector and Kenneth and everyone involved with Oliver's production, but then what? It's not like the killer would come out and admit to murdering Scott. And whenever I tried to talk to someone, they usually just blew me off, as they should. I wasn't a cop. I was just a nosy woman, looking to set things to rights.

"Hey, I should let you go," Vicki said, cutting into my thoughts. "Call Paul. Maybe you two can pick up wherever you left off before I interrupted you."

"No, really, it's okay."

She shook her head. "No, it's not. I was upset and wasn't thinking clearly. I should have thought it through more before calling."

"I'm glad you called," I said. "If Kenneth is trying to ruin the theatre, there's a chance it could somehow tie back to Scott's murder. It's better I know so I can tell Paul and he can do something about it."

"Maybe." She sighed. "But you should go anyway. I need to sit down and do some thinking of my own. If Kenneth *does* go through with litigation, I'm going to have to talk to the rest of the theatre so we can figure out how to deal with it."

I didn't envy her. "All right. Are you still stopping in at Death by Coffee tomorrow? If you need me to do it instead—"

"No, I'll be there for a little while. I need to get some inventory done. A few of the bookshelves up-stairs are looking a bit empty. I can't let Kenneth Purdy ruin that too."

I allowed Vicki to guide me to the door. "If you need anything else from me," I said, "call."

"I will."

We hugged, and I headed for my car, more unsettled than I was letting on. I didn't know what to think about Kenneth and his possible involvement in the murder. Did he have actual evidence of a crime? Or was he lying in the hopes of scaring the local actors into . . . what? Coming back to him? Allowing him to buy the new theatre? I couldn't fathom what he could possibly want from them other than petty revenge.

I reached my Escape and put my hand on the handle, so lost in thought I didn't realize I wasn't alone.

"Thanks for doing that."

I screamed and spun around, hand flying outward on reflex. It made a solid *slap* against Mason's cheek that echoed off the houses in the ultra-quiet neighborhood.

"Oh, my gosh! I'm so sorry, Mason," I said, covering my mouth with the offending hand. "You scared the life out of me!"

Mason rubbed at his cheek, but he was smiling. "It's okay. I shouldn't have snuck up on you like that."

"Where did you come from?" I asked him, swallowing my pounding heart as I rubbed at my hand, which was stinging from the slap. His face had to hurt worse, though he wasn't about to admit it. "I thought you went upstairs?"

Mason winked. "I'm sneaky." He dropped his hand, revealing a growing red welt on his cheek that looked worse than it probably was due to the harsh outside motion lights above their garage. "Vicki's really upset about that call she received earlier. I tried to calm her down, but I didn't know what to say. I'm really glad you came."

"She'll be fine. She's just worried."

"I know," he sighed. "I only wish I could have come up with something to say to make her feel better. You'll figure this thing out, right?"

I didn't know if he meant the murder or whatever it was Kenneth thought he knew, but I nodded anyway. "I plan on it."

"Good." He rubbed at his cheek once more. "I pity whoever gets in your way."

Mason returned to the house, and I climbed into my car and headed for home. I considered calling Paul on the way, but decided against it. By now, he'd probably already relieved Susie of her dog-sitting duties and was settling in for the night. And while I wanted to tell him about Kenneth's threats, it could wait. There was nothing he could do about it tonight, and I had a feeling that if the police were to get involved, it would somehow only make things worse.

Still, I worried all the way home. When I parked in my driveway, I shut off the engine, but didn't get out right away. I kept thinking about Scott, about how everyone seemed to be using his murder for their own gain. I didn't know how anyone could do something like that and not feel awful about themselves.

Could Oliver Quick have set it all up with the help of Kenneth Purdy? Could Hector Kravitz have killed Scott to ruin Oliver and Kenneth? And what about Austin and Drew and Link? They all had a history with Scott. And then there was Lydia and her note.

I felt as if I was getting nowhere, and the more I learned, the further from the truth I seemed to be drifting.

A thump on the drivers'-side window had my heart shooting into my throat for the second time within an hour. I managed a startled squeak as I recoiled from the window, only to find my neighbor, Caitlin Blevins, looking in at me, a chagrinned expression on her face.

"Sorry," she said when I opened the car door. "I didn't mean to startle you."

"It's okay," I said. "It happens." A lot more than I would like.

Caitlin stepped back. She was dressed for bed and looked cold as she hugged herself. "Could you stop over at my place for a second? I've got something to show you. It might not be anything, but . . ."

Oh boy. "Sure. What is it?"

Caitlin started walking. "I think it's best for me to show you."

We crossed the yard to her front door, which she'd left slightly ajar. The television was on, but it wasn't her usual video game. Instead, a scene was paused that appeared to show a bunch of darkly dressed people rolling around in mud, though the footage was somewhat grainy.

Could this be what she wanted to show me? It seemed strange, but, hey, right then, I expected just about anything.

"It's a documentary about Woodstock '99," she explained as she passed by the television. "That thing was a disaster."

I took her word for it as she crossed the room and picked up her phone, which was sitting on the couch beside a bag of chips. She tapped the screen a few times and handed the phone over without a word.

The screen was paused on what was clearly security footage from her window camera. Caitlin had once had a problem with a friend-turned-stalker and had cameras sitting in her windows, just in case that former friend ever found her. That meant she sometimes caught footage of happenings around my house, though the distance made it hit or miss.

This time, it was a hit.

"Press PLAY," she said as I studied the image, which showed a car sitting at the side of the road between our driveways. It was parked close enough to Caitlin's house that it was likely what had triggered her system to start recording.

I tapped the PLAY icon, and the image started moving. The car door opened, and a woman stepped out. From what I could tell from the grainy black-and-white footage, she was dressed smartly and had her hair styled so that it was long in the back, with bangs in the front.

And that was it. I couldn't make out her features otherwise, especially when she raised her hand and there was a flash that washed out the image briefly. She checked the item in her hand, which I assumed was her phone, and she started for my house.

I tensed and leaned closer to the phone, though it didn't help make the footage any clearer. The woman moved to the door, peeked in a window, raised her phone, and the flash of light came again as she apparently took a photo of whatever she might have seen past the curtains.

And then the video stopped.

I looked up at Caitlin, practically frantic.

"That's it. There's another short clip of her getting into her car and driving off, but you can make out even less because she's looking down the entire time. She stayed at your place for about two minutes, based on the timing of each alert." She flushed. "I was in the bathroom when she showed up or else I would have confronted her for you."

"No, it's better you didn't," I said. I tried to come up with a face that matched the person I saw, but no one came to mind. I didn't know anyone who had bangs like that.

"Do you know who it was?" Caitlin asked. "The whole thing seemed strange to me, and since I heard that there was a murder, I thought it best if I showed it to you, just in case it was connected."

Strange? How about terrifying?

"I don't," I said. "But I plan on finding out."

Caitlin nodded and was still hugging herself. She looked as unsettled as I felt. "Let me know when you do?"

"I will. Send the footage to me? I'll pass it on to Paul and see what he thinks."

Caitlin fiddled with her phone until my own pinged with an email alert. I checked it, made sure the footage played, and then thanked her before leaving.

As I walked across the yard, I got the distinct impression I was being watched. A glance back showed Caitlin at her window. She waved before letting the curtain fall closed.

And, still, the feeling didn't go away.

17

Morning barged in like a bully, forcing me out of bed after a night of tossing and turning. I'd lain in bed, covers tucked under my chin, waiting for my mysterious visitor to return. I jumped at every sound, no matter how small, expecting someone to come bursting in at any moment. With a cat, there were a lot of random noises, especially when he got the 2:00 a.m. zoomies.

I sludged my way out of the bedroom to the kitchen, where I fed Misfit, who was none the worse for wear after his late-night laps around the house. Yawning, I put on coffee and made for the bathroom to get my morning routine started. I wanted to crawl back into bed and sleep for a few more hours. Or maybe a week. Unfortunately, I couldn't indulge because Cassie was waiting for me, and there was no way I was going to leave her hanging. As Paul had said, friends are important.

The shower helped wake me up a little. The coffee, complete with a chocolate chip cookie soaking at the bottom of my to-go mug, even more so. It made me feel almost human as I headed out the door, dressed for a bout of exercise, despite not feeling all that up to it.

"Krissy!" Jules Phan called out from his open car door. "I'm glad I caught you." He hurried across the yard to where I stood, leaning against my Escape. As soon as he reached me, he held out his hand, palm upward.

"What's this?" I asked, even though I could see exactly what it was. Chalk this one up to my brain malfunctioning due to lack of sleep and insufficient caffeine.

"It's your missing key!" Jules said with a laugh. "I found it this morning. Apparently, I'd dropped it into a mug Lance and I keep in the kitchen for things we don't want to lose. I'm not sure when I did it, and I sure as heck don't know why I didn't think to look there the moment I realized it was missing, but there it was, waiting for me when I checked it this morning."

I took my key back and dropped it into my purse. "I'd completely forgotten about it," I admitted. "It's been so crazy lately, I'm barely able to remember what day of the week it is."

"Tell me about it." Jules crossed his arms and puffed out a breath. It was just cold enough that a faint wisp trailed from his lips. "The murder is all anyone can talk about. I know people like to gossip, but to do it in a candy store where impressionable ears can hear?" He tsked. "Save it for the dinner table if you must talk about it."

I smirked before asking, "Has anyone said anything interesting around *your* impressionable ears?"

Jules tapped his ears, which were starting to turn red from the early-morning chill. "Nothing useful so far. It's mostly just been gossip and speculation. If I do hear something that sounds remotely plausible, you'll be the first to know."

"Thanks." I checked my watch and winced. "I should get going. I'm meeting Cassie Wise at the new gym downtown this morning. She's probably already there, waiting on me."

"Good luck with that," Jules said with a grin. He knew how much exercise and I didn't get along. "Tell me how it is. I might want to check the place out sometime if it's halfway decent. I think the candy is starting to weigh on me." He patted his stomach, which looked flat to me. "Literally!"

"Will do." I started to turn away, but paused. "You haven't happened to see anyone lurking around my house recently, have you?"

"Lurking? No, I don't think so." Jules considered it a moment before he shook his head. "No, I definitely don't recall seeing anyone or else I would have told you. Why do you ask?"

"It might be nothing," I said, "but a woman came to my door and appeared to be taking photos of my living room through the window. It was strange. Caitlin caught most of it on her security camera, but I couldn't make out who it was."

Jules shivered. I couldn't tell if it was from the chill or from the thought of a stranger poking around the neighborhood, taking photos. "That's frightening."

"Yeah. It kept me up all night thinking about it."

"I imagine it would."

"I sent the footage to Paul, so hopefully he'll be able to figure who it was."

"I hope he does. I don't like thinking that there might be some crazy lady running around the neighborhood, peeking in everyone's windows. And you said she took pictures?"

"With her phone."

"Creepy."

I agreed wholeheartedly.

Jules and I parted then, the two of us climbing into our respective vehicles. Jules honked and waved as he backed out of his driveway. I returned the wave and followed him all the way downtown, and we only parted when I reached the gym and he continued on to Phantastic Candies.

Most businesses in Pine Hills were named with puns or a play on words in mind. Scream for Ice Cream, Fern's Perm, and even Phantastic Candies were all examples of that. When I parked out front, I fully expected to find the place to be named Jim's Gym or something similar.

Honestly, I wasn't too far off the mark.

"Weight of the Hills?" I said aloud as I stepped out onto the sidewalk. The letters were shaped into the pattern of a bowing barbell with a muscular silhouette holding it up. Two mounds I assumed represented hills took the place of the weights on the end. Little pine trees poked up from the top of the hills, three per side.

Large, frosted plate-glass windows fronted the gym.

I could just barely make out what appeared to be tread-mills facing the windows, though no one was currently using them. There was faint movement in the back, but the glaze made it impossible to make out much more than the motion.

I was debating whether to head inside or wait for Cassie when the woman in question pulled up next to my Escape. She climbed out of her car and rubbed her hands together as she joined me in front of the gym. "Sorry I'm late. I slept through my alarm. Are you ready for this?"

"Not in the slightest."

She laughed and clapped me on the shoulder, and together we entered Weight of the Hills.

Registration took only a few minutes, and after depositing our things in lockers situated in a small room in the back, we were soon checking out the machines. The treadmills, as I noted from the outside, were by the windows, along with a trio of rowing machines near the wall. Weights were situated at the back of the room, and a handful of fit, good-looking women in their twenties were lifting them and chatting amicably among themselves. Bikes and other machines with handles and pulleys were situated around the room, most of which I didn't know how to use.

"What do you think?" Cassie asked, eyeing the treadmills. "Start with a run?"

"Works for me," I said, already dreading the sore muscles that would follow.

We chose a pair of treadmills next to one another and began. Cassie, who was a natural runner, jacked

hers up to so that she was running at a near sprint. Me?
I opted for the low end of the scale, which was more of
a brisk walk than a run.

The first few minutes went great. I was focused on
not falling flat on my face, while Cassie had opted for
her earbuds, since there was no way I was going to be
able to chat while running. Once I got into a rhythm,
and with no music of my own to listen to, my mind
started to wander.

And what would I start thinking about?

Murder, of course.

The world around me vanished, and I was back at
Ted and Bettfast, surrounded by faces I now knew:
Drew, Link, Oliver, Austin, Shari, Richie, Lydia. The
list went on and on. Scott was connected to each, and
often not in a good way. He'd fought with Drew, fought
with Link, gotten on the wrong side of Austin. He'd
even annoyed Oliver at one point. Enough to kill?
Unlikely, but that didn't mean they didn't have a history that went further back, one that might have eventually led to murder.

Then there were the women: Shari and Lydia. Scott
seemed to get along with them well enough, but Shari
had abandoned him, along with Austin. And Lydia *had*
given him the note that took him to the logging camp
where he was murdered. Was it planned? A coinci-
dence? Could the entire production have been put together to kill one man?

Annoyingly, the more I looked at it, the more it
seemed like a possibility. A slim one, mind you, but a
possibility nonetheless.

My mind drifted to Hector and Kenneth. I considered whether they could possibly be involved, and I was right back to Oliver and his production.

Shari and Austin left Scott at the Banyon Tree. Scott somehow found a way to the logging camp, likely by having someone give him a ride. But a ride from whom? And when did he make the call? The security cameras never picked him up calling anyone or even getting into a car.

But someone might have seen it.

The thought hit me like a slap, hard enough that I missed a step on the treadmill. My toes somehow caught the belt, and despite my slower pace, my foot was jerked backward. I staggered, very nearly clunking my chin on the console as I pitched forward. I caught myself on the grips, so I didn't fall and go zipping off it, but my ankle twisted sideways when I tried to regain my footing, and I somehow managed to put all my weight on the awkwardly placed foot, causing it to buckle.

The pain was instantaneous.

I yelped, nearly putting my good foot back onto the belt, which would have sent me zipping backward to crash across the room, likely into the women lifting the weights. I somehow pivoted so that I was hanging off the side of the treadmill for a dizzying moment, before I dropped to the ground with a grunt. My injured foot buckled, sending lances of white-hot agony shooting up my leg, all the way to my knee. I went down, thankfully landing butt-first on a treadmill that wasn't moving.

Cassie, who must have caught the entire show out of the corner of her eye, stepped off to either side of her still spinning belt and asked, "Are you all right?" She hopped down and rushed over to where I sat, gingerly touching my ankle. "What happened?"

"I twisted my ankle." A gentle prod told me that not only had I twisted it, it was starting to swell.

Cassie knelt in front of me to examine my leg. She didn't touch it, thankfully, but she did make a pained expression. "You should see a doctor. That doesn't look good."

"I'll be fine." I tried to push myself to my feet, but a sharp bark from my ankle had me easing back down. "In a minute or two."

Cassie made a frustrated sound and glanced back toward the guy who'd signed us in. He was currently standing with his back to us, talking to the women lifting weights, completely oblivious to my distress. He had apparently missed my less-than-graceful dismount, for which I was kind of grateful.

"I don't think it's going to get better," she said, turning back to me. "Let me drive you to the doctor."

I wanted to agree, I really did, but I couldn't shake the thought that had caused my accident.

Someone might have seen who picked up Scott from the Banyon Tree.

And I thought I might know who.

"I'll go to a doctor," I said.

Cassie frowned. "Why do I sense a 'but' here?"

"But I need to talk to someone first."

She was shaking her head before I'd finished. "You shouldn't put this off. Can you even walk on that foot? Your ankle's starting to look like an overripe eggplant."

Ignoring the less-than-flattering description, I stood.

Gritting my teeth, I put weight on my injured ankle, which barked in pain but didn't buckle. I gave her a triumphant grin.

Cassie wasn't impressed. "Walking on an injured ankle could cause more damage. And what are you going to do if it gives out as you're going down a flight of stairs?"

"I'll be okay." I sat back down before I fell down. "It's just . . ."

"Don't tell me." Cassie rose from her crouch and stepped back, arms crossed. "You need to go poking around a murder investigation. I can see it written all over your face."

There was no sense in denying it. At this point, everyone seemed to think of me as the murder-lady. I might not like the title—or the implications—but it *was* warranted to some degree.

"I don't need to go anywhere," I said. "I can call from here."

"You can also call from my car on the way to see a doctor."

I could. But that meant I also would need to keep the call short. And if I lost reception along the way . . .

I knew I was making excuses to avoid seeing the doctor. It was likely I'd be told to stay off my ankle, would be given some pain meds, maybe a wrap, and then what? I supposed I could make the call afterward, but what if the pain medication was strong and it knocked me out? What if I was stuck in the waiting room for an hour or more and I missed my chance?

What if Scott's killer decided to kill again? Could I really put it off?

"It won't take long," I said. "Just a quick call." Or two, depending on who answered and what they had to say.

Cassie heaved a sigh. "Fine," she said. "But as soon as you hang up, I'm taking you to the doctor."

I flashed her a smile, which wasn't exactly agreement, but it seemed to suffice.

"Let me get your phone."

I handed over my locker key and waited while Cassie retrieved my phone. I tried flexing my ankle, but every little movement hurt. It wasn't world-ending pain, but it was enough that I was already jonesing for something to take the edge off.

She returned with not just my phone, but all of our things.

"Thanks," I said, digging my phone from my purse. "This should take just a second."

Cassie nodded and moved a respectful distance away.

A quick online search and I soon found Vivian Flowers's number. It was amazing what you could find online these days. I dialed, crossed mental fingers, and waited as it rang.

"Hello?" Vivian's voice sounded far away, like she was talking to me from a tunnel. "Who is this?"

"Hi, Vivian, it's Krissy Hancock. From Pine Hills."

"Krissy?" Her voice was clearer, and I detected curiosity in her tone. "What can I do for you on this *very* early morning?"

I winced. I hadn't even considered the time when I'd called. Vivian was of a retired age, and while I knew some older people liked to get up early, not everyone did. "I'm sorry about that," I said. "I was hoping we could talk."

"About the murder, right?"

"Sort of. It's about what you might have seen at the Banyon Tree."

"I'm not sure I'd be of much help," she said. "I've told you everything I know."

"It's about when Scott left," I said. "Do you recall seeing anyone pick him up?"

She was silent a moment while she considered it. "I can't say I do. But I wasn't looking that way. Sara, on the other hand, might have. You know what? What do you think about you coming this way? We can have brunch. I'll call Sara and Albert and have them meet us. If they know it's about the murder, I'm sure they'll make time."

I glanced over at Cassie, who was watching me with a concerned expression. "When?" I asked.

"It'll take you what? Thirty minutes to get here? How about we set it up for forty-five. This your cell?"

"It is."

"I'll have Sara pick us out a nice place to meet and she'll text you the address. Sound good?"

Forty-five minutes wasn't enough time for me to get to the doctor, get checked out, and then meet with them. But I really wanted to hear what Sara might have to say, especially if she'd seen who picked Scott up.

"Sounds great. I'll see you then."

Vivian clicked off. I tucked my phone back into my purse and started to work my way to my feet. Cassie hurried over and helped.

"Ready?" she asked once I was upright.

"Actually . . ."

Cassie's pretty features contorted as she scowled. "Krissy . . ."

"I know, I know, but I need to do this."

"Do what?"

"Meet with some friends. In Cherry Valley."

Cassie tapped her foot and looked down at my ankle—my right ankle. "And how are you going to get there? Can you drive with that foot of yours?"

"Maybe?" I shifted in an attempt to put more weight on my ankle and immediately sucked in a breath when it twinged. "Hopefully."

Cassie sighed. "Here's the deal. I know I won't be able to convince you to change your mind, so I'll drive you so you can talk to your friends. As soon as that's done, you're going to let me take you to the doctor's office to get your ankle checked out. No pit stops. Friends, then doctor. Got it?"

I nodded. "Thank you. I'll owe you one."

"A big one."

Cassie stayed by my side as I limped my way out of Weight of the Hills. At first, I thought that maybe it was getting better. The first few steps were painful, but doable.

About two steps out the door, however, and I'd changed my mind. The throb had turned into a sharp, stabbing pain that sent stars shooting through my vision. I wanted nothing more than to sit down and never get up again.

"I can't believe we're doing this." Cassie helped me into the passenger's seat of her car. The moment I was off my feet, I closed my eyes and leaned my head back.

It wasn't quite bliss, but it was as close to it as I could get in my current state. "Where exactly are we going?" she asked.

"I'll tell you as soon as I know." At her glare, I pulled out my phone and held it up. "I'm waiting on the text."

Cassie rounded her car and got in next to me. "This better be worth it," she said, glancing at my leg, as if she feared it might swell so much, I'd float away like a balloon.

"It will be," I said, hoping it wasn't just wishful thinking. Already, I was regretting the decision not to go to the doctor. I didn't think anything was broken, but, boy, I'm a wimp when it comes to pain.

"All right then, here we go."

And with that, Cassie pulled out onto the street, and we were on our way to Cherry Valley.

18

Cherry Valley was of a similar size to Pine Hills, but a downtown area full of fast-food restaurants and a shopping mall made it feel much larger. Pine Hills had none of that, which was part of its charm, though there is something to be said for having everything you could possibly want crammed into a centralized area.

"Sara said there's parking in the back," I said, as Cassie pulled into the mostly empty mall parking lot. Like most malls in smaller towns these days, stores were closing at an alarming rate, leaving only a handful of staples behind. Many of the stores that remained had their own separate entrance to the parking lot.

The Tiny Aloha, one such place, was our destination. The lot here was slightly more full, hinting that, unlike the stores inside, the restaurant was still popular. It also helped that it was early enough that we'd beaten the lunch rush.

I eased out of the car, thankful that Cassie had found a spot close to the entrance. I was careful not to put too much weight on my injured ankle, which was throbbing in time with my heartbeat. Cassie came to my aid, and together we hobbled to the doors and went inside.

Bright lighting and an upbeat atmosphere met us as we entered. There were at least a dozen televisions spaced around the room, all tuned to various sports channels, with no two set to the same one. A bar dominated the middle of the room, though no one was currently manning it.

I spotted Vivian and Sara immediately. They were seated in a booth on the far side of the room. Vivian was laughing at something Sara had said as Cassie and I crossed the restaurant to join them. There were only a handful of other customers around the room.

"What happened to you?" Vivian asked as I limped to her side.

"Exercise accident," I said. "I'm fine."

She chuckled. "I've been there, though it's been a few decades. Sit down before you fall down." She motioned to the seat across from where she sat next to Sara. "Have a coffee. The Aloha serves only beverages until noon, when they officially open, so if you're hungry, you'll have to go elsewhere."

"I'm good." I glanced at Cassie, who nodded. "It's nice here."

And it was. While it might be attached to a mall, the Tiny Aloha felt upscale. Not Geraldo's nice, but it was definitely an upgrade over the chains that populated most malls. It made me wonder what kind of prices I'd find on their menu if and when I got a chance to eat here.

"It is. Used to only open at lunchtime, but the mall

walkers changed that." Vivian thumped the table for emphasis. "We needed our morning fix, and once the cookie place closed down, this was our next best bet if we didn't want something from the pretzel shop."

"Don't mall walkers usually come in early?" I asked. "Like well before open?"

Vivian winked. "Your call interrupted my morning stroll. I had to let the ladies finish without me so I could set this little gathering up."

I was impressed. Dressed in a lily white blouse and capris, which exposed pale, veiny legs, Vivian didn't look much like a walker. I hoped I was as mobile as she was when I hit my eighties, though considering how I felt now, I wasn't counting on it.

"I'm Sara Huffington." Sara leaned toward Cassie. "Vivian sometimes forgets she's not the only person in the room when she gets to talking."

Cassie smiled. "Seems like she and Krissy have a lot in common."

"Very funny," I said, before going about introductions. There was no shaking of hands, just polite nods and smiles. "Where's Albert? I was hoping he could join us."

Sara rolled her eyes. "He's at a meeting with my dad."

"Your dad?" I asked. I only knew of Sara's father by reputation. He was the CEO of Huffington Mulch, which was surprisingly profitable. I didn't know anything about the mulch business, but the Huffington family was well off due to it. Go figure.

Vivian grinned so wide, it seemed to split her face in

half. "Big Joe isn't happy that an old fart like Albert Elmore is dating his daughter."

I couldn't help it; my mouth fell open in shock. *Albert and Sara?* Together? I couldn't believe it. Albert was older, yes, but he was also kind of awkward and, dare I say, unattractive. I mean, he wasn't ugly, but compared to Sara, he looked average at best. And Sara was . . . well, Sara. Rich. Dressed like she was worth the millions she really was. I couldn't imagine a scenario where the two of them got together, and yet, here we were.

Sara picked at a nail, seemingly bored with the topic, though I detected a hint of tension in her shoulders. "Dad'll probably pay Albert off, and that will be that. It wouldn't be the first time."

She tried to play it off like she didn't care, but it was clear the thought of Big Joe throwing a wad of cash at Albert to make him go away saddened her. Sara had once told me she didn't want to die a lonely old maid. If her father kept interfering with her relationships, I was afraid her fears very well might come true.

Vivian cleared her throat, took a sip from an off-white coffee mug sitting in front of her. "You didn't come here to talk about Sara and Albert. You want to discuss what we might have seen at that diner, correct?"

"I do," I said. "Especially about what happened once Austin and Shari left Scott behind."

Cassie seemed to shrink in on herself next to me. She didn't much care for talk of murder, and while we weren't discussing the body or possible murder weapons, it still made her uncomfortable.

"Like I told you over the phone, I can't tell you much," Vivian said. "I didn't see anything while I was there. I was mostly focused on my pre-nap lunch at the time."

Sara, seemingly still lamenting what her dad may or may not be offering to Albert, merely shrugged.

I considered where to go from there and decided to back up even further. There was one detail that I wanted to clarify from the night before.

"Sara," I said, drawing her attention, "you said you saw someone talking to Drew outside your window the night before the murder. You thought it was one of Oliver's assistants."

"Honestly, I don't know who it was. I could only hear the Drew fellow talking, and he's the only one I could make out with any clarity. The other person talked quietly, so all I heard was a faint murmur. It wasn't like I was eavesdropping, so I didn't really pay it much mind, to be honest."

"You didn't see the other person at all?" I asked, knowing I sounded desperate. "Maybe you overheard a snippet of their conversation and could figure out who the other person was from it? Could it have been Austin?"

She shook her head. "Sorry."

I'd hoped that mentioning Austin would trigger a memory of some kind. So far, all I had was Richie's assertation that Austin was the most likely candidate for meeting with Drew, but that wasn't proof.

I moved on.

"What about at the Banyon Tree?" I asked her. "Do you recall anything at all that might help? Scott went into the restroom, and then . . ." I left it hanging, hoping Sara would be prompted to fill in the gap.

"Then he left," she said, glancing at Vivian with an expression that made it seem like she was wondering why I was being so weird.

"Scott needed to get to the logging camp, where he was murdered," I explained. "He didn't drive. Austin and Shari took the car, leaving him stranded. Someone had to have picked him up. Did you hear him call anyone? See him get into a car?"

"I didn't see or hear anything," Vivian said. "And while he's not here to corroborate, I'll go out on a limb and say Albert didn't either. He was sitting with me the entire time and would have commented on it if he'd seen anything fishy."

Sara opened her mouth as if to agree, but a thought must have struck her because she left it hanging open without speaking. A thoughtful expression passed over her face, and she looked to Vivian, though the older woman didn't notice. A handful of seconds passed, and she nodded slowly.

"You know, I think I did see someone," Sara said. "I never saw Scott call anyone, but I suppose he could have done it while he was in the restroom."

"Seems like a crummy place to make a call," Vivian said.

"Unless you don't want anyone else to overhear what you have to say," Cassie added.

Sara was still nodding as she thought it through. "When he went outside, I remember him standing there, like he was surprised his team had actually left him," she said. "He looked confused. It was like he didn't know what to do or where to go next."

Beside me, Cassie leaned forward, despite her dislike of getting involved in murder investigations. If she kept hanging around me, she might not have any choice but to start to enjoy them.

"I'm not sure why I didn't think of it before," Sara said. "I got up to use the restroom myself. I'd waited because I didn't want anyone else in there with me. It would have felt strange to go with a man in there."

"No kidding," Vivian muttered.

"When I stood up," Sara went on, ignoring Vivian's comment, "Scott starting walking toward the road. I thought it strange, thinking he might have decided to walk back to town or something, but there was a car waiting for him."

It was my turn to lean forward. "Did you see the driver?" I asked.

Sara nodded. "I don't know his name, but his face did stand out since it was still all made up."

I just about screamed when she fell silent as she thought about it some more. The anticipation was killing me, especially since the driver was likely one of the last people to see Scott alive. If he wasn't the killer himself, he might have seen who was.

"Who was it?" Cassie asked, though she had no idea who anyone was. And, yes, there was a twinge of excitement in her voice and anticipation that surprised me.

Sara hesitated a moment longer, then finally told me what I wanted to hear. "The man driving the car was the actor who played the dead man at the start of our little game."

Lincoln Freel was the one who had picked up Scott!

I was practically bouncing in my seat as Cassie drove me back to Pine Hills and the dreaded doctor's visit that was to follow. It was the first solid piece of evidence I'd uncovered. It wasn't a smoking gun, but it was something. It put Link at the crime scene, which was something I couldn't do for anyone else, not even Lydia, who'd given Scott the note that sent him there.

"You really enjoy this, don't you?" Cassie asked. "Asking questions, getting answers."

I wanted to tell her no, I didn't enjoy solving murders, because in order for me to do that, someone had to die.

But that would have been a lie. I might have hated it when I first started nosing around in murder investigations, but now, despite what I wanted to tell myself, I was enjoying it. It still upset me anytime someone was killed, of course. I was sad for the deceased, for their loved ones.

Yet the exhilaration at finding a clue, of taking that next step toward discovering who the culprit was and why they'd done it—it was like a drug. No matter how hard I tried to keep out of it, the addiction to the thrill always pulled me right back in.

I imagine I had my dad to thank for that. James Hancock was a mystery writer who loved telling stories of murder and crime solving. It wasn't much of a stretch to think that his fascination with it had passed down to me, even though he only ever wrote about fictional murders, while I'd had to deal with real ones.

"I guess I do," I admitted.

"I can see the appeal," Cassie said. "I'm not saying I ever want to put myself in a position where I'm helping solve a crime, much less a murder, but I can see why you do it."

"Before long, you'll be my trusty sidekick." I said it with a grin.

Cassie snorted and focused on her driving without further comment.

We arrived at the doctor's office a few minutes later. Cassie helped me through the door and patiently sat in the waiting room while Doctor Lipmon checked me out.

"Chasing killers again," Paige said as she gently turned my ankle, causing me to suck in a pained breath.

"Not this time," I said, which was true when it came to my ankle. "Treadmill got me."

She glanced up at me out of the corner of her eye. "Exercising? That's good to hear."

"Yeah, well, my ankle disagrees."

She chuckled, wheeled over to the computer in the corner of the room, and started typing. "I'm going to prescribe you some pills for the pain. I'd suggest crutches, but I have a feeling that you wouldn't use them. You shouldn't be out of commission for too long, but if you don't take care of yourself, it'll be longer." She wheeled back around. "No running. Keep walking to a minimum. Try to keep your weight off it, okay?"

"I'll try," I said, knowing that would last right up

until the moment when I decided to follow my next lead.

"Well, try hard." She stood. "And if you have any questions, feel free to call."

"Will do." And then, because I couldn't help myself: "You don't have any insights about the murder, do you? Like an idea of what kind of weapon was used, who would have had access to it, or anything like that?" A long shot, I knew, but, hey, it couldn't hurt to ask.

The scowl that Paige shot me would have burned if I hadn't been prepared for it. It lasted about two seconds before she sagged. "Nothing substantial. I wasn't there when it happened, and I never saw anything that I found suspicious."

I wasn't surprised, but thought I'd take a shot. "Thanks, Doc." I eased my way to my feet.

Paige started for the door. She hesitated with her hand on the knob. "If I'm hearing right, the victim had his face covered."

"He did," I said. "I saw it myself." I suppressed a shudder.

"Don't quote me on this, because I'm not a psychologist or anything, but that often indicates that the killer was someone who knew the victim. Maybe a lover. Maybe a friend. They covered his face because they felt some semblance of remorse. It's also possible someone close to the victim had found him and covered his face, but why they wouldn't have reported the crime, I wouldn't know."

As I rejoined Cassie in the waiting room, my mind played over that little tidbit.

Link knew Scott. But so did Lydia and Austin and a whole mess of people.

But how many of them cared about him enough to feel remorse for killing him?

We left the doctor's office, and Cassie insisted on driving me to pick up my prescription, which I appreciated, though I felt I was starting to take advantage of her kindness, despite the fact that it was Cassie who'd suggested it. We had to wait ten minutes at the pharmacy before my prescription was ready, and we left, sans crutches, and she returned me to my car, which was still parked in front of Weight of the Hills.

"Looks like we'll be putting a hold on further exercise plans," Cassie said as she helped me to my car.

"For a week at least," I said, though I wasn't as sad about it as I tried to make it sound.

She laughed. "I'm guessing it'll be at least two." She watched as I groaned my way behind the wheel. "Make that three weeks before you'll want to come back."

"We'll see about that," I said, tentatively tapping the brake, just to see if I could push on it without crying. I managed it, but barely. "I'll be running circles around you in no time."

Cassie had the grace not to laugh in my face as she took hold of the door. "If you need me to drive you home, I can do that. I can even call a friend and have them pick me up at your place so I can come back for my car."

"No, I think I'll manage okay," I said. "I'll be sure to go slow."

She didn't look convinced—or happy about it. "All right. If you need anything, just call."

"I'll do that." Though my stubborn streak disagreed. I'd crawl around my house, whimpering in pain, before I asked anyone to wait on me. "Thanks for, well, everything, Cass."

"No problem. Drive safe. Text me when you get home." She stepped back and closed my car door.

I shot her a thumbs-up and started my car. Another tentative test to make sure I could press down on the brake and hold it, and I pulled away from the curb, honking to Cassie, who was watching me go, hands on her hips.

What I should have done was head straight home, where I could sag down onto the couch, put my foot up, and spend the rest of the day mindlessly watching television while my ankle healed. I could call Paul, ask him to come over to make me feel better. And while he might not be able to stay long, thanks to the murder investigation, even an hour of Paul time would be enough to work its magic on me.

It was a good idea, but, as I've said before, when did I ever take good advice, my own or otherwise?

19

"It's disrespectful. And not to just us, but to Scott."

Shari's voice hit me like a brick wall as I limped through the front door of Ted and Bettfast. I jerked to a halt, half-convinced she was yelling at me.

"Quitting is disrespectful!" Oliver shot back at her, with his finger leveled at her face. "Walking away from a golden opportunity is disrespectful."

Neither Oliver nor Shari noticed me as I stopped just inside the doors. Across the room, Lydia and Richie were watching the argument with nervous agitation. Richie's gaze met mine briefly, and I thought I caught a flash of relief, as if he thought I'd find a way to defuse the situation. He eased closer to Lydia so that they were almost, but not quite, touching.

"To you, maybe," Shari said. Her fists were clenched at her side, and every so often, she'd squeeze, as if attempting to channel her anger through her fingers so as not to punch Oliver in the face. "But to demand we remain here, in this sleepy little town, when we all have real lives to get back to, just so you can take advantage of another man's death? I don't think so."

"Then leave if you think it would make things better for you," Oliver snapped. "We both know you could use the good press. But, hey, if you want to throw away a chance to pull your reputation out of the gutter, be my guest."

"You know—" She raised a fist and finally caught a glimpse of me watching. Some of the anger bled out of her, and she dropped her hand to her side.

Oliver laughed. "That's what I thought."

This time, I was almost positive Shari was going to hit him. Her teeth snapped closed loudly enough, I heard them clack clear across the room. Through them, she eked out, "Go screw yourself, Oliver," before she stormed past him, toward me. Our eyes met, but unlike Richie, who'd appeared glad to see me, Shari's gaze only expressed her rage. She didn't quite bump shoulders with me as she passed, but it was a near thing.

Oliver waited until the door slammed closed behind her before he said, "That woman," and turned to Richie and Lydia. "What are you two doing still standing there? We have a lot to do." He clapped his hands together. "Get moving!"

Both his assistants jumped into action, with neither quite sure where they were supposed to go. They spun in a pair of quick circles, as if searching for something to do, before they both fled to the back. Oliver heaved a put-upon sigh, turned, and made a face like he'd tasted something foul as his eyes landed on me.

"Hi, Oliver," I said, trying not to take offense, but I couldn't help it. The man oozed disrespect, and it was hard not to feel insulted by it.

"Ms. Hancock. I'm rather busy at the moment—"

"I won't take up too much of your time." I limped toward him, doing my best to disguise how bad my ankle hurt. I really should have taken something before coming. "I was hoping I could ask you a question or two."

"You've already taken more than enough of my time," he said. "If you need something, speak to Mr. Husted or Ms. Ray. Preferably when they aren't busy assisting me."

"It's about Link," I said as he started to turn away.

Oliver hesitated, his expression going cold and hard. "What about him?"

"What can you tell me about him?" I came to a stop and leaned against a nearby chair for support. A bead of sweat had risen across my brow, and the drafty air in the room caused it to chill.

"He's one of my better actors," Oliver said. "And he's loyal, which is more than I can say about some of my other acquaintances." He shouted the last, eyes aimed toward the door where Shari had gone.

"I heard that he may have picked up Scott Flanagan from the Banyon Tree and driven him to the logging camp where he—Scott—was murdered."

"That's preposterous," Oliver snapped. "He was with me the entire day."

"He was with you? Did you pick Scott up?"

Oliver rolled his eyes and turned away. "That's such a stupid question, I'm not even going to dignify it with a response." He walked toward the back, already barking orders to Lydia and Richie. I was dismissed.

I remained leaning against the chair a few moments longer, not quite sure what to do next. There was a chance Link was somewhere in the building, but where? I could go room to room, hoping to stumble upon him, but there was no guarantee he'd even answer the door if I came knocking. Chances were also good that Oliver would have a conniption fit if he saw me wandering around without his leave.

And then there was the issue of the stairs leading up to the rooms. I wasn't so sure I could make it up them without resorting to crawling.

I continued to linger, hoping either Link or one of Oliver's assistants might wander through, and to give my ankle a little more time to stop barking at me, but no one appeared, and the pain didn't abate, so I pushed away from the chair and headed for the doors.

Shari was waiting for me outside.

"Sorry you had to see that," she said, managing a smile, though her anger was still evident in her posture. "Oliver just . . ." She made a frustrated sound.

"No worries. I feel the same way about him." I winced as I put all my weight on one leg. Boy, was I ever a wimp when it came to pain. "Is he still trying to continue with his production?"

"Honestly? I don't know what he's trying to do. He's attempting to convince those of us who stuck around thus far to continue to power through, but I don't see why any of us should. I'm only still here because I thought the police might want to ask me more questions about Scott since we were teamed up, but I'm now regretting that decision."

"They still might," I said.

"Yeah, well, I'll leave them my number." Shari ran her hands through her hair, pushing it away from her neck. In doing so, she revealed the upper corner of the tattoo I'd noticed when I'd first met her. It appeared to be a wing, though it was still hard to tell with so little exposed.

Shari saw me trying to get a better look, and instead of letting her hair fall back, she tugged the collar of her shirt down so I could see more of the tattoo. It was some sort of bird of prey, wings and talons spread—the left wing being the one I'd seen earlier. If it was reaching for something farther down on her chest, it was covered by her shirt, and I wasn't about to ask her to undress so I could see the whole thing.

"This is what Oliver was referencing when he alluded to my past mistakes," she said, letting her hair fall back into place.

"It's well done," I said, and I meant it. The tattoo looked professional.

"Thank you. I don't regret getting the ink, but I sometimes wish it had happened under better circumstances. Let's just say I made a few mistakes over the years, and not everyone in my life has forgiven me for them. The tat wasn't one of the mistakes, but it was tied to a major screwup that I'm still paying for to this day. If Scott ever talked about me like he did the others, he wouldn't have had to concoct a story to garner attention. The truth is bad enough."

"Did you know Scott well?" I asked, recalling how

she'd been the one to come to his defense when Drew had gone after him.

"Well enough, I suppose," she said. "We weren't close, which I assume was pretty obvious. I hate that he was killed, but honestly"—her sigh was sad—"I'm not surprised."

"If you weren't friends, how did you end up as team-mates?" I asked. "And how did Austin get involved? None of you seemed to have much in common."

Shari laughed. "It was an odd pairing, that's for sure. We . . ." She trailed off as she thought about it. "It all came together by chance, really. Austin and I knew each other and were both interested in taking part in this thing for our own selfish reasons. We weren't friends, but rather acquaintances. I mean, we got on well enough, so it wasn't too big of a stretch for us to work together." She paused, thought about it some more. "I believe Drew was the one who turned Austin on to Oliver's production."

"They know each other," I said, though I still didn't know how.

Shari nodded, but didn't expand on their relation-ship. "Austin and I decided we should team up since Drew didn't have room for him on his team, but we still needed a third. I knew Scott a little, and I think Austin did as well. Neither of us chose him, however. He was placed on our team."

My heart did a little leap. "He was placed?"

"Yeah. I think it was Lydia Ray who made the call, but I can't be sure. I'm only assuming that because Scott and Lydia got along. I don't think he was friends with anyone else here. But Lydia . . ."

"Were they dating?"

Shari considered it and shrugged. "They might have been, but if they were, I never saw them together. I mean, there were rumors, of course. Scott said a lot of things, and at some point, you just sort of tuned him out." Her expression fell. "Honestly, I wish I would have paid more attention to him. Don't get me wrong; I tried to be friendly with Scott, and I didn't like how Drew and some of the others were treating him, but we never really clicked beyond what we already were."

"What about Austin?"

"What about him?"

"Why was he angry with Scott?" I asked. "When I saw the three of you at Death by Coffee, Austin seemed pretty upset."

Shari sighed. "I'm not completely sure what happened." She paused, reconsidered. "No, that's not true. Like me, Austin wanted to get along with Scott for the sake of the team, but he couldn't let some of what Scott said go. And Drew fed Austin some crap, claiming Scott was talking about him, which, knowing Scott, was probably true. It was clear, at least to me, that Drew was just trying to get us to start fighting among ourselves. I tried to keep the peace, but Austin wasn't having it. And then, when Scott said he wanted to run off somewhere alone . . ." She shook her head.

"You left him."

"I hate that we did." A tear formed in the corner of her eye. She sniffed and wiped it angrily away. "One of us should have gone with him. Or followed him. I don't know. All I know is that, once we got to that hotel on the edge of town, Austin was beside himself. He kept ranting that Scott was screwing us over, and that Drew was right about him. It got bad enough that I finally snapped and told him that if he didn't like it, he could give up and go home, that I'd finish the dang thing alone."

A car pulled into the lot. A small woman with dark hair and stylish glasses climbed out of the vehicle and power walked past us, into Ted and Bettfast, without so much as a hello.

"India's here," Shari said with a scowl. "Looks like Oliver's calling in the big guns."

I wanted to ask her who India was exactly, but I didn't want her to get off track. "What happened then?" I asked instead.

"What do you think? I was upset that everything was falling apart and didn't really mean it, but Austin took me literally. He said some things I might have taken the wrong way in my own frustration, so I said a few other choice words I wouldn't ever want repeated. Long story short, Austin left me stranded at the hotel, and I had to hitch a ride with another team when Oliver called us all back here after Scott was found."

"Wait," I said, excitement growing. "Austin left you?"

"He did."

"Do you know where he went?" I mentally did the math, trying to make it all fit. Austin and Shari left the Banyon Tree before Scott. They might even have reached the hotel before Scott found his ride. Could Austin have left Shari and, in his anger, tracked Scott down and killed him?

But if so, how did he know where Scott was if Scott

didn't tell him where he was going? Could he have known about Lydia's note? Or had he found the clues and left, thinking he would finish solving Oliver's mystery on his own, and happened upon Scott at the logging camp? Or could he have had contact with Link, who was on his way to pick Scott up and learned about it from him?

I had to be missing something.

"Before he left, Austin made a call," Shari said, cutting into my thoughts.

"Do you know who he called?" I asked, with Link's name blazing in fiery letters in my head.

"I don't," Shari said. "All I heard before he walked off was that Austin told someone that something needed to be done about Scott." Her jaw flexed as her eyes started to water. "I don't want to think Austin could have had anything to do with Scott's death, but the more I think about it, the more I wonder."

Austin and Drew were caught talking the night before Scott's murder. And in that conversation, Drew told Austin "You know what you have to do." Or something akin to that. Could we be dealing with a conspiracy from the start? Lydia might have gotten Scott placed on Shari and Austin's team. She gave Scott the note to meet at the logging camp. Drew and Austin were clearly working together to some degree, might even have met outside Sara's window to discuss their plans.

And what about Oliver and Link? Kenneth Purdy and Hector Kravitz? How did they fit in, if at all? And did Drew's teammates Tony and Curtis know anything? As far as I knew, they could already be gone.

"Look, I've got to get out of here," Shari said, wiping at her nose with the back of her hand. "I can't take this anymore. I just want to go home." She started to walk away, stopped. "If you talk to Austin, don't tell him I told you anything, all right? My life is hard enough these days. I don't need the extra drama."

"I won't," I promised, though I would need to tell the police. This felt like something Detective Buchannan needed to hear.

Shari stared at me a long moment before nodding and walking back into Ted and Bettfast, presumably to grab her things before she headed back home.

I returned to my car but didn't call Buchannan right away. I needed to think about what I'd learned and see if I could put the pieces together in a cohesive story. If I went to Buchannan with only speculation and assumptions, he'd tell me to stop poking my nose around in his investigation, and that would be that.

Besides, I wanted to check in on Vicki at Death by Coffee to see how she was doing after last night's excitement. I could always stop by the police station later. And who knows? Perhaps talking to Vicki would somehow give me the breakthrough I needed.

20

"The usual?" Beth asked as I entered Death by Coffee and approached the counter.

I almost told her that, yeah, one coffee with one chocolate chip cookie floating inside would be fantastic, but changed my mind. "Actually, I think I'm going to have a caramel macchiato." Like Richie before me, it made me feel as if I were honoring Scott by drinking one of his favorites. "I can make it."

"No, you're the customer today. I've got it." Beth turned and started making the macchiato before I could object.

"Thanks." While she worked, I went ahead and picked up stray trash in the dining area and tossed it into the bin. It was obvious I'd just missed a rush and no one had gotten a chance to fully clean beyond a cursory pass. The tables had been wiped down, but the floor needed to be swept, and one of the chairs had what looked like chocolate drizzle on it.

Vicki's black-and-white cat, Trouble, meandered

over to the top of the stairs, eyed me a moment, then went to lie down within the stacks. That meant Vicki had been here, though since she wasn't upstairs with the books or behind the counter with Beth, I was afraid I'd missed her.

"Here you go," Beth said, handing the macchiato over as I returned to the counter. "It's been a hectic day already."

I took a sip. The coffee was good, but I still missed the cookie. "Beyond being busy?" I asked, half-afraid something bad had happened because, well, with how the week had been, why wouldn't it?

"No, I suppose not. Vicki was here to help, so it wasn't really all that bad. At least, I don't think so. We'd just gotten through the rush and had started to clean up when Vicki got a call that upset her."

Uh-oh. "Any idea what it was about?"

Beth shook her head. "Whatever it was, she appeared pretty frazzled before she ran off to the back."

I could hazard a guess as to what the call was about. "Is she still here?"

"She's in the office. She hasn't come out since she got the call."

I thanked Beth for the information and the coffee, and headed into the small, overpacked office behind the counter that we mostly just used for storage. I nearly bumped into Vicki on her way out.

"Oh!" she said, startled. "Krissy? When did you get here?"

"Just a few minutes ago." I eyed her purse and jacket. "Something come up?"

She blew a strand of hair out of her face. "I got a call from Angela Cartwright. You remember her, don't you?"

"She's one of the play directors at the community theatre, right?"

Vicki nodded. "She's called a meeting at the theatre so we can try to sort out this mess with Kenneth Purdy before it gets out of hand."

"Kenneth is going to be there?"

That caused her to laugh. "No. But because of his threats, there's real concern. If he goes through with a lawsuit, we're going to need to figure out how to handle it. I honestly don't know if we can. The hope is that we can convince Hector to back off and maybe apologize for being, well, Hector, so that Kenneth might reconsider. I doubt it will work, but, hey, it's worth a shot."

I considered that. I wanted to talk to Hector Kravitz to discern if he was somehow connected to Scott's death, just so I could rule him out and focus on those who were more likely. The meeting would be the perfect place to do so. "Do you mind if I tag along?" I asked. "I don't want to get in the way, but . . ."

"Sure. You're just as much as part of the theatre as I am."

While that wasn't exactly true, I *had* taken part in a play at the old community theatre, thanks to Rita's urging. Did that make me an actress? Somehow, I doubted it.

"You heading there now?" Dumb question, but it seemed impolite to assume.

"Yeah. I'm actually running a little late. They've probably already started without me."

"Then we'd better go." I spun to lead the way, but my ankle buckled, causing me to nearly fall. I braced myself on the doorframe, nearly spilling my macchiato in the process.

Vicki grabbed hold of my elbow to help steady me. "Whoa. What happened? Are you all right?"

"I'm fine. It's my ankle," I said. "Exercise accident. Don't ask."

Vicki at least attempted not to grin, but couldn't help herself. "I figured you might have had another mishap with Misfit tripping you."

"Ha-ha." Deadpan. "Don't go blaming an innocent cat because I'm a klutz."

"Sorry." She contorted her face a few times, and the smile almost faded. Almost. "I'll drive."

I almost told her that I'd be fine, but, honestly, I wasn't sure that I would be. Me being me, I still had yet to take my pain meds, mostly because I was afraid they'd knock me out or make me dizzy or lightheaded. And I suppose I was simply being stubborn. "Sounds good. Let's go."

Vicki kept a steadying hand on me as we left Death by Coffee. She helped me into her car, not letting me go until I was safely seated, which made me feel like a total wimp. I mean, people got hurt all the time and didn't need someone babying them. You really couldn't call it "toughing it out" if you were being carried everywhere.

The drive to the community theatre was a short one, so I didn't get much time to think about how I was going to go about confronting Hector before we were there. I climbed out of the car and limped my way to the door, waving Vicki off when she tried to help. Despite my protests, she still held the door open for me, sticking out her tongue at me when I tried to complain.

"Thanks," I muttered, resigned to my fate, though it was drowned out by the raised voices coming from the room beyond.

"We have to put our foot down!" a man was shouting. "If we let him walk all over us, then we deserve whatever happens. We have to fight back!"

"I understand that, Hector." I recognized Angela's voice. "But if we are too aggressive, it'll only antagonize him. You know what Kenneth is like."

Vicki and I paused at the doorway, neither of us wanting to interrupt.

"I do," Hector shot back. "And that's why I think we need to push him. He's not going to back down on his own. We have to make him understand that we won't take this lying down. If that means showing up at his house in the middle of the night, then that's exactly what I'm willing to do."

"We have to be united." This from a woman with graying hair and a mole just under her left eye. "If half of us are running around town, causing mayhem, it'll make those of us who want to do this diplomatically look bad. Then there'll be no chance of us working this out."

Hector made a disgusted sound. "You always shy away from conflict, Reyna. You'd much rather sit back and let people walk all over you instead of standing up for yourself."

"Perhaps you should have followed my example,

Hector," she retorted with some heat behind her voice. "Maybe then we wouldn't be in this situation."

I eased the rest of the way into the room, with Vicki right behind me. A few eyes shifted our way as Hector continued to plead his case. And by plead, I mean scream it at the top of his lungs.

"What do you think will happen if Kenneth is left free to do as he pleases? He'll ruin us simply because we allowed him to do so. I told you all what I saw. He's working with Oliver Quick. He's the reason we were dropped from Oliver's production. Do you think he'll stop there? No. Even if he doesn't go through with his threats, he will continue to sabotage us any way he can. He has sway in this town. You all know it. We'll lose licenses. We'll probably get hit with sanctions of some kind. We'll be forced to close within the year, and who will we have to blame? Not Kenneth if we don't try to stop him. It'll be *our* fault." He punctuated the last with a thump to his chest.

"I understand your concerns," Angela said, patting the air, in a vain effort to remain diplomatic, "but we need to talk about how best to proceed. We can't just blunder ahead with no idea of what we're getting ourselves into, and with no direction outside of *attack*."

"Blunder ahead?" Hector shouted it. "This is our theatre. We are family. We should stand united against anyone who would do us harm. I don't think it's too difficult to see what we should do next."

"What we should do is sit down and talk about this civilly," a tired-looking man leaning on a cane said.

"Andre is right," Angela said. "Let's all calm down, take a breath, and discuss this properly."

Hector scoffed. "You can all sit around and talk until you're blue in the face, but nothing will get done until we take action!" He spun on his heel. "Have your little chat. I need air."

I shuffled aside as Hector stomped between Vicki and me. He used both hands to slam the door open before he stepped outside, muttering under his breath. The door swung closed behind him, cutting off whatever he had to say.

"That went well," someone said to a round of nervous chuckles.

Vicki started forward to join the rest of her colleagues. She hesitated and gave me a questioning look when I didn't follow.

A quick internal debate, and I said, "I'm going to talk to Hector. I'll be right back."

She made a face. "Good luck with that."

"Thanks." From the sounds of it, I was going to need it.

I slipped out the door as talks resumed, this time in a far more respectful tone than when Hector had been shouting at everyone. I was half-afraid to find that Hector had decided to cut his losses and abandon the meeting, but when I stepped outside, I found him pacing the far end of the parking lot, muttering angrily to himself. I limped over to him.

"I heard what you said in there," I said, and when he glanced at me, I added, "I'm Krissy Hancock. Vicki's friend."

Hector eyed me with distaste. Up close, I got a good look at him and saw that the finely trimmed stubble from his photo had grown to be a little less refined and that he wasn't wearing eyeliner. He looked less like a movie star and more like, well, everyone else.

"I'm sure you were sent to talk some sense into me," he said, before turning away. "You can march right back inside and tell them that my mind is made up. We can't sit back and let this happen to us without fighting back."

"No one sent me," I said. "And I don't think they're saying that they don't want to fight back. They just want to do what's right for the theatre."

"That's exactly what I want to do!" Hector spun on me so violently, I nearly stumbled backing away from him. "Oliver and Kenneth are working together to ruin us. I just know it! They want us to be afraid and to hole up here when we should be out there, screaming our defiance at the tops of our lungs." He flung a hand in the general direction of town.

"How do you know Oliver is involved with Kenneth?" I asked.

"I saw them together."

"This was before Oliver's production started?"

"And after," Hector said. "They thought they could pressure me into silence, but I wouldn't have it! If the police hadn't shown up and ruined everything . . ." He trailed off with a scowl.

"This was on the day of the event?" I asked, very nearly mentioning the murder. If Hector was somehow involved in that, I didn't want to spook him by bringing it up.

Hector nodded. "I was here protesting with a few like-minded individuals who aren't afraid of a little conflict." He raised his voice on the last bit, as if he was trying to be heard all the way inside the theatre. "I'd been here all of fifteen minutes before Oliver showed up with Kenneth right behind him."

"Oliver was here?" I asked. "In person?"

"Of course it was in person." Hector gave me a look like I was a complete moron. "He showed up whining that I was going to ruin his little play." He laughed. "As if I needed to do anything to turn it into a joke. That man thinks he's the biggest star this side of the sun, but he's really just the biggest—"

I cut him off before he finished *that* thought. "What time was this?" My heart was thumping in my ears. Oliver had said he was at Ted and Bettfast all day on the day of the murder. But if he'd lied about that, what else could he have lied about?

"I wasn't keeping track of the time," Hector said. "It was early."

Early, as in just after we'd all started running all over town, looking for clues? Or early, as in around the time Scott was killed? I was almost afraid to ask.

"Were the two of them alone?" I asked instead. "Kenneth and Oliver. Was someone with them?"

"No. It was just the two of them." Hector spat to the side as if talking about Oliver and Kenneth left a bad taste in his mouth. "I can't believe they have the gall to blame us for that murder. I know for a fact that one of them must have done it. Look at what Oliver is doing now! I saw him on the news last night, hamming it up for the cameras. It's all part of his plan."

While I was also appalled by what Oliver was doing in using Scott's murder for his own benefit, I wasn't entirely convinced he'd taken part in the murder. I mean, the thought *had* crossed my mind. But if Oliver was here, arguing with Hector, he couldn't have been with Link, who'd presumably picked up Scott at the Banyon Tree.

There was always a chance that Link was here, of course. He could have waited in the car while Oliver and Kenneth confronted Hector, and once that was done, he and Oliver could have driven to the Banyon Tree, picked up Scott, and driven him to the logging camp together.

But Sara hadn't mentioned seeing Oliver. Could he have hidden in the back seat, waited for Scott to appear, and sprung up and . . . what? Killed him? For what reason? And how did Lydia's note fit in? Scott's issues with Drew and Austin? Two people working together, I could believe. But five? Six? I seriously doubted it.

"I'd better get back inside before the rest of them do something rash," Hector said, sounding resigned. "If you're Vicki's friend, maybe you can talk some sense into her for me, yeah?" He looked me up and down, and sighed, as if disappointed in what he saw, before he headed back inside the theatre, head shaking.

I remained in the parking lot a few minutes longer, still trying to sort through the timing. I didn't know exactly when Scott had died, only that he'd left the Banyon Tree sometime before I'd arrived. How long was it before he'd been killed? Could Rita, Wendy, and I have just missed the killer, possibly even passed him on our way there?

I tried to remember if I'd seen a car, but came up blank. I hadn't been paying attention to anyone who'd passed; I didn't have a reason to.

But if I knew where each team was at the time of the murder, perhaps I could put together a better timeline, all while eliminating suspects. I mean, if Austin was still with Shari at the hotel at the time of Scott's death, he couldn't have killed him. The same went for Oliver when he was here, Drew with wherever he was, and so on.

As much as I hated to admit it, it was time I talked to Detective Buchannan.

21

I was back at the logging camp, foot caught in a bear trap that was inexplicably placed in the middle of the back room. Scott was alive and standing across from me, caramel macchiato dripping from his face. He didn't speak. Instead, he raised a hand and pointed to a spot just over my shoulder. When I tried to turn, my head refused to move. And then, a sound . . .

A rapid series of knocks caused my heart to leap from my chest as I jerked awake, sending Misfit careening off the coffee table as he bolted for the bedroom. Disoriented, I looked around the room, head thumping in time with the thunderous pounding of my heart. I wasn't sure if what I'd heard was real or imagined.

"Wha?" I managed through gummy lips and a thick tongue. Whatever those pain meds Doctor Lipmon had prescribed me were, they'd hit me like a truck.

The knocks came again, a steady, rapid beat that

was almost musical. It took me a moment, but I soon realized that they were coming from the door.

I stood and swayed my way across the room, still trying to piece together what exactly was going on. I remembered calling Buchannan once the meeting at the theatre had concluded, but he hadn't answered. I left him a voicemail, and after Vicki had dropped me off at my car, I'd come home to wait for his return call. I vaguely recalled taking my pain medication and sitting down on the couch with Misfit curling up in my lap as soon as I was settled, and I'd clearly fallen asleep, considering the unsettling the dream that I'd been having right before the knocks had jarred me awake.

Since it was only the late afternoon, and because my brain was still malfunctioning, I didn't think to peek out the window or call out to see who my visitor might be, despite the fact there was a killer on the loose and someone had been lurking around my house recently.

Instead, I stifled a yawn that felt like it had come straight from the depths of my soul and opened the door, only partially aware that I could be making a grave mistake.

"Ms. Hancock? What can you tell me about the murder of Scott Flanagan?" A hand flew toward my face, holding a black object that took me a moment to recognize as a phone. "Do you have any suspects? And could this murder be connected to prior killings in the area?"

"Wha?" I took a step back, which was yet another mistake. The woman moved forward with me, putting her inside the threshold of my home.

"Have you spoken with the victim's family? Could

they be involved?" The woman brushed her hand across her forehead, fluttering her bangs.

Wait . . . *bangs*?

Flashback of black-and-white images of a smartly dressed woman with bangs poking around my house while I wasn't home. A quick glance behind her showed me that the same car I'd seen in Caitlin's security footage was now parked in my driveway behind my Escape.

"Who are you?" I asked, some semblance of mental control returning. "Why were you at my house last night?"

"I'm Sabrina Mayfield with the *Levington Online Herald*. I'm doing an exposé on the murder-lady of Pine Hills. *You*." She smiled as if she thought I approved of being called "the murder-lady."

"The who with the what?" Okay, maybe I wasn't as in control as I thought. My overmedicated brain was still playing catchup.

"Sabrina Mayfield. I'm a reporter for the *Levington Online Herald*. You're Krissy Hancock?" The last came out uncertain, as if she feared she'd gotten the wrong address.

If I'd been thinking straight, I might have denied it, but instead, the words, "Yeah, but—" came out of my mouth before I was cut off.

"Scott Flanagan was murdered in Pine Hills, which is quickly becoming the murder capital of small towns in not just the state, but the entire country! There have been what? Eleven? Twelve murders within the last decade? And *you*, Krissy Hancock, have been at the center of each and every one."

As if I needed reminded of that fact. "I . . ." Had no idea what to say.

"They call you the murder-lady . . ."

"Where did you hear that term?"

She ignored the question. ". . . of Pine Hills. Do you have insights on the latest murder? What can you tell me about your process? My readers would love to know how it is you do what you do."

I blinked at her, unable to come up with anything to say. Of all the people to show up at my house, a reporter doing an exposé on me? I never would have imagined it in a million years. Nor was I thrilled by the prospects. Unlike Oliver Quick, I had no intention of using Scott's death for my own benefit.

Regaining my composure, I straightened to the best of my ability, looked her in the eye, and said, "No comment."

Undeterred, Sabrina pressed on. "Do the police come to you for aid? Or do you go to them with the information you've gathered on your own time and money?"

"No comment."

"It's important that my readers understand how you are able to do what you do," Sabrina said. Her phone, likely set to record, was still shoved under my nose. "What makes you tick? How do you manage to investigate without getting in the way of the police? Do you have their blessing to examine the scene?"

"Look, I've really got to go—"

"There's talk that you found the latest victim yourself, and that you are training a new wave of crime fighters. A . . ." she glanced down at a small notebook she'd produced from her pocket. "Wendy Wilcox? What can you tell me about her?"

"I'm not training anyone." Flustered, I nearly backed up another step, but caught myself when Sabrina leaned forward, ready to pounce. I feared that if she got all the way inside the house, I'd never be rid of her.

"What about"—another look at the notepad—"Rita Jablonski. Is she your assistant? She's worked with you before, has she not?"

"I'm sorry, I need to go." I tried to close the door, but Sabrina refused to budge. She wasn't a big woman, but even though my ankle felt better, thanks to the pain meds, I still couldn't put my full weight behind it so I could push her out of the way.

"I've spoken with people involved in the most recent crime," she said, putting her shoulder against the door and leaning into it so I couldn't push her out. "There is a lot of speculation about your part in the murder, and if you would only talk to me, we could clear a lot of it up."

"What speculation?" I asked, and then, realizing that would only give her an opening to pepper me with more questions, I added, "I have no comment. If you want to know anything about Scott's murder, talk to Detective John Buchannan. He's the lead detective on the case." And the only detective in Pine Hills, for that matter.

"I plan to do just that." An almost eager gleam came into her eye then. "You are in a relationship with the police chief's son. Is that how you've gained access to sensitive information?"

"I—"

"Krissy!" Jules appeared like an angel from above, though he'd only come from next door. He wedged himself past Sabrina, managing to not-so-subtly force her out of the doorway in the process. "We should talk." He turned to face the reporter. "I'm so sorry. I need Krissy here for a few minutes. I'm sure you could, I don't know, never come back."

And with that, he slammed the door in her face.

I sagged down onto a dining room chair, both mentally and physically exhausted. My head was spinning, and I wasn't entirely sure it was due to the pain medication. "Thanks," I said. "She woke me up and ambushed me."

"I saw that," Jules said. "Well, I saw her invading your space and decided to come over and make sure everything was okay. You looked panicked."

"Was it that obvious?"

"I was still in my car, and I could see the petrified look on your face."

Petrified? Was I really handling it that badly? "I hurt my ankle," I said, as if that would explain everything. "The pain medication knocked me out and made me feel all kinds of weird."

Jules walked past me, into the kitchen, "Let me put on some coffee. That'll perk you right up."

Coffee sounded fantastic right about then. "Thank you."

As Jules busied himself in the kitchen, I rubbed at my temples in an attempt to kick-start my brain. Sabrina Mayfield had obviously talked to someone who'd known Scott since she'd used the term *murder-lady*, but who? Richie was the only other person who'd come close to calling me that, outside of Scott himself, so did that mean he was the one who'd talked to her? Or had it been Oliver who'd let it slip? Since he was the one who was talking to reporters, I assumed he was the best bet.

"There," Jules said, coming over to join me at the table. "It'll be done in just a few minutes." He looked me up and down with a frown that said he wasn't too sure I'd make it that long. "How are you holding up?"

I seesawed my hand, leaned back with a groan. "It's been a long couple of days."

"Tell me about it." Jules sighed. "You know how I told you about how Lance was off to Colorado to deal with his cousin's crisis? Things have been going . . . Well, poorly is such a massive understatement, but I don't know how else to phrase it without saying something I might later regret."

"That's all right. I understand."

"Lance is on his way home now. He called me while I was at Phantastic Candies a little while ago, and what he had to say about how they treated him had me so rattled, I closed up shop early." He smiled. "It's a good thing I did, or else that woman would still be here, pestering you."

"Thanks again for saving me," I said. "She was asking about the murder." At Jules's raised eyebrows, I explained. "She's a reporter for an online paper or something. As soon as I answered the door, she launched right in, catching me completely off guard."

"Ah." He shook his head. "It's crazy how the press is getting involved in this one. I'm not sure I've ever seen it like this before. Did you know that Pine Hills was actually trending on Twitter or X or whatever it's called these days?"

"It was?"

Jules nodded. "I only gave it a quick peek because, most of the time, that stuff is full of such bile, it's not worth the time." The coffeepot beeped. He stood to pour our coffees and kept talking. "They're saying all sorts of things on the internet, most of which seem not just inappropriate, but flat-out wrong."

"Like what?" I asked, half-tempted to look for it myself, though I wasn't sure I actually wanted to see it. I didn't know what I'd do if I saw the term *murder-lady* plastered all over the net with my name connected to it.

"There was speculation that the victim was a part of a cabal or some such. Another post mentioned that he deserved what happened to him because he was 'woke,' as if that was an insult." Jules handed me a coffee and sat down again with one of his own. "It's honestly not worth your time, or mine. Every time something bad happens, people can't seem to help themselves, and they just have to put in their two cents, even if they have nothing productive to say."

I took a sip of my coffee and just about melted into my chair. Boy, did that ever hit the spot. "You know how I asked you this morning if you saw someone lurking around my house recently?"

"I do." His eyes widened. "That was her?"

"I think so." Small bubbles rose to the top of my mug, along with tiny chunks of sugary goodness. Jules had included one of the chocolate chip cookies I kept near the coffeepot. "She didn't confirm it, but she looks just like the person I saw in the video, and I'm pretty sure it's the same car."

"Wow." He clucked his tongue as he shook his head. "Well, I suppose it's better that it was a reporter rather than some crazed killer stalking you."

"Very true." A new thought. "What if she goes to Death by Coffee and starts harassing my employees?" And what if other reporters joined her? I imagined a dining room full of men and women, shoving their cell phones and microphones into the faces of Beth and Jeff and the others and half-rose out of my chair, intent on rushing over and putting a stop to it.

"I'm sure they'd be fine if she tried," Jules said. "You've trained them well."

I eased back down, not entirely convinced, but it wasn't like I could do much of anything if she did start harassing them, other than calling the cops. Speaking of which . . .

I rose and retrieved my phone from where I'd set it on the coffee table before passing out. A quick look at the screen showed me no texts or missed calls from Buchannan or anyone else. Mild irritation washed over me as I returned to the table.

"So," Jules said as I sat back down. He was smiling in a mischievous way. "Tell me about this injured ankle of yours."

Thankful to be talking about something other than a murder or a nosy reporter, I told him about how I'd fallen off the treadmill at Weight of the Hills, and my subsequent adventures around town, including my trip to the theatre.

"I suppose we should expect drama from those who are dramatic," he quipped.

We polished off a pair of coffees each, and I munched on the gooey remains of my cookie before he rose and headed for the door.

"I'll keep an eye out for our reporter," he said. "If she comes sniffing around again, I think I might show her that we aren't interested in being harassed."

I chuckled. "You do that. If you managed scare her off for good, the entire town would owe you one."

"You'd better believe it."

We said our goodbyes, and I spent the next ten minutes puttering around the house, mindlessly picking up. I was awake and feeling better, but I couldn't settle my mind. I couldn't stand by and let Oliver—or whoever it was who had talked to Sabrina Mayfield about me—bring the media circus down on Pine Hills.

No, it was best to nip that in the bud before things got out of hand and I *did* find Death by Coffee swarming with reporters and lookie-loos.

Without another thought, I gathered my purse and keys, gave Misfit a pat on the head, and was out the door.

22

I was surprised to see one of the employees of Ted and Bettfast, Jo, sweeping the front room when I entered. She glanced up, saw me, and went right back to work without acknowledging my presence. She looked distraught, which I chalked up to the pending sale of the bed-and-breakfast, which would directly impact her employment status. I made a mental note to talk to Robert about keeping on the old staff if he did indeed buy the place.

Oliver was nowhere in sight. In fact, no one, other than Jo, was. I was worried the emptiness meant that the production was finally dead and that Oliver and his cast and crew had gone home. I wasn't looking forward to the prospect of driving to Levington to talk to him, especially with a bum ankle.

The door opened behind me. I turned, and relief washed through me as Austin Helms entered, a troubled expression on his face. No, it wasn't Oliver, but it *was* someone involved with Scott.

Not wanting to pass up a good opportunity, I plastered on a smile and stepped in front of him.

"Hi, Austin," I said. "I'm glad to see you're still here."

He jerked to a stop, seemingly confused by my sudden appearance. "I, uh, yeah?"

"It's Krissy," I said. "Krissy Hancock. I was on one of the teams."

"I know." He frowned. "What are you doing here?"

"I was hoping to talk to Oliver about some of the stuff happening around town. Is he still here?"

Austin's eyes roved the room before he gave me a pointed look. "Apparently not. He's probably locked away somewhere, talking to India." He spoke her name with a hint of fear. "I wouldn't expect to see him again until sometime tomorrow."

"Is India his boss?"

Austin made a face reserved for talking about the boogeyman or other such horrors. "She's something, all right," he said. "I'd steer clear. She doesn't like it when people poke around where they don't belong."

That wasn't exactly an answer, but I let it go. "I talked to Shari about Scott and what happened at the Banyon Tree. She was pretty upset by everything and said she was going home."

Austin's face went carefully blank. "Really? I can't imagine she had much to say. It wasn't a big deal, though home does sound nice. Now, if you'll excuse me . . ."

He started to step past me, but I moved to intercept. "You left him there," I said. "And you left Shari at the hotel on the edge of town, knowing she had no way to get around. That doesn't make you look very good."

Austin's gaze flickered toward the stairs. "Okay, yeah, it was a jerk move, but I was upset."

"Upset enough to confront Scott about it?" I asked. "Where did you go when you left Shari?"

A flash of anger crossed Austin's face. It was quickly replaced by frustration. "That's none of your business."

"But the police might want to know," I said. "Wouldn't it be better to tell me, rather than wait for them to take you in for questioning?"

A beat, and then, "Is that a threat?"

"No." I decided to ease off lest I antagonize him to the point where he'd refuse to cooperate. "But I know the local cops, and they'll be wondering the same thing as me. You left both Scott and Shari, and no one knows where you went. That is the definition of suspicious."

Austin ran a hand over his mouth. I could see the wheels spinning behind his eyes as he considered whether to tell me or to take his chances with the police.

Apparently, dealing with me won out.

"Look, it's not what you think," he said in a near pleading tone.

"Then tell me what it is I *should* be thinking," I said.

Austin's toe tapped on the floor in a rapid staccato before he answered, measuring his words. "I admit that I was upset. Scott was acting all weird, demanding he go off on his own, which would leave Shari and me hanging. I didn't like it, and I made sure to tell him that. Then, once we left him, Shari got on me about it, and I decided I'd had enough. I left her and called Link to tell him that Scott should be kicked off my team. That's it."

"Where did you go after you left Shari?"

"Where else? I came back here and pouted in my room until I got the text telling everyone to come back. I was being dumb, and I guess a bit of a crybaby, but I swear that's all that happened."

I searched his face. I believed most of what he'd told me, yet I still felt he was leaving something out. "On the day of Scott's murder, I saw you at Death by Coffee. You were already angry with Scott. This was before the Banyon Tree and before he started demanding you separate."

This time, Austin's gaze shot toward the back door, as if he was considering making a run for it. He bit his lower lip, foot still tapping so quickly, it was making *my* leg tired.

"Austin," I pressed when it didn't appear that he'd answer, "you should tell someone. The more you hide, the worse it looks for you." And then I used my proverbial ace in the hole. "Someone overheard you talking to Drew the night before the game began. *'You know what to do.'* Sound familiar?"

Austin paled, and the strength seemed to go out of him. "It's not what you think," he said. It was fast becoming his mantra.

I didn't bother responding this time. I was pretty sure I had him. I could see it in his eyes, the way his shoulders slumped. Was he about to confess to murder? Or, at the minimum, being part of a conspiracy to kill Scott Flanagan?

Across the room, Jo finished sweeping. She glanced our way, frowned, then slipped upstairs, broom still in hand.

That left us alone, which seemed to calm Austin ever so slightly.

"It was about what Scott had said," he said.

"About you and your neighbors?"

Austin reddened. "No. That was a rumor started *by* my neighbor." When I looked at him like I didn't believe him, he sighed. "Dixie—my neighbor—wasn't getting along with her husband. She wanted to make him jealous. I was single, living next door, and, I suppose, an easy target. She told everyone she knew that I had seduced her in the hopes it would get back to her husband."

"Did it?" I asked, interested despite myself.

"Heck yeah, it did. Dude got angry, but after I talked him down, he realized I had nothing to do with it. His wife eventually copped to the story, letting me off the hook, but Scott wouldn't let it go. He took Dixie's story and twisted it to be, I don't know, more scandalous than it really was."

"You weren't upset with him about that?" I asked.

He started to shake his head, caught himself. "I suppose I was. It's probably why I—" He cut himself off, scowled. "He was talking about Lydia."

Now, that caught me by surprise. "He was telling stories about Lydia?"

Austin's foot stopped tapping. "No. Yes." He made a frustrated sound. "Kind of? In our room the night before the game started, Scott claimed he and Lydia were seeing one another. You know, dating."

"Were they?"

"I doubt it. I mean, no one believed him. Not me, not Shari. I'm sure he bragged about it to others, and maybe he started believing it himself, but there's just no way."

I got that Scott was awkward, kind of nerdy, and that Lydia was attractive and, well, seemingly the opposite of Scott. But did that really mean there was no chance that they could have hit it off? Look at Sara and Albert. They were nothing alike and yet seemed happy with one another.

"Scott rarely told the truth," Austin went on. "He had to have been lying about this. Lydia is a good person. We all like her." His already red face deepened another shade. "*I* like her. She doesn't need the kind of scrutiny, the sort of ribbing, she'd get if everyone thought she was seeing Scott, even in a friendly manner. I was angry because Scott insisted it was true and refused to back down."

My mind was racing. Scott and Lydia. Her note. What if he was telling everyone about their relationship—real or not—and she didn't like it? Could it have angered her enough that she thought she had to do something about it? Could she have asked him to meet, begged him to stop talking about it, and, when he refused, killed him for it?

"Drew concocted a plan," Austin said, after a moment's thought. "He made up an elaborate story about Scott, one so embarrassing that Scott would stop talking about everyone else in his shame. It was stupid, and I'm not going to tell you what it was he wanted to spread because it embarrasses me even thinking about it. I only went along with the plan because Scott irritated me so darn much. That night, Drew and I went outside to hash out the details, and in the dark, with no one around, it sounded reasonable."

So *that* was who Sara saw outside her window that night.

"Drew wanted me to be the one to start the rumor because, coming from him, it would have been dismissed almost immediately," Austin said. "Everyone knew Drew and Scott didn't get along. I was annoyed enough, I was going to do it, but after Scott started talking about Lydia, I don't know, I started thinking that it wasn't worth my time. Besides, it was childish. How could I justify making up stories about Scott when it frustrated me when he did the same thing? It would have been hypocritical."

"So you left him at the Banyon Tree."

"I regret that. Maybe if I'd stayed . . ." He didn't finish the thought, didn't need to. "Drew was angry that I didn't follow through with it, but after we learned about Scott, I guess we were both happy that I didn't. And then, when I saw Lydia . . ." He sucked in a breath that trembled ever so slightly. "His death hit her hard. Seeing her like that made me wonder if I was wrong and Scott was telling the truth about their relationship the whole time. Could we really have been that wrong about him?"

It was clear Austin felt guilty about what happened to Scott, but looking at him, I was pretty sure the guilt was more about leaving him behind where a killer caught up to him instead of, you know, actually killing him.

"Do you know where Lydia is?" I asked, instead of pressing him further. I had a feeling that if I didn't let him go soon, Austin would break down. That wasn't something I wanted to see. "I haven't had the chance to express my condolences."

Austin rubbed at his face, let out a sigh that sounded almost relieved. "Last I saw, she was out back, by the pool. That was something like twenty minutes ago, so she might be somewhere else by now."

I thanked Austin and finally let him head to his room. The look he gave me as he passed was one of pure remorse. I was struck by how it was possible that someone who didn't commit the crime likely felt worse than the one who did.

Once he was upstairs, I headed for the back door that led to the pool. As soon as I reached the door, I saw that Lydia was indeed still out there, bundled up in a heavy coat that seemed to swallow her as she sat in one of the chairs. Richie was seated next to her, arm draped over her shoulder. He had his head close to hers and was talking to her in what appeared to be a soothing tone. The pool, as expected for this time of year, was covered.

I opened the door and joined them on the back deck. A chill breeze blew from the surrounding trees, causing me to shiver. It wasn't pleasant back here, but it was quiet, which I assumed was why Lydia was out here now.

Richie glanced back as I stepped outside. He said something else to Lydia, patted her on the shoulder, and then stood. He gave me a "be gentle" look before he went inside, leaving the two of us alone.

"Hey, Lydia," I said, sitting down next to her. "How are you holding up?"

She glanced over at me. Her eyes were red and puffy. "Krissy, right?" When I nodded, she gave me a sad smile. "How do I look?"

Flashback. Sara Huffington sitting in nearly the same exact spot, mourning the murder of her boyfriend at the time. She'd tried to act strong, but there were cracks. The image was so strong, Sara's face appeared superimposed over Lydia's own for a heartbeat before the cold wind blew it away.

"Like someone who is mourning the loss of a loved one," I said.

The sad smile dropped. "Scott and I . . ." A shuddering breath. "We were keeping it a secret because we didn't want the scrutiny, especially here. No one knew about us at first, but he was so proud, he started telling people."

"They didn't believe him."

Lydia's laugh was void of humor. "I'm not surprised. Almost everyone wanted Scott to fail. I understand that they didn't like how he talked about them, but it wasn't like he was trying to hurt anyone. Scott wanted everyone to like him, he really did. But as soon as he got into a social situation, he didn't know what to do. He'd talk. You know, like he thought he was gossiping with his buddies. No one saw it that way, of course. They thought he was being insulting."

"But you saw him for what he was."

"I suppose." She shrugged. "I don't know. He was different. He cared. He treated me like I was special, didn't force me to do anything I didn't want to do."

I searched her face, looking for any signs of deception, but saw none. Lydia seemed genuinely upset about Scott. If she'd killed him, would she still feel that way?

"You gave him a note to meet," I said, trying to keep my tone as gentle as possible so as not to upset her too badly. "On blue paper. I found it at the Banyon Tree."

Lydia flinched, and her face bunched up. For an instant, it looked as if she might burst into tears before she managed to stuff her emotions back into whatever box she was keeping them in, but barely.

"I did," she said. "I heard about what Drew and Austin were planning and realized I needed to talk to him."

"You heard about the rumor they were going to spread about Scott?"

She nodded, a flash of anger passing over her features, before dissipating. "They thought they were being sneaky, but Curtis told me. He's a good guy, despite being friends with Drew." She paused a moment, seemed to consider that, before going on. "I wanted to warn Scott, but was afraid to text him. Scott doesn't always check his messages right away. And if I'd tried to call, with Oliver around . . ." She shook her head. "So I gave him the note, asked him to meet."

"Why at the logging camp?" I asked. Neither Scott nor Lydia were from Pine Hills, so it seemed like an odd choice. "Why not just talk to him at Death by Coffee? And why not talk to him about it right away? Two hours is a long time to wait if it's an emergency."

"I warned him when I gave him the note," she said. "About Drew and Austin." Likely when she whispered to him when she gave him the note. "Oliver had me running errands, or else I would have talked to him there. And . . . I had another reason for wanting to talk to him."

The urge to ask her what that reason might be was strong, but I kept silent and let her talk.

"I wasn't sure where to go at first," she went on, "but then I remembered Richie talking about how his uncle ran a logging company and that he'd come here to take down some trees, but was forced to shut down. He said the camp was still here and that it was abandoned, so I asked him where it was."

"Richie knew where you were going?" I asked.

Lydia considered my question before speaking. "No, I didn't tell him what I was planning." Her face, which was pale from the cold, colored. "He wouldn't have understood. No one would have." A moment passed, and she spoke at nearly a whisper. "I asked Scott to leave with me. To just drop everything and get into my car and we'd just drive. I thought we could . . ." She swallowed, shook her head.

I suppose that explained why she wanted to meet him so far out of the way. Not only would no one be around, but if she was able to convince Scott to leave, no one would see them go. They'd just be gone.

"He told me that he wanted to go," she said, "but couldn't. He said that he couldn't abandon his team, that him coming to meet me already had upset them. He was going to make everything right."

"Who else knew about the camp?" I asked, trying to think it through. Richie knowing about it looked bad for him, but if someone else had overheard . . .

"No one, as far as I know," she said. "Well, Link and Oliver were there and would have heard. And that weird guy who's been hanging around. Robert?"

Weird was right. "Anyone else?"

"I mean, Richie might have told someone else, but when we talked about it, it was in the office and just a few of us were there. I never heard it mentioned again." Her lower lip trembled. "Scott was fine when I left him. He told me to go, even though I offered him a ride. And I went."

This time, she couldn't hold back. Lydia burst into tears. She covered her face with her hands, her entire body wracked with sobs.

Unsure what to do, or if Lydia would even want me to do anything, I gently patted her on the back. I felt for her. I couldn't imagine what I would do if something were to ever happen to Paul. The thought alone was nearly enough to give me a panic attack.

I sat there and waited her out. It felt cruel, but I still needed to ask her one more question. I was pretty sure the police had asked her before me, but I couldn't be positive, not when they might not have known about her relationship with Scott or the meeting.

When her sobs eased, I asked, as gently as possible, "Did you see anyone else at the camp? Scott's driver? Another car?"

"No." She sniffed, dabbed at her eyes with her fingertips. "I wish I had. And I didn't even think to ask him how he got there. If I'd known he hadn't driven himself, I wouldn't have left him alone. I would have . . . I'd . . ." She took a deep, trembling breath. "I'm sorry, but I think I want to be alone right now."

"Of course." I stood, hesitated at the door. I had to ask. "Why don't you go home? Get away from it all?"

A hard look came into her eye then, one that made me nearly regret asking. "Oliver, that's why. He's paying me for this job, and I can't afford not to get paid. I'll lose my apartment if I don't."

She didn't say it, but it was clear that she feared Oliver would withhold her earnings if she were to leave before he allowed it.

"Thank you for talking to me," I said, and then, because it needed to be said, "I'm sorry for your loss."

Lydia gave me a sad, wan smile and lowered her head. As I walked back into Ted and Bettfast, she began to cry all over again.

23

The phone rang twice before Paul answered with, "Hey, Krissy. Sorry, but I can't talk right now."

"Still at work?" I asked, glancing at the clock. It was already past seven, and he'd been working since early that morning.

"No. I'm with Chief." There was a long pause. "I'll see you tomorrow at Ted and Bettfast, all right? I'll tell you about it then."

A brief flare of panic flashed through me. "Is she okay?" There was something off in Paul's tone that had me on edge.

"She's fine. Like I said, I'll tell you all about it tomorrow. I've got to go."

And with that all-too-brief goodbye, he was gone.

I frowned at my phone before tossing it onto the table. Paul was with his mom, which, okay, that's fine. But why the secrecy? Sure, a son could spend time with his mother, but Paul had always been open with me. Could they be closing in on a suspect in Scott's murder and he didn't want me to get involved? That would constitute work, however, and I didn't think he'd lied to me.

You're overthinking it.

The voice in my head was probably right. I had to clamp down on the contrary part of my brain that had further questions, such as why did he say he would see me at Ted and Bettfast tomorrow? Did he know something I didn't?

Misfit was lounging on the coffee table, watching me as I paced. He'd already had his dinner and had finished his post-meal wash, so now he was just waiting for me to settle in so he could get his pre-bed lap time.

But I was too agitated to sit. Even with a bum ankle that was screaming at me to get off it, I couldn't make myself relax. I'd already been worried about killers and reporters lurking around Pine Hills, and now I was worried about Patricia Dalton. Could she be sick? Was "fine" code for "in the hospital, but stable?" Nothing he said had given me that impression, but still . . .

No, Krissy, focus on the reporter.

I picked up my phone and did a quick search for the *Levington Online Herald*. The site was rather plain, with a basic black-and-white header with the online paper's name and nothing else accompanying it. No graphics, no fancy font. The articles were posted in blog format, with a single paragraph leading to a link that took you to the full story. I skimmed through the headlines of the first dozen or so articles, and not seeing my name or Pine Hills listed, I deduced that Sabrina Mayfield had yet to post her exposé or a teaser for it.

Real detective work there, Ms. Hancock.

Okay, it was time to ignore the condescending voices in my head, though without someone to talk to, it was hard to do.

I considered calling Dad to talk things through. These were the sorts of times when his calming voice and mystery-writer insights paid dividends. Sometimes, even if he had nothing more to contribute than kind, supportive words, hearing his voice was enough to center me. I suppose it was a dad superpower.

I'd just opened my contacts and placed my finger over Dad's name when there was a knock at the door. Frowning, I tucked my phone into my back pocket and went to the window. Peeking outside, I noted the car in the driveway, recognized it, and considered hiding under my bed until my unwanted visitor went away.

"Ms. Hancock, I know you're in there." Detective John Buchannan's voice was terse. "I can see you in the window."

I ducked back, but it was already too late.

Sure, I had information for him and had left him a voicemail to call me back so I could tell him all about it, but the key word there was *call.* In person, I had to deal with his scowls and hard stares, not to mention the fact I couldn't just hang up on him when he was standing in my kitchen.

I took my grand old time limping over to the door to open it. And, yeah, maybe I played my injury up a bit as I stepped back from the door, hoping Buchannan would take pity on me and treat me with a little more care than usual.

If he noticed I was hurt, he sure didn't show it as he

stomped into my house without so much as a how do you do. In fact, the first thing out of his mouth was, "What in the world were you thinking? I should haul you in right now and force you to sit in a cell for a few hours as payback."

Payback for what? I did a quick mental rewind, but all I'd done was talk to a few people around town. That wasn't a crime.

I opened my mouth to say just that when Buchannan plowed ahead.

"I have a murder to investigate. It's my investigation, Ms. Hancock. Not yours. They're never yours, no matter what you tell others. What were you thinking when you claimed that you're the only one solving crimes in Pine Hills? Do you truly believe the police do nothing but sit on our hands while murderers are running free? Is that how you see us?"

"What? No!"

"Then why are you telling reporters that we do?" His chest heaved as he glared at me.

Uh-oh. I scrambled for something to say, something that might defuse the situation before it got out of hand, but all I managed to come up with was a pathetic, "That's not what I said."

"And what exactly did you say?"

"Nothing! The reporter came to my door and asked me a bunch of questions. I told her I had nothing to say." And then it hit me. I looked down at my feet when I said, "I suppose I told her that if she wanted to know something about the case, she should talk to you."

"You suppose?" Buchannan seethed. "That woman called me out of the blue and started hounding me for answers. And when I hung up on her, she had the gall to show up at my house! My wife was at home, and because she's a good, kind person, she let her in, unaware that she was about to be interrogated like a common criminal. It wasn't until I got home that we were able to get that woman to leave!"

Still looking at my shoes, I muttered, "Sorry."

"Sorry." Buchannan threw his hands into the air, spun in a frustrated circle. "You're sorry. That'll fix it."

I let him stew without comment. I understood his frustration, though I didn't appreciate him targeting his anger at me. It wasn't my fault that Sabrina Mayfield was writing a story about me. Sure, I might have sent her Buchannan's way, but I didn't tell her I was the only one solving crimes. I'd just been trying to get rid of her. And I surely didn't want her bothering Elsie Buchannan, who was indeed a good, kind person.

Buchannan composed himself, and his customary scowl settled into place. "You called me earlier."

"I did."

"What did you want? If it's about that reporter . . ."

"It's not!" Ignoring his skeptical glare, I told him about what I'd learned throughout the day, leaving out my mishap at the gym. For one, it wasn't important to the story. For another, he wouldn't care.

Buchannan listened, his scowl never leaving his face. In fact, it only deepened the longer I talked. When I was done, he stood staring at me, nostrils flaring as he fought to keep from erupting at me once again. Clearly, he'd had a stressful day and was looking for an outlet for his frustration. I was a convenient and, in his eyes, a deserving target.

"Is that all?" he finally managed. "Have you spoken with anyone else I should be made aware of? I don't know, maybe the killer." His anger built as he kept talking. "I mean, if you are the genius you make yourself out to be, and since you have reporters interested in your story because you are *so* much better than us, perhaps I should have you watched some more so I could learn a thing or two from you."

I blinked at him. *What?*

Buchannan's breath caught, and for an instant, I saw a flash of what I could only describe as horror in his eye.

"You're having me watched?" I asked.

"That's not what I meant."

"Then what did you mean?"

Buchannan's jaw worked a moment as he tried to come up with a way out. He chose a change in subject.

"You're not the only one talking to reporters, you know?" he said.

"Big whoop." I planted my hands onto my hips. "What did you mean by having me watched some more?"

"Oliver Quick is hosting a sit-down interview at Ted and Bettfast tomorrow," Buchannan pressed on. And was the sudden color on his cheeks due to embarrassment? "You are to be there."

Now that caught me by surprise. This time, my "What?" was verbalized.

"You are to be at Ted and Bettfast at eleven in the morning. Actually, you need to be there at least twenty minutes early so they can prep you."

"Back up. Prep me for what?"

Seeing a lifeline, Buchannan grabbed hold, regained

some of his command. "An interview with a reporter from a Levington news station. She is conducting an interview with Mr. Quick, and I've arranged it so you will take part since you seem to love talking to reporters."

"Whoa, whoa. I'm not doing an interview."

"Yes, you are." Buchannan actually smiled. "You're going to go in there, sit down, and talk nice about Pine Hills and the local police department. You are going to be our PR, and you're going to like it."

"But—"

"No buts. You did this to yourself when you sicced that reporter on me. I had Elsie pull some strings with someone she knows at the Levington station. She had to call in a lot of favors to make this happen, so don't mess it up."

I stared at him. He couldn't possibly expect me to go in there and talk about Pine Hills and its police department when the reporter was going to want to talk about the murder and how it affected Oliver. Heck, they might even prefer to discuss my involvement, considering my history.

"Officer Dalton will be there," Buchannan said. "He's not going to be on camera, but will be there for moral support and to keep the peace, just in case things start to get out of hand, as they are wont to do around here."

Paul's earlier comments about seeing me at Ted and Bettfast now made sense, but it didn't make me feel any better. "Why not have him talk to the reporter?" I nearly whined it. "He's a cop. He could put on a good face and show everyone how not scary you guys are."

Buchannan glared at me in a very scary way. "Yes, but you took part in Mr. Quick's little game. You were part of the team that found Mr. Flanagan. You've already talked to a reporter. You insist on inserting yourself into my investigation. Do I need to go on?"

I could have pointed out that Buchannan himself also took part in the "little game," as had Officer Garrison, but had a feeling it would get me nowhere.

"Fine," I said, resigned. "Is there anything specific you want me to do?"

"Just . . . don't screw this up."

It was my turn to scowl.

"Do what you do," he said. "Listen. Keep watch. You know what happened. See if Mr. Quick alters his story. See if the reporter asks something she shouldn't know, which indicates someone else is talking." He pointed that finger of his at me. "And if anyone so much as suggests the police aren't doing their jobs, I want you to set them straight."

A part of me still wanted to protest, but really, was being there for the interview going to be so bad? I wanted to talk to Oliver. To Link. It would give me excuse to poke around some more, ask some questions under the guise of wanting to get my story straight for the reporter.

Still, I couldn't just accept having it thrust onto me without making Buchannan squirm at least a little.

"I'll do it," I said. "But only if you tell me what you meant by having me watched some more."

"It's not important—"

"It might not be, but I want to know." It was hard to look strong and imposing when you couldn't put your full weight onto one of your feet, but I did my best. "Otherwise, I might have to start asking questions. In fact, I might just call Paul right now and see what he might know about it. He's with Chief Dalton, so he might ask her . . ."

"Don't do that," Buchannan snapped. His eyes darted around the room, as if looking for an escape, but there was none, not unless he wanted to sprint out the door behind him. That, he knew, would give me too much satisfaction.

Seconds passed where he actually did squirm, before he licked his lips, ran his hand over his face, and spoke through his palm, causing his voice to be muffled, though I could still make out what he said.

"I had people text me your location during the game."

Even though I'd heard him just fine the first time, I asked, "What was that?"

Buchannan dropped his hand and glared at me so hard, I felt it. "I had people text me your location during the game," he snapped.

"That's how you knew I was at the logging camp!"

He nodded, teeth grinding. "I got the text while at the hotel. Someone overheard you say that's where you were going. If I hadn't been so far away, I would have beaten you there and would have found the body myself."

The hotel was about as far from the logging camp as you could get and still be in Pine Hills, so it was no wonder it took him so long.

"You cheated," I said, practically giddy from it. "You

had me watched so you could try to beat me." A giggle burbled up, slipped from my lips.

Buchannan's embarrassment had him seething. "Eat it up," he said. "Have your little laugh. Then show up at Ted and Bettfast tomorrow and do the right thing."

I was still stifling giggles as Buchannan stomped his way out of my house. He slammed the door hard enough that Misfit, who'd watched the entire encounter from the coffee table, shot from the room in an orange blur.

After a rough day, this was exactly the sort of laugh I needed.

And the only thing better than enjoying a moment like this alone would be to share it with someone else.

I picked up my cell and dialed. It rang only once before Dad answered with, "Hey, Buttercup, what's happening?"

"Hi, Dad. You're not going to believe what just happened . . ."

24

I was up bright and early the next morning, but not by choice. I spent most of the night lying in bed, staring up at the ceiling, visualizing what I was going to say when I was face-to-face with the reporter. I'm not a celebrity. Dad, in a roundabout, author-like way, was, and he'd done his best to prep me for my time in front of the camera—something he'd experienced a couple of times with local morning talk shows asking about his books.

I was so not ready for this.

My stomach was in knots as I forced down a piece of toast with my coffee. Next came a pain pill since my ankle was still barking at me, though the swelling had gone down. As I ate, I considered everything I knew about Oliver Quick, his production, and Scott's murder. Buchannan might want me to show up and talk pretty about the Pine Hills police department, but I had an ulterior motive in mind.

I was going to solve the case.

How? No idea. But I did know that step one required more information, and I had just enough time before I was due at Ted and Bettfast to get it.

I picked up my phone and dialed.

"Well, look who it is," Rita said, answering on the first ring. "Here I thought that I'd surprise you at Death by Coffee, and wouldn't you know it, I get here and you're nowhere in sight!"

"You're at Death by Coffee?"

"Didn't I just say that?" And then, fainter, as if she'd moved the phone away from her face, "Didn't I just say that, Wendy?"

I could just barely make out Wendy's "You did."

"Wendy and I thought it would be a good idea to put our heads together this morning," Rita said, returning to full volume. "We've been hearing all sorts of crazy theories about the murder, and so we thought it would be smart to talk about what we knew, what we might remember about that day, and see if we could come up with some sort of consensus on what we think might have happened. Isn't that right, Wendy?"

This time, I had to imagine her response because I couldn't hear it.

"Have you come up with anything?" I asked.

"Not yet we haven't. We got here about ten minutes ago, so we've really just started."

I was already picking up my purse. "I can be there in fifteen minutes." Barring traffic, of course.

"Well, you'd better hurry, dear. We can't just sit around waiting for you forever."

Though, knowing Rita, she'd do just that if she thought it would help. "I'm on the way." I clicked off, pulled the door closed behind me, and was indeed on the way.

Rita and Wendy were sharing a table by the window at Death by Coffee. Rita, who must have been watching for me, waved for me to hurry as soon as I'd climbed out of my car. I did my best, limping my way through the door, and to them, without so much as a "Hi" toward Eugene behind the counter.

"Did you come up with something?" I asked, dropping heavily into a chair. The urge to reach down and massage my ankle was strong, but I held back, not wanting Rita to notice, lest the entire town hear about my mishap by midday.

She eyed me a moment before speaking, "We may have, but we want to hear what you have to say first. No sense in us feeding you our speculation before you have your say. It might alter your perception, and then where would we be?"

I considered where to start, and then simply launched in. I laid out everything I knew. About Lydia and Scott seeing one another. About Austin and Drew. Shari. Everything I could remember about the main culprits, though I was certain there was something I was forgetting.

Rita nodded along, as if I wasn't telling her anything she didn't already know. Every once in a while, she'd glance over at Wendy, who'd give her a meaningful look, which further suggested there was something they were keeping from me and I was only verifying their suspicions.

"Is that everything?" Rita asked when I ran out of steam.

I thought about it and said, "There is talk about Hector Kravitz causing a stink and Kenneth Purdy looking to sue the theatre. Kenneth claims he has evidence that one of the local actors is responsible for Scott's death."

Rita waved a hand in front of her face as if the mere suggestion that anyone local could have had anything to do with the murder stunk. "Kenneth has nothing."

"He called Vicki and—"

"And he made up a bunch of hogwash because he's a petty man who was looking to take advantage of a horrible situation because, as I said, he is a petty man," Rita interrupted. "The way I heard it—this from Georgina, mind you—is that Kenneth had a sit-down with the locals and has since backed off his accusations and threats. He'd made up the whole story about evidence and suing and what have you in the hopes of pressuring the actors to, I don't know, take him back? Honestly, I don't know what he was thinking."

"Has Hector backed off?" I asked.

"He has nothing to complain about anymore," Rita said. "Well, I mean, he's not thrilled about all the attention Oliver Quick is getting, but who is? I saw that man on television last night. Can you believe it? Every time I turn around, there he is, boo-hooing about how the whole thing is an attempt at ruining him." She rolled her eyes. "As if anyone would care enough."

"A reporter showed up at my place last night," Wendy said.

"Sabrina Mayfield?" I asked. "Bangs. From a Levington online paper?"

She nodded. "I avoided her. Haley chased her off and threatened to call the police if she showed up again."

"I can't believe how the media is feeding on us like this," Rita said. "A man is dead, and what do they care about? Ratings. They help Oliver use the murder as a promotional tool and to massage his ego. And for what? Some overdone production? Pah!"

I almost commented on Rita now calling the production overdone, considering how she'd scoffed at me for saying the exact same thing that first evening, but thought better of it. "I talked to Vivian Flowers and Sara Huffington yesterday," I said instead. "Did you know Sara and Albert are dating?"

I'd been hoping to catch Rita by surprise and have actual gossip for her instead of the other way around, but she waved off my comment. "Everyone knows that."

"You knew? When?"

"Albert called me after their first date. He was rather smitten and wanted the entire world to know." She leaned forward. "Big Joe Huffington tried to pay Albert off so he'd stop seeing his daughter, but wouldn't you know it, Albert declined! Told him he could keep his money and walked right away. I think that's just about sealed the deal for Sara. I wouldn't be surprised if they ended up married within the next year." She gave me a meaningful look. "I expect they shouldn't be the only ones?"

There was no way I was stepping on that landmine,

so I avoided the question. "I spent some time thinking about who had a reason to kill Scott," I said, "and after some consideration, I'm definitely leaning toward Link."

Rita and Wendy shared a look, with Rita, of course, taking the lead. "That's what we were thinking too. It fits. After his moment in the spotlight, he didn't have anything to do."

"He could have snuck out without anyone knowing," Wendy said.

"There was a point where the only people left at Ted and Bettfast were Link, Richie, and Robert," I said.

"The rest of us were out investigating," Rita said. "And even if a team were to have followed clues to the logging camp, that would have put three people there. It seems unlikely that we are dealing with a trio of killers."

"So, we just have to figure out who wasn't with anyone at the time of the murder," I said.

"And we could narrow it down from there," Rita said.

I thought it through, speaking out loud as I did. "We know that Scott parted with his team at the Banyon Tree. Austin and Shari have a fight at the hotel. Austin abandons her there, calls Link."

"Who knows now that Scott is alone," Wendy said.

"Oliver, likely right around this time, went to the theatre to confront Hector, leaving Richie in charge."

"Which means that poor assistant was probably too busy to notice Link slip out," Rita said. "I know Oliver, and he wouldn't just leave. He'd heap as much work on that boy as he could possibly manage."

I nodded. That sounded about right. "Link hears from Austin, realizes that Scott is stuck at the Banyon Tree, and heads there under the guise of giving him a ride. He stays in his car, calls him over so he won't appear on the security footage, and then takes him to the logging camp, waits for Lydia to leave, and kills him."

"He might not even need to wait around," Rita said. "He could have promised Scott that he'd pick him up after his tête-à-tête with Lydia, driven around for a little while, maybe even popped in somewhere so that he'd be seen, and then he could go back to kill him."

Wendy was frowning. "Something's not right."

Both Rita and I looked at her. "What was that, dear?" Rita asked.

"I'm not sure." Wendy considered it, spoke slowly. "If Link found out that Scott was alone at the diner through Austin, would he really have gone there to pick him up and risk being seen if he planned on killing him?"

It was my turn to frown. Sure, he'd avoided the security camera, but was that enough to assume he'd gone there with foul intent in mind? It was hard to imagine it being anyone else, honestly. Lydia didn't seem to be a fit. Most of the teams were together. Oliver was at the theatre. Austin had left Shari, sure, but would he have had time to get all the way to the logging camp and kill Scott before I'd arrived? As Buchannan had pointed out, it was a long way.

"We know Link picked him up," I said. "Sara saw him. She claims Scott never made a call."

"Which means he might have known Scott was

there even before Austin called," Rita said. "I mean, he'd have to, right? The timing would be off otherwise."

Could Link have been on the way to Scott already? If so, why? To make amends? Doctor Lipmon had said Scott's face being covered could indicate someone who knew him and felt remorse. Was it possible that Link picked Scott up, tried to talk to him, and then killed him when it didn't work out as he hoped?

"It's really starting to feel like this whole thing was planned," Rita said. "You just don't randomly show up somewhere, right when someone needs you."

"Detective Buchannan did," Wendy said. "After we found the, uh, ..." She swallowed back the word *body*, and honestly, I didn't blame her.

"Actually, Buchannan's appearance wasn't random," I said. This time I did have information neither of them had. "He had someone watching us who texted him our location."

Rita's eyes just about popped from her head. "He was cheating? Oh my Lordy Lou! I knew it! He couldn't beat us fair and square, so he used underhanded tactics in order to win." She smacked the table with the flat of her hand. "And we were still ahead of him!"

"Could it be possible that Link had someone watching Scott?" Wendy asked. "A spy of some sort?"

"Possibly," I said. "But who?"

We all thought about it, but came up blank. Link wasn't a resident of Pine Hills. As far as I knew, he didn't know anyone, though I supposed it was possible he had a relative or friend who lived in town. Could either

Shari or Austin have been feeding him information? I mean, Austin did call him. Could he have sent him a message earlier, telling him where Scott was?

"What about one of the assistants?" Rita asked. "They were supposed to be keeping an eye on things anyway, so it stands to reason one of them might have been watching Scott specifically."

"It'd have to be Richie, I would think," Wendy said. "If Scott was sweet on Lydia, she probably wouldn't spy on him for anyone."

"But Oliver was keeping them busy," I said. "He had Lydia out running errands, which is why she settled on the logging camp and waited as long as she did."

"What about the actors?" Wendy asked. "They could have been relaying information back to Oliver and his assistants as teams made their way through the production."

"And since Link had little else to do, he could have been listening in on those reports," Rita said. "Let's assume the actors were indeed reporting everyone's location to Richie and Lydia. If Lydia was indeed running errands before meeting with Scott, perhaps Link offered to take her calls, since, as we noted before, he wasn't doing much else."

I doubted that Oliver would have allowed that, but it did make some sense.

"There wasn't an actor at the Banyon Tree, though," Wendy said.

"You're right." Rita tapped her chin. "But maybe he still had someone watching so that the clues didn't up and walk off."

The door opened behind me. I glanced back out of

reflex and was surprised to see Drew MacDonald enter. He went straight for the counter to order.

"What do you think, dear?" Rita asked me.

"Maybe," I said, my attention focused on Drew, who had ordered and was now tapping his toe impatiently as Eugene went about putting together his drink. Drew looked agitated, and I was dying to know why.

There was only one way to find out.

Rita was saying something else, but I'd completely missed it. Eugene was nearly done with Drew's drink, and once he was, Drew would leave and I might miss my chance to talk to him before the interview.

"I've got to go," I said, rising. "I'll tell you how it goes."

"How what goes?" Rita asked.

I nodded absently, not hearing a word she'd said, and limp-walked my way over to where Drew stood.

"Good morning," I said. "Hi, I'm Krissy Hancock. We haven't officially met." I stuck out a hand.

Instead of scowling at me, as I suspected he might, Drew surprised me by shaking. "Drew MacDonald. You were one of the locals, right? Took part in Oliver's thing."

"I did."

"Right mess that was," he scoffed. "I'm done with it. I'm getting a coffee and heading home."

"You're not sticking around for the interview?" I asked.

There was the scowl I'd expected. "No, I'm not. I never should have taken part in this stupid thing from the start. I only wanted to mess with Oliver. It's why I—" He glanced at me side-eyed, then shrugged. "Who cares now, right? I was cheating, yeah. Wanted to finish so quickly, it would make Oliver look like he couldn't put together a mystery worth solving. Dumb, yeah, but so was Oliver's plan."

"Scott almost ruined it," I said, thinking back to how he'd caught Drew snooping when we were all supposed to be locked in our rooms.

Eugene slid Drew's coffee across the counter to him. Drew picked it up and took a large gulp before speaking. "It is what it is. I was never a Scott Flanagan fan, but, hey, I didn't want to see the pipsqueak get killed." He sobered. "He was annoying, but aren't we all in our own way?"

I didn't know what to say to that. When I'd come over to talk, I'd expected Drew to be belligerent and confrontational, not thoughtful and, dare I say, almost respectful.

"Look, this whole situation is one that got out of hand," he said. "I'm sorry we brought our drama to your little town. It's a nice enough place. I let my emotions get the best of me and lashed out a bit. Then someone had to go and kill the guy. It sickens me, and I just want to go. Oliver can . . ." He shook his head, unwilling to voice what he was thinking.

"Do you know who might have done it?" I asked. "Killed Scott, I mean."

"I wish I did." Drew's hand tightened on his cup so much, I was afraid he'd pop it. "People like that don't deserve to walk the streets free. I'd . . . well, I wouldn't be treating them with much kindness if I found out who did it, that's for sure."

Somehow, I believed him.

Drew took another drink of his coffee, saluted me with it, and walked out the door. I stared after him, somewhat dumbfounded by his candor. Drew might have his issues, but as he'd said, don't we all? Just because he'd gotten angry a few times, gotten physical with Scott, and had a history of being rude to patients at the hospital, it didn't make Drew MacDonald a bad guy, let alone a killer.

Besides, at that point, Lincoln Freel was my best, and very nearly only, worthwhile suspect when it came to the murder of Scott Flanagan.

And I hoped that sometime within the next hour, I'd be able to prove it.

25

I'm not sure what I expected to find when I arrived at Ted and Bettfast. Perhaps hulking television cameras with those big, bright studio lights placed around the room, which would be full of makeup artists, reporters, assistants, and so forth.

Instead, I entered to find a single camera aimed at a pair of chairs near the back door. A woman I took to be the reporter was doing her own makeup in the corner, while her cameraman leaned against the wall, eyes closed, seemingly snoozing while standing up. Oliver was pacing near where the small, dark-haired woman, India, was lecturing Richie and Lydia. A few Levington people remained, all of them Oliver's actors. Robert was gnawing on a thumbnail by the office door, looking nervous and out of place.

And there was, of course, Officer Paul Dalton.

He noted me enter and immediately broke out into a smile, which helped ease some of the tension. "Hey, Krissy," he said. "You ready for this?"

"Not in the slightest." I tried my best not to limp when I joined him. "I can't believe I let Buchannan talk me into this."

"You'll do fine," Paul said, eyeing me. "Are you okay? You look stiff."

"Let's just say I might not be running on a treadmill again anytime soon and leave it at that."

Paul laughed. "Noted."

"How's your mom?" I asked. Across the room, India finished laying into Richie and Lydia and turned on Oliver, who immediately lowered his head and took it like an oft-chastised child. "Is she doing okay?"

"She's fine," Paul said. "It was her wedding anniversary. It always hits her hard. After Dad passed . . ." He trailed off, though he didn't appear upset, just thoughtful.

Still, I felt bad for bringing it up. It was likely just as hard on him as it was her. "I'm sorry."

"Don't be," he said. "Chief doesn't like to let it show how much certain things bother her. I guess I should apologize for not being able to talk last night. Was there something you wanted?"

"No, it's okay. Don't apologize for being a good son."

He put an arm around me briefly and kissed my temple. "Thank you for understanding."

I flushed with pleasure. "You know, maybe I should invite her over one night soon," I said. "You and your mom. Dinner, at my place."

Paul's eyebrows rose. "You sure you'd want that? You know she can be intense sometimes."

"I know." I also knew how important she was to him

and, by extension, me. "It wouldn't be anything fancy. I'm not much of a cook."

"You're not *that* bad," he said with a grin.

I smacked him on the arm, but not hard. "Keep it up and you can join Misfit and eat on the floor."

He chuckled. "Who knows? That might be fun."

Across the room, Link stepped away from the rest of the actors, who were talking among themselves. He stared at Lydia and Richie a long moment, frowned, and then spun away and started for the stairs.

Snap decision. "I'll be right back," I said, and then, before Paul could stop me, I hurried over.

"Link," I called, as his foot hit the bottom step. "Hold up a sec."

He glanced back, and for a second, I thought he might sprint up the stairs to escape me. Instead, he eased back down with a sigh. "I only have a moment. They'll be starting soon." He motioned toward the reporter, who had roused her cameraman, and they were busy messing with the camera.

"This will only take a minute," I said, and then, seeing no reason to beat around the bush, I hit him with it. "You drove Scott to the logging camp."

Link flinched, and then paled. "I'm not sure where you're getting your information—"

"I'm not done," I said. I already had him on the ropes and intended to press my advantage. "A few years ago, you and Scott got into a fight. You hit him, which sent him to the doctor. He claimed it was a misunderstanding, but that doesn't mean you thought of it the same way."

"Ms. Hancock?" the reporter shouted. "We have ten

minutes until we're rolling. I need you so we can get you ready!"

I held up a finger for her to wait. That earned me a huff from her and a scowl from Oliver, but I wasn't going to let Link off the hook that easily.

"Why would you drive Scott to the camp?" I asked. "Did he call you? Or were you already on the way to him because you had ulterior motives?" He opened his mouth to say something, but I cut him off. "And don't try to lie to me."

Link gave me a look full of attitude that crumbled after only a few brief moments. "Okay, fine," he said, sounding almost relieved. "I drove him."

Bingo! I immediately wanted to pepper him with a dozen hard-hitting questions, but held back. Sometimes, simply letting someone talk was better than leading them along.

Link glanced over to where the rest of the actors were laughing at something Claudia said. None of them were paying us any mind, yet he lowered his voice when he said, "I admit, Scott and I had a history. Everyone knew about it, so it's not like it was a secret. The whole thing was stupid. Scott got on my nerves, and I let him get to me more than I should have. I made a mistake and struck him when I should have walked away. But we didn't hate one another. You have to understand that, while I might not have liked him, I didn't want to see him dead."

Oliver cleared his throat. Loudly. He was already seated in one of the chairs across from the reporter. India was at his side, glaring at me like I was ruining their moment.

But this was too important. They could wait.

"When I got the text to pick Scott up—" Link went on, but I cut him off.

"You got a text?"

"I did," Link said. "Scott told me he was with his team and they were on the way to that diner—J&E's Banyon Tree, I think it's called—and that he planned on parting from them there. We'd spoken for a few minutes the night before, and I told him I'd like to bury the hatchet and had given him my number so we could talk. When he texted, I figured it would be a good time to do just that, so I agreed to drive him, even though Oliver would have pitched a fit if he'd known."

My mind spun as I attempted to work out the timeline. "Austin called you," I said.

Link nodded. "He was upset. I guess he wanted me to remove Scott from the game because of what happened. Scott was sitting right beside me when he'd called, and I'm pretty sure he could hear what Austin was saying, but he didn't seem upset by it. I told Austin that I'd let Oliver know and hung up."

"So you'd already picked up Scott by then?"

Link swallowed, and tears formed in his eyes. "I drove him to that camp. He told me to drop him off, drive around a bit, and come back in twenty minutes." He shrugged. "I didn't have anything else to do, so that's what I did."

I searched his face for deception, saw nothing.

Link went on.

"Once I got back, I waited outside for like ten minutes, but he never showed up. I thought about just leaving him, but realized that if I really did want to make things right between us, I couldn't do that. So I went inside." His lower lip trembled, and his nostrils flared. "I found him lying there, already dead. I didn't see anyone else, but knew . . ." He coughed, sucked in a breath. "I knew he was there to see Lydia."

"He told you that?"

"I saw her car when I dropped him off," Link said. "Scott told me they were together, and while I was skeptical about their relationship, I couldn't deny that she was there, waiting for him."

A glance across the room showed Lydia with her head down, hands folded in front of her. Richie was watching her with concern.

Could she have killed Scott? It was looking more and more like she was the last person to see him alive.

"You told Oliver you were afraid I knew something," I said, turning my attention back to Link. "Someone overheard your conversation with him after the murder."

Link sniffed, then heaved a sigh. "I was afraid you knew that I drove Scott and that I'd found him. Scott talked about you, you know? He said you'd solved some murders, which gave you an advantage with Oliver's mystery, and when I realized that you might look into his death, I thought you'd figure out that I touched"—he squeezed his eyes closed—"I covered his face. I thought that it would be horrible if Lydia came back and found him like that, so I covered his face with a towel I keep with me in case I'm all made up, like I was that day. I sit on it so I don't get anything on the seat of my car."

Which explained where the towel had come from. I

should have wondered about it before now. I hoped that Buchannan already had.

"I panicked," Link went on. "I told Oliver that I found Scott and that I didn't know what to do. He made me promise not to tell anyone. Not that I wanted to. I knew how it would look to the police since we did have that history, and I didn't have much of an alibi. I played it off like I didn't care, but I swear"—his voice broke—"I didn't kill him."

"Ms. Hancock!" the reporter called. "It's time!"

As much as I wanted to ignore her, I couldn't. Still, I hesitated, asked one more question. "Did you see anyone else there when you dropped Scott off or when you returned to pick him up?"

Link shook his head. "I wish I had. I really do."

And with that, he abandoned any thoughts of heading upstairs and instead returned to group of actors, which had moved so they could watch the interview from directly behind the camera.

I walked over to my chair in something of a daze. I sat down, and the reporter immediately launched into a set of instructions that went in one ear and out the other. No one came over to do my makeup, nor did the reporter especially seem to care whether I was listening or not.

All I kept thinking was that Link was my best suspect, yet I believed what he'd told me. He had a history with Scott. He drove him to the logging camp. Lydia never saw him, but that didn't mean much if she was already inside. Could Link have lingered and waited until Lydia left before he struck? Who else had a motive? I mean, Drew seemed angry at Scott, but if he had abandoned his team so he could kill him, his team-mates would have said so. As Rita had said, I doubted we were dealing with a trio of killers.

It had to have been Link. Or perhaps Lydia, if Link was telling the truth. Who else could it have been?

The atmosphere in the room shifted. The reporter was seated across from Oliver and me, while everyone else, Paul included, stood behind the cameraman, who counted down from ten, going silent during the last three numbers, and, quite suddenly, we were live.

"I'm Belinda Wainwright, here with Oliver Quick and Kristina Hancock, discussing the tragedy that has befallen the small town of Pine Hills." She turned to Oliver. "Tell me, how did this whole event come about?"

"Well, Belinda, let me first say that I'm heartbroken about what has happened. I . . ."

His words turned into a buzz in my ear as I scanned the group watching us. Most of the actors were excited, as if this was their moment, despite not being in front of the camera. Link looked distraught, while Paul was watching me, a faint smile on his lips. Robert, who was lingering near the back of the group, was still gnawing on his thumbnail. India was mouthing words to Oliver, who read her like a teleprompter.

And then there were Lydia and Richie.

Oliver's assistants flanked India, but from my angle, I had a good view of them. Lydia still had her head down, hands folded in front of her. She was trembling ever so slightly, and her eyes were red and damp. Richie whispered something into her ear and then reached out for her hand. He squeezed it, but didn't release it. Instead, his thumb caressed the back of her hand as he continued to console her. She tensed, shook her head, and then pulled her hand free of his grip.

"While the teams were busy with their investigations, I managed things from here," Oliver said, catching my attention.

"You left," I cut in. "You went to the theatre."

A beat, and then, "Well, yes, I did briefly." Oliver sounded annoyed. "But I was able to keep an eye on everything from there, just as easily as I could have from here. I—"

"Who did you leave in charge?"

"Pardon?"

"When you left," I said. "Who did you leave in charge, just in case one of the teams returned or needed assistance?"

Oliver looked to India, who was glaring at me with an intensity that I could feel. Belinda Wainwright leaned forward, seemingly as interested in the answer as I was.

Oliver cleaned his throat and after some fidgeting, he answered. "Well, I have two assistants who would have assumed control during my absence."

"But Lydia wasn't here," I said. "One of my first stops was at Death by Coffee, and she was there. You had her running errands, and she wasn't here when you left."

"Then Richie would have handled everything," Oliver snapped. "That's why I have two assistants."

Mousy, quiet Richie. Richie, who'd wanted to talk to me and painted Drew as a bad person. Richie, who clearly had a thing for Lydia, who had been seeing Scott before his death.

Richie, whose uncle owned the logging company, and who had pointed Lydia in the direction of the abandoned camp.

"Link picked up Scott at the Banyon Tree," I said, speaking out loud more for my own than anyone else's benefit. Gasps met my proclamation. "He dropped him off at the logging camp so he could meet Lydia."

All the blood left Lydia's face when she turned to face Link.

"I didn't kill him," he told her. "I swear."

"He didn't," I said, growing more and more certain of that as I spoke. "Oliver left for the theatre. Lydia ran her errands and then met Scott, who was driven to the camp by Link, leaving one person here alone."

Or almost alone.

"Robert was here," I said.

He jerked his thumb from his mouth and hid his hand behind his back. "Uh, what?"

"You were here," I said, this time with more confidence. "When everyone else had left, you remained behind so you could keep an eye on the bed-and-breakfast."

Confused, he nodded.

"Where was Richie?"

The room went silent as all eyes turned toward the man in question.

"I was here," he said. "Mr. Quick put me in charge."

I ignored him. Instead, I kept my attention on Robert, whose face had scrunched up in thought.

"I don't see what this has to—" Oliver started, but Belinda shushed him.

"Robert?" I pressed. "Do you remember seeing Richie after everyone else had left?"

The oh-so-slow wheels were turning in his head. When he spoke, he did so with some hesitation. "No," he said, "I don't think so."

Close enough. I turned to Richie. "You have a crush on Lydia," I said. "A big one."

His eyes widened. "What? No. That's not true."

She looked down at her hand, the one he'd so recently grabbed, and then back at him. "You told me about the camp," she said. "You made sure I knew that it was private and out-of-the-way."

"It was for you!" Richie said. He seemed to realize how that must have sounded because he tried to backtrack. "I realized you wanted to talk to Scott privately. I told you about the camp so you'd have someplace to go because I . . ." He floundered.

"You followed them," I said. "Or waited for them. One or the other."

Richie shook his head, took a step back.

"You heard about Scott's relationship with Lydia," I pressed. "You saw them sneak outside together that first night and realized that something was up. Lydia is the one who got Scott placed on Shari and Austin's team. It caused friction between competitors, which helped distract the police. Drew fought with Scott. Austin was angry with him. Link had a history with him. With so many people frustrated with him, it made it easy for you to slip under the radar."

"One of them must have done it," Richie said. "I told you about Drew!"

"Exactly," I said. "You were trying to deflect, to pin

someone else for a murder you committed." I had no evidence, but it fit. Richie had a crush on Lydia, needed to get rid of Scott. He tells her where they can meet, possibly even tells Scott to wait for him there after he meets with her. Lydia leaves and Richie swoops in, kills him, all before Link can return to pick him up. Perhaps Richie had hoped that Link would be blamed for the crime. Considering how Rita, Wendy, and I had been thinking, there was a good chance Detective Buchannan was leaning that way as well.

"Richie?" Lydia asked, taking a step away from him. "You killed him?"

"I . . ." He looked to Oliver for help, and seeing none, he turned back to Lydia. "If you'd let me explain, I know I could make you understand."

I don't know if Richie planned on grabbing her and using her as a hostage so he could escape, or if he was going to take her hands so he could plead his innocence to her while on his knees, but he never managed to do either.

He took a pair of lunging steps toward her, arms outstretched. Lydia didn't hesitate. She reared back and, putting everything she had into it, punched him square on the nose.

It was like he'd hit a brick wall. Richie's feet went out from under him, and he crashed down hard, out cold.

"Scott," Lydia said, before she fell to her knees, cradling the hand she'd hit Richie with.

And then she broke down into tears.

26

I ripped tape from the cardboard box with gusto. A fresh shipment of books awaited to be shelved at Death by Coffee, and I was looking forward to spending the next hour or two doing it. It was late in the day, inching closer and closer to closing time, and I was feeling upbeat, giddy even. I had the slightest of limps, but the pain was a distant memory.

A week had passed since Richie Husted had been arrested for the murder of Scott Flanagan. Details had trickled out, slowly at first, and then in a landslide as the media regained interest in the story. I followed it online, though I refused to comment whenever a reporter called. I had no intention of using Scott's death to raise my own celebrity.

It was a simple story, really, one Richie had no problem discussing with the police once he'd broken down and admitted to the murder. Richie and Lydia had met when they'd both started working at Kohl's in the Levington mall after they'd graduated from high school.

They became friends, but were not as close as Richie wanted. He was too shy to ask her out, so it wasn't a surprise that Lydia never picked up on his interest. Richie figured he could bide his time and wait her out, that she'd eventually see him for the great guy he thought himself to be. When she signed on to become Oliver's assistant, he was quick to follow suit.

And then Scott came along.

No one, and that included Richie, believed someone like Scott Flanagan could win the heart of a pretty, well-liked woman like Lydia Ray.

But he did. And soon Richie realized it.

He might not have been assertive, but Richie was observant. He watched Lydia and Scott, deduced that something was up between them, and after hearing Scott's claims that he was dating Lydia, decided he needed to do something about it.

So he followed her.

Richie watched Scott and Lydia talk at the camp. He saw them embrace, which told him everything he needed to know about their relationship. Once Lydia left and before Link could return, he confronted Scott, demanding he leave Lydia alone because, as Richie put it, he wasn't good enough for her.

Of course, Scott refused. Richie, frustrated, grabbed the caramel macchiato from Scott's hand, which was still piping hot thanks to the travel mug he used, and he threw it into Scott's face. When Scott started screaming, Richie claims he feared that Lydia might return and hear the screams, so he grabbed an old axe handle that had been abandoned in the corner of the room and hit Scott with it in an effort to get him to stop.

The blow, meant only to quiet him, killed him instead.

The details were hazy from there. Richie fled, likely escaping right before Link arrived. Link found Scott's body, panicked, thinking he'd be blamed for it, and covered his face with a towel from his car. They all then trickled back to Ted and Bettfast and pretended like nothing had happened.

There were some questions still, but I was content. Even when Sabrina Mayfield's rather light puff piece on me was released, there wasn't much info in it. I'm not even sure anyone but me read it.

I was okay with that. Unlike Oliver Quick, I wasn't interested in the attention.

I was sorting through the box of mystery novels when the door to Death by Coffee opened. I glanced up and was surprised to see Lydia Ray walk through the door. Her hand was in a cast, though she wasn't using a sling. She looked around, and then, spotting me sitting on the floor upstairs, she walked my way.

"Lydia?" I asked, pushing my way to my feet with a groan. "I thought you went home?"

"Hi, Krissy," she said. "I did. But the police needed me to come back so I could clear up a few details. Dot the i's and cross the t's and what have you."

"You look good." And she did. Her eyes were bright, and there was a bounce to her step that had been lost after Scott's death. She wasn't over him, of course, but she was getting through it.

"Thank you," she said. "It hasn't been easy."

"No, I imagine not."

"I still can't believe Richie did it." A crack formed,

and I could briefly see the pain hidden beneath her strong exterior before the mask was back in place. "I don't care that it was an accident. You don't hit someone like that and not expect them to get hurt."

I didn't know what to say to that, so I remained quiet.

Lydia took a breath, managed a smile. "I just wanted to stop by and thank you for what you did. I'm not sure Scott would have found justice if you hadn't figured it out."

"I got lucky," I said. "If he'd denied it, I'm not sure anyone would have been able to pin it on him. There simply wasn't any evidence." From what I'd heard, the police still hadn't found the axe handle, which Richie said he'd pitched out the window—along with Scott's wallet and cell phone—on his way back to Ted and Bettfast.

"Yeah, well, lucky or not, I appreciate it."

Feeling somewhat awkward with the compliment, I changed the subject. "How's your hand?"

This time, her smile was not just genuine, but satisfied. "Broken, but I'm okay with that."

"You pack a mean punch."

She laughed. "I suppose I do. I never knew I had it in me, to be honest."

And, I imagined, neither did Richie.

Lydia sobered. "Anyway, I'm heading back home. Thanks again for helping and not giving up on Scott."

"It was my pleasure."

She stepped forward and gave me a one-armed hug. Then, she turned, walked down the trio of stairs that led from the bookstore portion of the store into the dining area, and she was gone, out the door and heading back to Levington.

I went back to work on the books, though I'd lost some of the enthusiasm for it. Lydia was doing well, which was great, but she'd be feeling Scott's loss for a very long time. You didn't ask someone to run away with you if you didn't care for them deeply. It might be years before she was truly happy again.

As I worked, my mind drifted to Wendy, who was also doing better now that the killer had been found. As with Lydia, it was going to take some time before she got over the murder, though for another reason entirely. She no longer blamed herself for Scott's death, but still couldn't shake the memory of finding him and not re-alizing he was dead right away. She'd eventually work through it, but it was a process.

Just as I finished shelving the last book, the door opened again, and someone else entered the store. He didn't need to look around to know where to find me. He immediately crossed the dining area, ascended the stairs, and wrapped me in a strong, warm embrace.

Any sense of melancholy I might have had now van-ished.

"Paul!" I said, hugging him back with a fierceness that surprised me. "I didn't think I'd see you tonight."

He released me and stepped back with a grin. "I'm done for the night. It was a long day, but a good one."

"The case is closed?"

"As good as," he said. "We were worried Mr. Husted might recant after talking to a lawyer, but he doesn't appear to want that. I think, like the rest of us, he just wants it to be over with. He did leave us with a few interesting tidbits, however."

"Oh?"

"You might not believe this, but you know the guy who was running that whole show? Mr. Quick?"

I nodded. "Oliver."

"Well, apparently, he believes in alternative remedies for stuff like aging and what have you. Mr. Husted pointed us to some . . . unorthodox materials in Mr. Quick's possession. Nothing that would get him arrested, but it's strange enough that it will tarnish his already shaky reputation once it gets out."

I was dying to know if Scott had been right and Oliver was using actual blood remedies, but decided it was too icky to ask. I was sure that Rita would eventually hear about it and would rev up the gossip engine she was known for.

"So . . ." I said, dragging out the word as the last customer walked out the door downstairs, leaving just the two of us—and Beth, who was closing up the kitchen and dining room as we spoke—alone. "Have any plans this evening?"

"Actually, I do," Paul said, sidling up closer. "You see, there was this one evening not too long ago where my plans were oh so rudely interrupted."

My entire body warmed, and when I spoke, it came out as more of a purr. "What plans might those have been?"

Paul's smile was mischievous and very sexy. "Well now, that would ruin the surprise, wouldn't it?"

"It would."

"Have you eaten?"

No, I hadn't, but right then, I wasn't interested in food. "How about we skip dinner tonight and move right to where we left off the last time?"

Paul's eyes gleamed when he said, "That sounds perfect." He removed his phone from his pocket, showed it to me, and turned it off. "No distractions."

I stepped back from him long enough to pick up my phone from the counter where I'd left it when I'd sat down to start working on the books. There was a text from Rita, asking me if I'd heard anything new about the murder, and that she had some juicy tidbits to share about . . . well, right then, I didn't care.

I held the POWER button down until the screen went black and showed it to Paul, a grin of my own plastered across my face. "No distractions," I said before shoving it into my back pocket.

As for what happened during the rest of the night . . .

Well, I'll leave that up to your imagination.